THE MENAI BRIDGE
KILLIN

By Sim

A DI Ruth Hu

B

First published by Stamford Publishing Ltd in 2021
Copyright © Simon McCleave, 2021

Your FREE book is waiting for you now!

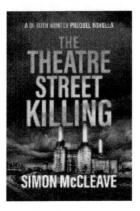

Get your FREE copy of the prequel to
the DI Ruth Hunter Series NOW
at www.simonmccleave.com[1]
and join my VIP Email Club

For Simon, Kate, Lucas and Milo x

PROLOGUE

WALKER, NEWCASTLE UPON Tyne
July 2008

It was a scorching hot day. A stolen red Fiat Punto, occupied by three young boys, drove into view through the heat haze. The car screeched around the corner of Scrogg Road in Walker, a deprived suburb to the east of Newcastle city centre. With the smell of burnt rubber in the air, it straightened up and continued on its journey. It was the last week of the summer term and the boys were on the wag. Finn Mahoney, the driver, and his mate Declan were ten years old and in the same class at St Cuthbert's Primary. Finn's younger brother, Steven, sat in the back of the car holding on for dear life. Steven had only just turned seven.

The boys wouldn't be missed, what with Finn and Steven's parents likely to be in bed for the day. They had been up drinking, taking drugs and partying with friends until dawn. Thursday was benefits day, which meant the house would be a chaotic mess of booze and smack until Monday - if the money lasted that long. Food was low down on the essentials for the house. If they were lucky, Finn and Steven would be tossed fifty pence to go and share a bag of chips from Mag's Chippy down the road for their tea.

Normally the boys would have been shouting and honking the horn down the street. After all, stealing cars was a buzz and most Walker boys were skilled at their favourite hobby. But today they drove in silence. Finn had other things on his mind. After what happened to Steven last week, he knew what had to be done. There was no other way. Revenge.

Acorn Street was only a five-minute drive from their home. That's where he lived. That dirty filthy pervert. He had done the same to Declan and Finn when they were bairns. Everyone knew what that nonce Paul Catteridge did to little boys but, because he was a copper, no one had stopped him. Not even that bitch of a wife of his, Doreen. Bloody coppers. Looking after their own. Even a kiddy fiddler like that bastard Catteridge.

Finn's parents said Steven was making it up, but of course they would. They didn't want any trouble. They were fiddling their benefits so didn't want the bloody coppers coming round to the house, poking their noses in where they weren't wanted. When Finn argued with them, he got a smack across the face for his trouble.

Finn and Steven shared a bedroom. Newcastle United scarves and posters on the walls. King Kevin Keegan was now their manager. Finn's grandad said Keegan was going to save United and stop them being relegated. And he bloody did. Keegan! Keegan! Keegan! But Finn had watched his little brother cry himself to sleep every night for the past few days. He had even wet the bed. It made Finn so angry.

As the car entered Acorn Street, Finn slowed and glanced down at the red metal jerry can that nestled by his feet. He had stolen it from his neighbour's shed. The petrol inside was making a weird sloshing sound. He wrinkled his nose as he got a whiff of the pungent fumes.

The three boys continued on in an uneasy silence. Finn had told Steven to stay at home, but he had refused. To be honest, Steven was safer with him than he was at home.

A builder's van came down the road towards them. The driver slowed down and peered over at them.

They all froze.

Finn could already feel his stomach twisting with anxiety. He's going to stop us or report us!

The van driver roared with laughter at the sight of Finn driving, then gave them a wink and revved the engine before driving away and out of sight.

Phew!

Glancing back at Steven, he could see how scared he was. 'You wanna go back? You don't have to come.'

Steven shook his head and stared out of the window.

Number 34 Acorn Street loomed into sight. Finn began to steel himself. He looked over at Declan, who was as cool as a cucumber. But that was Declan. Mr Bloody Joe Cool.

'What if he's in?' Steven asked quietly.

'Don't be soft, lad. He's a copper and it's the middle of the day. And that bitch he lives with works at Asda during the day,' Finn replied.

'Aye, I've seen that fat lass on the fish counter,' Declan said.

Finn stopped the car but left the engine running.

His heart was thumping in his chest. He took a deep breath.

This is it then, Finn thought. *No going back.*

He turned the steering wheel and carefully positioned it so that the car would head for the garage at the side of the house.

Next, he put the car into neutral and told the other two to get out.

Finn took the petrol can from the car and placed it on the pavement.

Taking a brick and a roll of gaffer tape from the boot, he crouched in the footwell by the pedals.

His hands were shaking.

Wrapping gaffer tape around the accelerator, he then placed the brick against the pedal and wedged it so that the engine roared.

Getting a car to drive on its own and then smash everything in its path was Finn's party trick. He'd done it in Walker Park three or four times before and drawn a big crowd of onlookers.

However, this time the consequences of what they were going to do were far more serious.

Going around to the passenger side, he leant in.

He glanced up and down the road to check no one was watching.

His anxiety was making him feel sick.

Here goes.

Cautiously, he clicked the automatic gearstick into drive and jumped back.

The car lurched forward at speed.

Finn dived out of its way.

The car mounted the pavement, ploughed through the garage doors, and smashed into the BMW that Finn knew was inside.

CRASH!

Bloody hell! Belter!

The BMW was Catteridge's pride and joy. He never stopped bragging about it. Fuck him. It was going to be a write-off.

Finn scanned up and down the street. Even though the car driving into the garage had made a huge bang, the street was still empty. Maybe they were just used to it?

But the work wasn't finished.

Finn surveyed the road again to check that the coast was clear and grabbed the petrol can from the pavement. 'Come on.'

The three boys scurried up the garden path.

Crouching down by the front door, Finn could feel his heart beating in his chest. 'Steven, keep an eye out. Dec, give this bloody letterbox a push, will ya man?'

Declan pushed the letterbox open. Finn poured the petrol through a nozzle into the Catteridge's house. The fumes went up his nose and started to make his eyes water.

I hope we burn down everything that dirty bastard paedo owns in the world, Finn thought as he gave the jerry can a final shake.

'Stand back, Steven,' Finn warned as he took out a match box. He looked at his little brother. He was doing this for him. And for himself and Declan - and all the other boys Catteridge had 'interfered with' at the Walker Park Rovers football club where he coached kiddies' teams at the weekend. A copper, a football coach, and a trusted pillar of society. Bastard.

Finn struck the match.

CHAPTER 1

TAKING A CIGARETTE from the packet, DI Ruth Hunter of the North Wales Police shielded her lighter from the wind with her cupped hand, lit it and took a long, deep drag. She blew the smoke into the thick misty air that already filled the cemetery, making the whole scene feel unearthly.

First ciggie of the day is still the best, she thought.

It was about six-thirty in the morning. The sun was starting to rise slowly to the east over the plum-coloured ridges of Snowdonia. The uneven edges of the horizon glowed with a tangerine orange that was gently being diffused by burning yellow and celestial blue. The sound of melodic birdsong – robins, goldfinches, blackbirds and nuthatches – filled the air, welcoming the dawn of a new day.

A few feet in front of her, in the middle of the grass that sparkled with morning dew, lay Sian's beautiful Welsh slate gravestone.

Sian Gwyneth Hockney 7.5.1985 – 12.4.2020
'A woman of grace and courage,
The song in our hearts.'

Resting against the headstone was a fresh bunch of blue and yellow irises. They were Sian's favourite flower so her brother must have visited in the last day or two.

It had been over three months since Sian had been murdered in a police operation that had gone horribly wrong. Ruth hadn't even begun to process it properly. Even though they had been split up at the time, she and Sian had been tentatively back on the road to making their relationship work when she had been killed. That was the cruel irony.

'I should have stopped you going up there. If I'd stopped you going, you'd still be here,' Ruth said in a whisper.

There was no one around to hear her, but she still felt awkward talking out loud.

She stared intently at the ground beneath which Sian's body now lay. She remembered seeing her, lying on the bed of the Intensive Care Unit. The oxygen tube had been removed from her mouth and the monitors switched off. Her skin had still been warm when Ruth held her hand and kissed her face. She still tormented herself with the fact that she hadn't managed to get to the hospital before Sian had passed.

Ruth drew in a short breath as her eyes began to fill with tears. How could she be dead? It still didn't feel real. There were cruel moments of respite when Ruth woke in the morning, and for a few seconds expected to feel Sian's soft breath on her neck or back. And then the devastating realisation of what had happened came thundering in, overwhelming her with grief, anxiety, and anger.

As she stubbed out her cigarette on the stone pathway, Ruth wiped the tears from her face and gazed at the imposing silhouette of Chirk Castle, a 13th century fortress with four medieval turrets, which sat on top of a steep hill. It was somewhere Sian used to love to go for a Sunday afternoon stroll. The giant Baroque iron gates. The dark stone turrets and rounded towers from where Welsh archers had defended the castle from the English. Sian would joke that they must *take a turn* around the formal Jacobean gardens. For a moment, Ruth smiled at the thought of her and Sian, arm in arm, as they strolled through the beautiful rose garden.

'I need to go now. But I'll come again next week,' Ruth said under her breath.

As she turned to go, she saw an old man at a grave close to the path. He was in his 70s, with a dark overcoat and a flat, tweed cap.

As Ruth took a few steps back down the path towards her car, the man must have heard her. He turned and squinted. 'Good morning.'

'Morning,' Ruth said, but her voice broke a little as she cleared her throat.

She stopped and glanced at the grave that the man was tidying – *Mary Ann Bale b. 1936 – d. 2017. Loving nain, mother and wife.*

'It's lovely and peaceful at this time of the morning,' the man said with a kind smile. His face was dark and leathery, with creases in his forehead that were as deep as cuts.

Ruth smiled back at him. 'Yes, it's my favourite time to come here.'

'Mine too ... See you then.'

'See you,' Ruth said as she turned to go.

CHAPTER 2

IT WAS NINE O'CLOCK in the evening by the time Finn had packed his suitcase. He closed it slowly, zipped it up, and laid it down neatly on his bed. Everything he owned in the world was in there.

Not much for twenty-three years of life, he thought to himself sadly.

Finn slowly surveyed the shadowy room for the last time. It had been his bedroom for nearly two years, but it had never felt like home. He checked the cupboards and the rickety pine wardrobe to make sure that he hadn't left anything behind. Resting at the bottom was an old, vinyl album of Paul Young's *No Parlez* that had been there when he arrived. He had no idea who Paul Young was but his spiked hair, baby face, and shiny silk suit made him appear ridiculous. Glancing at the walls, he gazed at the rectangles on the cream paintwork where the colour was much brighter. When he first moved in, he had guessed they had been made by the posters or drawings of the previous occupant. Finn had never had the inclination to paint the bedroom because it didn't feel like his. They never did.

He went over to the basin in one corner of the room, turned on the tap and splashed his face with cold water. That afternoon, he had scrubbed the sink clean until it gleamed. Force of habit, he presumed. Twelve years in a Young Offender Institution will teach you that kind of rigour. Finn was also aware that cleaning and tidying just made him feel less anxious. Order, neatness and control.

He gazed at his reflection. The straight nose, thin lips and pointed chin. The long and shaggy hair that he sometimes pulled into a ponytail. It made him, as it always did, uncomfortable. Was that normal? Did everyone struggle to look at their own reflection? He just didn't like what he saw looking back at him. Maybe it was because he had started to resemble his father.

Taking his suitcase from the bed, Finn thought he heard a noise from outside.

What the hell was that?

He knew the neighbours' fence rattled when there was strong wind. Finn used to listen to it in the darkness when he couldn't sleep. Sometimes he played his life forward as though he had never been to Ockley Cross. What if he, Declan, and Steven hadn't ventured out that day in 2008? How would things have turned out for them?

He listened again. The sound had gone.

He was probably just hearing things. Events in recent days had certainly made him paranoid.

A figure appeared at the doorway.

Finn was startled for a second.

'All set, Finn?' the man asked. Michael Bartowski was his witness protection officer from Northumbria Police. Now in his fifties, Michael had known Finn for over four years.

'Yeah, ta,' Finn mumbled in his thick Geordie accent, despite the fact it had been over thirteen years since he had last set foot in Newcastle. And according to his sentence, he would never be allowed in his home city again.

Finn followed Michael into the darkness of the hall and through to the living room. The lights in the flat were all switched off as a safety precaution. After the threats that had been made against Finn's life, it was safest to pretend that he wasn't home.

Michael walked over to the table, picked up a folder, and showed it to him. 'Right sunshine. New passport, National Insurance number, employment details.'

Finn rolled his eyes. 'Not another care home job?'

He had spent a year clearing up after old people in a home just outside Norwich and it wasn't his idea of fun.

'DIY warehouse,' Michael said.

That sounds very boring.

'Bloody hell,' Finn grumbled.

'We're not gonna put you in a bloody boy band, are we son?' Michael said dryly as he tapped the folder on Finn's shoulder. 'And I don't want to be doing this ever again, understood? Keep out of bloody trouble.'

He liked Michael. He was the nearest thing he had ever had to a proper father and he felt guilty that he had let him down.

Finn had been so drunk that he couldn't even remember bragging about his true identity in a pub in the middle of Norwich. However, it wasn't long before tabloid journalists had started to snoop around. Finn's victims' family had made a statement in the press saying that it was "... disgusting" that he had been granted lifelong anonymity. And then Norfolk Police found evidence online that Finn was going to be targeted and attacked by vigilantes. He needed to be moved for his own safety.

'I'm sorry Michael, you know?' he said quietly.

'Yeah, well you need to be careful or one day you're gonna end up badly hurt or dead,' Michael said grimly. Michael wasn't known for mincing his words.

'Got everything?' he asked.

Finn gestured to his suitcase. 'Yeah, that's it.'

Michael motioned to the back of the house. 'Car's waiting out the back. I thought it would be safer.'

Finn heard the sound of footsteps running on the pavement at the front of the house. Then angry shouts. It wasn't the first time he'd heard noises like that. He froze.

Michael shot him a look, then put his hand on his shoulder and guided him towards the door. 'Come on. Let's get out of here.'

Suddenly, the large living room window exploded with glass as two house bricks sailed through the panes.

"You fucking murderer!" came a shout from outside.

Then another smash. In a split second, the curtains and carpet were awash with orange and blue flames.

Someone had thrown a petrol bomb into the house.

"Hope you fucking fry you little bastard!"

Michael grabbed Finn by the shoulder and pulled him out through the door and into the hall. The air was already thick with smoke and petrol fumes.

They fled to the kitchen, headed out of the back door, and ran across the untidy garden.

'Jesus Christ! Come on!' Michael growled with a growing sense of urgency.

As they sprinted out of the rear gate, Finn could see an unmarked police car parked up. He threw his suitcase into the boot of the car, went to the rear door and got in.

A second later, the driver hit the accelerator.

Finn felt himself pushed back into the seat as he fastened his seatbelt.

'Where are we going, Michael?' Finn asked as he gripped the back seat.

'Llancastell,' Michael replied.

'Where the hell is that?' Finn asked.

'North Wales.'

CHAPTER 3

IT WAS SUNDAY MORNING, and Ruth had travelled to London. She had finally tracked down Fiona Parsons. In the past three months, Ruth had left several phone messages, texts and emails asking Fiona to get in touch. She hadn't responded and so Ruth felt she had no choice but to doorstep her – however ridiculous that might seem.

Ruth's head had been churning around the final words that Fiona had said to her in The Dorchester Hotel room on Park Lane three months earlier. She had seen Sarah three or four years ago. However, no one on the planet had seen Sarah for seven years. Fiona might have been mistaken. But three or four is a long way from seven. Ruth was aware that she was clutching at straws. She had been doing that ever since Sarah had disappeared.

The date was etched in Ruth's mind like the chiselled date on a tombstone - *5th November 2013*. Ruth's partner and love of her life, Sarah Goddard, had disappeared. She had boarded the 8.05am commuter train from Crystal Palace station to Victoria but never arrived. She vanished. No contact, no note, no idea where she had gone. As a copper, Ruth had made sure the CCTV footage from that day had been scoured. Every station on that line had been searched. There had been television appeals and articles in the press. There had been sightings of Sarah from all around the world. Ruth had found herself following women she thought looked like Sarah. But she had simply disappeared off the face of the earth.

Ruth had recently discovered that Sarah had had an affair with a man named Jamie Parsons, who ran the elite Secret Garden sex parties in London. Ruth had been hurt by the revelation that Sarah had cheated on her. In an attempt to discover more about Sarah's clandestine other life, Ruth had attended a Secret Garden sex party, drank too much, and had spent the night with Jamie Parsons' sister, Fiona. It was the following morning that Fiona had made what had seemed a totally innocuous comment about seeing Sarah three or four years earlier.

As Ruth walked briskly along a residential road in Fulham SW6, she pulled a cigarette from her coat pocket. She stopped and lit it. She had found Fiona's address through the PNC - Police National Computer - which was a central database for criminal records and information across the whole UK. She didn't care that this misuse of police information could get her into trouble. She passed the Lillie Langtry pub. If she remembered correctly, Lillie Langtry was a famous Victorian actress or music hall star who slept with a royal.

A few minutes later, Ruth was outside the large, immaculate Victorian house where Fiona lived. A black and white mosaic path led to the front door.

Christ, it's posh around here, she thought to herself. *You wouldn't be getting much change out of £3 million for a house on this road. Where do people get £3 million to spend on a house?*

Ruth took a breath as she headed for the front door. *Come on, Ruth, you can do this.* Of course, she had no idea if Fiona would be in. However, mid-morning on a Sunday was as likely a time for someone to be home as any other.

Ruth rang the bell and took a few steps back. The door was newly painted in a duck egg green, with a shiny, silver letter box, knocker, and doorknob. The brickwork at the front of the house had been painted in a light grey that appeared white in the sunlight. Perfect wooden window boxes of dark pink fuchsias rounded off the illusion of urban sophistication and wealth. If only people knew some of the dark and sinister things that went on behind these facades.

As she waited, Ruth took another step back. She didn't want to startle Fiona. A few seconds later, the sound of locks being turned.

Here we go.

The front door opened. Fiona peered at her and then frowned. She was dressed in a fawn, cashmere sweater and dark, chocolate brown trousers.

'Ruth?'

'Fiona.'

Fiona now had an indignant expression on her face. 'What are you doing here?'

'I have left you several messages.'

'Yes. And me not answering is a sign that I'm not interested in renewing our brief friendship,' Fiona explained in a cross, haughty tone that Ruth had come to expect of the London's upper-middle classes.

'Neither am I. But you didn't leave me much choice but to come here today.'

'Listen, I don't know what the issue is, but turning up on my doorstep is pretty bloody creepy. I'd like you to go. And don't contact me again or I'll get the police involved,' Fiona snapped and went to close the door in her face.

Having already anticipated Fiona's reaction, Ruth pulled out her warrant card and showed it to her. 'I am the police, Fiona. I'm a Detective Inspector in CID.'

It had the desired effect. Fiona stopped in her tracks. She seemed thoroughly confused and pulled the door open again.

'Right. I see. I ...'

'And I do need to speak to you urgently,' Ruth said calmly.

Fiona pushed her blonde, shoulder length hair away from her face and behind her ear. 'Is this part of an investigation or something?'

Ruth wasn't sure where to start.

'Sort of. My partner, my girlfriend, Sarah Goddard, vanished in November 2013. No one has seen her since. She's the woman you identified in the photo on my phone. You told me you saw her three or four years ago. If that's true, then you are the only person on the planet to have seen her since she disappeared.'

Fiona's whole demeanour had changed. 'Oh my God ... I ...'

'I need to find out if you definitely did see her,' Ruth explained.

'I'm so sorry. If I'd known any of that ...' Fiona beckoned Ruth inside. 'Come in, come in.'

The interior of the house was immaculate. Shades of Farrow & Ball, original artwork on the wall, the smell of freshly made coffee. It could have been straight out of a glossy interiors magazine or a Sunday supplement.

'I really am sorry to just turn up like this,' Ruth said. The information that Fiona had given was the first decent lead in Sarah's disappearance, and the anticipation of learning more was making her feel sick with anxiety.

'No, no. It's me that needs to apologise. I just had no idea why you wanted to talk to me,' Fiona said as they went into a gigantic kitchen space with glass doors that led out to a symmetrical, well-tended garden. 'And in my misguided vanity, I assumed you wanted us to sleep together again.'

'Sorry ... I didn't want to go into detail in an email for all sorts of reasons,' Ruth explained.

'Of course. I completely understand. Coffee?'

'Please,' Ruth said as she went and sat on an aluminium stool by the granite breakfast bar. Her stomach felt knotted and uncomfortable. She didn't want Fiona to think that she had been mistaken about seeing Sarah, and for all Ruth's hope to disappear in a flash.

Fiona switched the kettle on. 'Gosh, how awful. I can't believe you've been through all that.'

'That's why I need you to really think about when you actually saw Sarah and who she was with.'

'Of course. I can tell you who she was with right now.'

Ruth felt a little uneasy. 'Why's that?'

Fiona gave her a knowing look. 'Sergei Saratov. It looked like she was part of his entourage.'

I've no bloody idea who that is.

'Why do I know the name Sergei Saratov?' Ruth asked, not wanting to appear completely ignorant.

'Oh you must know. Sergei Saratov, the Russian billionaire, darling. Made all his money from nickel and gold deposits in the Ukraine. Surely you've read about him in the papers?'

Ruth was none the wiser. 'I don't think that I have.'

'Sergei was arrested two years ago. He owns two luxury hotels in Verbier, Switzerland,' Fiona said, as though Ruth should know it. 'The ski resort?'

'I've never been skiing,' Ruth said, realising that although she shared the planet with the rich and privileged, they really did live in a different world.

'The rumours were that the hotels were full of very expensive escorts from all over Europe. And Sergei held parties there for all his friends. He was effectively acting as a pimp. The criminal charges didn't stick but he's disappeared since.'

'And Sarah was with him and his friends?' Ruth asked in disbelief. It didn't make any sense. *What the hell would Sarah be doing with a Russian billionaire?* She was beginning to think it was a mistake.

'Yes, I'm positive. We were in the main bar at The Dorchester.'

'And you spoke to her?'

'Yes. Nothing more than a hello really. I think she asked after Jamie.'

Ruth got out her phone, pulled up the photo of Sarah and showed Fiona again. 'And it was definitely her?'

Fiona nodded. 'Yes, darling. We'd met before after all.'

'And you said this was when?' Ruth asked. Part of her hoped it was after 2013 because that meant Sarah could still be alive. But part of her also hoped it wasn't. It would mean that Sarah had deliberately disappeared and never contacted her. And that would be an incredibly difficult and painful thing to deal with.

'Sorry, it's so hard to remember. I'm trying to think who I was with ... Stephen Moore. That's it. I was having dinner with Stephen Moore, the Conservative MP,' Fiona said, nodding as she remembered.

'Does that narrow it down in terms of dates?'

Fiona thought for a second. 'Actually, yes it does. Stephen had just lost his seat in the general election.'

'Which general election?' Ruth asked, trawling her memory for the years of recent elections. All she knew was that there had been several.

Fiona tapped on her phone. 'Actually, I can give you the exact date ... Here we go. Saturday 9th May 2015. Two days after the election. Does that help?'

Ruth's stomach lurched and rolled.

That's eighteen months after Sarah vanished.

CHAPTER 4

FINN SAT STARING AT the back of the toilet door where there was an advice poster about the early signs of bowel cancer – *Wipe. Look. Flush.* He finished his ham sandwich and took a sip of his Diet Coke. The liquid fizzed in his mouth and the gas went up his nose.

He supposed that some people might think that eating your lunch in the toilet was disgusting. For Finn, it was just a form of self-preservation. He wanted to keep out of the way and avoid interaction with the other workers at the *BDG DIY Warehouse* on the Llancastell Industrial Estate.

Christ! Llancastell, North Wales. What a dump. I can't even pronounce it!

Why they couldn't have relocated him a week ago to a decent city was beyond him. It was too far to walk from the DIY warehouse into the centre of town, so the only other alternative was the staff canteen. He was new, and his accent always gave away the city of his birth. That would mean an awkward conversation about who he was, where he was from, and what he was doing in North Wales. Witness Protection had given him a credible story to tell people, but having to continually tell a pack of lies made him feel uncomfortable.

Finn took a sigh and stared at his chocolate bar. He would save it for his afternoon coffee break when he would return to the same toilet stall and stare at the list of *The first signs of bowel cancer.* He knew them by heart.

Finn's grandfather had died from bowel cancer when he was away at Ockley Cross, the Young Offender Institution he had been sent to in Kent in 2008. Finn had made an appeal to return to Newcastle to go to the funeral but it had been turned down by the Home Office. He had a new identity. There would be reporters watching the funeral to see if he would be there. It was too much of a risk.

Finn loved his paternal grandfather, Bill. He was the only adult in his life that had taken an interest in him and his brother Steven. He would take them fishing at Fontburn Reservoir where they tried to catch rainbow trout. He remembered Steven catching one that grandad Bill had said was over eighteen inches long. Finn could still see the look of sheer joy on Steven's face that day.

Finn placed his lunchbox into his small rucksack and zipped it shut. He then flushed the toilet in case anyone suspected that he had just been sitting in there eating his lunch for the past twenty minutes. He unlocked the door and was relieved to see that the other cubicles were empty. Going out to his locker, Finn put the rucksack away. As he closed it he saw Matty, the store's assistant manager. Finn already had his number. Matty was the kind of over-friendly person who needs to be liked by everyone and anyone. In short, a dickhead.

Matty came over and patted him on the shoulder. 'There he is. I was looking for you in the canteen, mate.'

Please don't touch me. And why are you calling me mate already?

'I went outside for a ciggie,' Finn explained.

Matty chortled, 'And a bit of fresh air, eh? Never asked you - you've got a Geordie accent, haven't you?'

Great. Here we go.

This was just the type of conversation Finn was desperate to avoid. Even though he hadn't been on Tyneside for over a decade, there was still more than a noticeable trace of the accent.

'Aye, that's right,' Finn said and then gestured to the door. 'Better get back.'

'Black and white, or red and white?' Matty asked. He was referring to Newcastle United and Sunderland football teams who were bitter rivals.

'Oh, I'm a Geordie not a Mackem,' Finn replied. Mackem was the slang for someone who came from Sunderland. Finn thought it had something to do with all the ship building they used to do in Sunderland, but he couldn't remember the derivation exactly. To mix up a Mackem with a Geordie and vice versa was incredibly insulting.

'Oh right. Newcastle then,' Matty said, keen to let Finn know that he knew the difference. 'Used to love watching Shearer play, even though I support Liverpool.'

Jesus. Just let me get back to work, will you?

'Yeah. I'll see you later, eh?'

'Holly wants to see you.' Holly was the store manager and Finn couldn't help but feel anxious about why she wanted to speak to him.

'Don't worry mate. There's some new girl started and she wants you to show her around seeing you've just done all the health and safety bollocks yourself,' Matty reassured him.

'Although if you ask me, I think Holly wants to get into your pants.'

Finn felt embarrassed as Matty chuckled and walked away into the toilets.

He put his green work baseball cap back on. His thick, shaggy hair made it feel tight and uncomfortable on his head. *Bloody thing!* He went out through the double doors into the giant warehouse store.

'Finn, can I borrow you for second?' a voice asked. It was Holly, who seemed to believe that running a DIY store was on a par with running a multinational company such as Microsoft. Her dark hair had been cut into a short bob that made her look a lot older than she was. Her face was shiny, plump and rosy red.

Finn then noticed the girl standing next to Holly. She was in her late teens, with long, blonde, curly hair and a nose-ring.

She's nice. Lovely blue eyes, Finn thought before reminding himself that he was keeping a low profile.

'Finn, this is Kat. It's her first day and I thought you could show her the ropes?' Holly said.

'Hiya,' Kat said quietly.

Finn forced a half smile. He couldn't work out if she was just nervous.

'Right. I'll leave you two to it then. Don't worry, Kat. Finn doesn't bite, or at least I don't think he does,' Holly laughed as she turned to go.

GRABBING A BISCUIT and a strong coffee, DS Nick Evans of Llancastell CID walked to the other side of the community centre. The room was brightly lit, with rows of people of all ages sitting talking and laughing with one another. On the wall hung two long scrolls – *The 12 Steps* and *The 12 Traditions.*

It was his usual mid-week meeting of Alcoholics Anonymous and this is where he felt at home. He said a few hellos, shook a few hands, and sat down.

Glancing over at the two large padded chairs at the front of the room, he saw Mary who was chairing the meeting. Mary was about thirty years sober. She gave him a smile and a little wave. In the other chair was Nick's partner Amanda. She seemed nervous. He didn't blame her. It was her first ever 'main share' at an AA meeting and he knew it had been making her anxious all week. He caught her eye and gave her a supportive wink. He remembered his first main share and how he had dried up after about fifteen minutes, forgetting all the things that he had wanted, and planned, to say. It didn't matter. There was no judgement in these meetings.

He watched Amanda take a deep breath and sit back, and he saw her with fresh eyes. She really was beautiful. Her big brown eyes, rosebud lips, and delicate features. The woman he had fallen in love with a couple of years ago. The mother of their beautiful daughter, Megan.

'Good evening everyone. My name's Amanda and I'm an alcoholic,' she said calmly.

'Hi Amanda,' everyone responded.

'Even though I'm nervous as this is my first ever main share, it's really good to be here. When I first came into the rooms, I was a complete mess. I sat at the back, terrified. And I cried. And I never, ever thought that I could stay sober long enough to be sitting up here, talking to you. So, that's a miracle, and I'm incredibly grateful.'

Nick smiled to himself and relaxed now she had started. It was so lovely to see her up there. And he was incredibly proud of her.

For the next half an hour, Amanda continued her share. She talked of having an alcoholic father and having a difficult childhood. How she drank to anaesthetise her crushing insecurity and self-loathing. And finally, how she had got sober and how she was trying to stay sober.

Towards the end of the meeting, Nick found himself drifting away and contemplating his own sobriety. He had no idea how it had happened. Four years ago, he couldn't go even a few hours without a drink. How had he got through the doors of AA and managed to stay there? There were thousands that didn't. He had seen them come and go. Some were dead, some insane, and some were in jail. Of course, there were those that managed to stay sober, but Nick didn't know how they did it without any support. Someone had told him that for every member of AA in the UK, there were a hundred alcoholics who were out there drinking themselves into an early grave and destroying other lives in the process. And with that thought, Nick knew how lucky he was.

As the meeting ended, Nick went and hugged Amanda, congratulating her on a brilliant first share. They walked hand in hand to the car.

Before they got in, Nick took Amanda in his arms. 'I'm so proud of you.' He kissed her and pulled her closer to him.

'Thanks,' Amanda said. She kissed him back lightly and moved away from him. It wasn't the first time in recent months that she had seemed uncomfortable when she was close to him. Nick was worried that she had become a little distant. In fact, they had hardly made love in recent months and he wasn't sure what to do. He knew he needed to be patient. Amanda had suffered with severe post-partem depression after the birth and it had taken her a long time to seem back to her old self. But now Nick was starting to question whether there was something more concerning afoot.

He frowned. 'You okay?'

Amanda smiled as she went around the car to the passenger door. 'Of course. I'm just exhausted. All that nervous energy.'

Nick got into the car, clicked in the seatbelt and put on the radio. *Wish I Didn't Miss You* by Angie Stone was playing.

Nick grinned. 'Hey, it's our song.' In the early days of their romance, they'd had sex to this song in the car.

Amanda raised an eyebrow. 'Don't get any funny ideas, buster. I want to go home, have a cup of tea, and make sure Megan is okay.'

'It's all right, I've stopped getting funny ideas,' Nick said under his breath.

CHAPTER 5

FINN HAD DECIDED TO go for one pint in The Crown pub on the way home from work. He made a mental note to make sure that it really was just one pint. The pub was showing Champions League football on various screens dotted around the walls. He couldn't remember if it was Chelsea or Liverpool playing. He didn't really mind. Anything was going to be better than sitting in his dreary bedsit.

He sat on a padded stool at the far end of the bar. He drew his finger down the condensation on his pint glass and felt a little sorry for himself. The pub was old fashioned and had dark red threadbare carpets that looked as if they'd been there since the 80s. The sudden noise of someone winning money on the fruit machine made him flinch. A decade at Ockley Cross had taught Finn to live on his nerves. It made him permanently jumpy. Intimidation and violence on a daily basis. He had been assaulted and hospitalised three times while he was there. No one knew who he was but there were rumours about his identity. That meant there was always some nutter willing to have a pop at him to bolster their reputation. The last time, Finn had been kicked unconscious and nearly died from internal bleeding.

After a few years, Finn would befriend the new inmates, especially the ones who had never been inside before and were obviously terrified. He would take them under his wing and explain the unwritten rules of a Young Offender Institution. Then he would show them where to buy chocolate and sweets, or get credits for the tearful phone calls home. Eventually the screws came to Finn and asked him to keep an eye on any of the new prisoners that seemed '... a bit wobbly ...'.

'Hello Finn,' said a voice that broke his train of thought.

It was Kat, the new girl from work.

'Oh, hi. Kat isn't it?' Finn asked, even though he knew it was. He already felt a bit awkward in her presence.

'Drinking on your own?'

Oh god, this is embarrassing.

Finn gestured to his drink. 'Yeah. Quick pint on the way home.'

'I'm with my mate Liv. She's over there,' Kat said in a lively voice. 'You gonna buy us a drink then?'

'I don't know, am I?' Finn said with a bemused smile.

She's very different to how she was in work, he thought to himself.

Kat frowned at him. 'You've got a funny accent, haven't you?'

'Geordie.' Finn could see that Kat didn't know what that meant. 'I'm from Newcastle.'

'Oh yeah, like Ant and Dec. What are you doing in Llancastell?'

'Long story. What do you and your mate want to drink?' he asked. He felt a little tingle of excitement. Maybe he could spend the evening getting drunk with them? Then he remembered that he needed to be careful. The last time he went on a bender he had mouthed off about who he really was. Even though no one had believed him it wasn't long before a journalist, and then the local police, had begun to snoop around.

'Two Bacardi Breezers, ta. I was gonna get me and Liv shots. D'you wanna shot?'

Finn shrugged. 'Aye. Why not, eh?'

Kat laughed and mocked his accent. 'Aye. Why not, eh?'

Finn raised an eyebrow. 'That's a pretty good Geordie accent.'

'Thanks. I'm dead good at accents,' Kat said as she opened her purse. Finn caught sight of a photo of a little boy inside.

'Who is this little fella then? Your son?' Finn asked.

Kat seemed offended. 'No way! That's my little brother Henry when he was a baby. Cute, isn't he?'

'Sorry ... Aye, looks like a right little smasher,' Finn said with a smile.

'You've got really nice eyes, you know that? ... I mean kind eyes, you know.'

Finn could feel himself starting to blush.

Bloody hell, she's very direct.

'Thanks. You're not so bad yourself,' Finn said.

Kat giggled. 'Oh, I didn't mean it like that. You gonna come and sit with us, or stay here like some Billy No Mates?'

For a moment, they looked at each other.

'Yeah, that sounds like a laugh.' Finn tried to get the attention of the barman.

IT WAS GONE EIGHT O'CLOCK in the evening when Ruth finished up her paperwork in the Llancastell CID office. She had found it difficult to concentrate on anything since Fiona had confirmed that she had seen Sarah in 2015.

Ruth took her phone to find the number for Stephen Flaherty, the case officer from the Met regarding Sarah's disappearance. Stephen was a kind and gentle man who had been a huge support at the time of Sarah's disappearance. For the next few years, they had contacted each other once or twice a year just to check in. Most of the time, Stephen had little to report except that Sarah was still missing and her case file was still open.

More recently there had been some significant developments. Missing persons officers from the Met had used CCTV at Victoria station and eye-witness statements to identify a German banker, Jurgen Kessler, who was seen by various passengers talking to Sarah on that train. He was probably the last person seen talking to her. The case took a darker turn when Berlin police linked Kessler to the murder of two young women in the city a couple of years ago. Kessler had vanished but had then been traced re-entering the UK on a false passport.

The phone rang and then Ruth heard Stephen's calm, quiet voice. 'Hello, Ruth. How are you doing?'

'I'm okay. You in the middle of something?' she asked, aware that it was getting late.

'No, no. Spot of gardening. How can I help?'

'I'm trying not to get carried away, but I think I have a significant lead on Sarah's case.'

'Okay. Let me just go into the house ... What have you got?'

'Jamie Parsons has a sister called Fiona. She's a regular at the Secret Garden parties. I went to see her on Sunday in London. She is convinced that she saw Sarah in 2015,' Ruth said, feeling her pulse quicken even as she said the words.

There were a few seconds of silence.

'Really? Do you believe her?' Stephen asked.

'I would have been sceptical, but she knows for certain that she was in The Dorchester Hotel in London with a Tory MP who had lost his seat in the 2015 General Election two days previously. It's so specific to that date that I think there might be something in it.'

'Right. That is very specific. If she's right, that's the most significant lead we've had in seven years,' Stephen said, still sounding a little incredulous.

'Apparently, Sarah was with some Russian oligarch called Sergei Saratov.'

'Saratov?'

'You know him?'

'He was on the Met's radar for years,' Stephen explained.

'What for?'

'Soliciting, sex trafficking, you name it. From what I hear, Saratov was going to be served up like a Russian Jeffrey Epstein.'

'What happened?' Ruth asked, her mind already putting more pieces of the jigsaw together.

'Never enough evidence to bring charges. Then he disappeared.'

'What do you mean?'

'He vanished. I guess if you're a billionaire, you can disappear relatively easily. There was a rumour that he was living in Paris under a new identity but that's never been substantiated.'

'Is there anything we can do?'

'Leave it with me, Ruth. I'll have a dig around and I'll get back to you.'

CHAPTER 6

NOW NICELY DRUNK, FINN tripped a little on the kerb as he and Kat made their way back through Llancastell. Kat roared with laughter as if this was the funniest thing she had ever witnessed. Feeling a little stupid, Finn reached over to take a chip from the bag they were sharing.

'Oi, greedy,' Kat said as she flicked his hand away with a grin.

'I'm starving man,' Finn said as he pushed the lukewarm chip into his mouth. It had been drowned in vinegar and took him back to a day when his grandad had taken him to Whitley Bay on the coast. He couldn't have been much older than five or six, but the redolent smell and taste took him straight back there.

'I'm starving man,' Kat said, mimicking his Geordie accent with a giggle.

'Where are we going?' Finn asked, looking around. They were in the centre of Llancastell and now he was lost.

'We can't go back to mine. I live with my mum and my stepdad. They'd go mental,' Kat said.

'Do you not get on then?'

'My stepdad is a fucking creep. I hate him. Mum's all right. Where do you live?'

Finn started to feel a little anxious as he pointed towards the cathedral. He was pretty sure it was that way. 'I think it's down here.'

Kat reached out and took him by the hand. 'Come on then!'

They weaved through the side streets, hand in hand, laughing and giggling. Kat started to sing *Salute* by Little Mix at the top of her voice. Finn didn't know the words and just watched her. As she smiled and sang, he realised how much he liked her. And even though he was drunk, Finn was feeling very uneasy.

What are we going to do when we get back to my room? he wondered.

With the exception of a drunken snog in a club in Norwich, Finn had no experience with girls. He had spent his entire adolescence in a Young Offender Institution with nearly a thousand other teenage boys and young men. Of course, there had been relationships between inmates, but that wasn't his thing.

I actually feel sick with nerves. I really fancy her.

Kat stopped and pulled Finn under the amber glow of a streetlamp. She turned to face him with a smile.

'Aren't you going to try to kiss me tonight?' she asked.

'I ... I don't know,' Finn said, feeling his stomach lurch.

'Oh well, that's bloody nice,' Kat said with mock offence. Then she leaned up and kissed him on the mouth. It was soft at first and then more intense.

Wow. That was amazing!

Finn looked at her. In the amber light she was beautiful. Her big eyes glistened as she gazed back at him.

Kat giggled and pulled him again by the hand as she skipped down the road.

Ten minutes later they were in Finn's bedsit. It was clean and tidy. A decade inside had made an immaculate room second nature.

However, Finn was starting to go into a panic. He was trying to avoid the inevitable question – *are we going to have sex?* Maybe he could find an excuse.

'This is nice,' Kat said as she twirled around the room.

What the hell am I doing here? I'm so scared my stomach actually hurts.

'It's all right,' Finn said, but his mind was elsewhere. He couldn't concentrate.

What if she can tell that I'm a virgin? What if I get it all wrong? What if she thinks I'm an idiot?

Kat took Finn by the hand and pulled him over to the bed where they both laid down. They gazed at each other and then began to kiss. Soft and urgent. Then with tongues and open mouths. Lost in the moment and the passion.

Kat took off her top revealing just a bra. She reached over and pulled Finn's t-shirt up over his head and dropped it on the floor.

Finn was starting to forget all his fears.

Maybe this is going to be okay? Maybe I can do this?

As Kat ran her hands across his back, he felt her hand stop and hesitate.

Bloody hell. My scars!

Kat frowned. 'Are those scars?'

Finn nodded. He wasn't embarrassed about them, but he was worried that they were a sign of where he had spent his years as a teenager.

Kat traced a delicate finger over the three deep scars across the middle of his back which were over a foot long. Wayne Bentley had managed to smuggle a Stanley knife out of the DT building and went for Finn in the canteen. He had been in hospital for a week.

Finn shrugged. 'It's nothing. I was in a fight years ago.'

'Poor you,' Kat said as she kissed him again. She reached behind and unclipped her bra.

Finn began to kiss her breasts and her nipples like he had seen in the porn films he had watched. Kat moaned with pleasure.

'I want you, Finn. I want you inside me,' she whispered into his ear.

Finn moved up, kissing her neck and her ear.

He felt her hand reach down to his trousers. She began to unzip them and reach inside.

From nowhere, Finn felt a wave of anxiety sweep over him. He couldn't help it. He didn't know what to do. What did she mean by that? Well, he knew what she meant, but what was he supposed to do? Thoughts raced round his head and he began to shake as his stomach clenched in a tight ball.

I don't think I can do this!

Kat stopped kissing him and pulled away, looking at him quizzically. 'Are you all right?'

Finn took a deep breath and shook his head. The fear that had so powerfully invaded his body was overwhelming him.

'Yeah, ... erm .... just give us a minute,' Finn murmured. He couldn't look at her.

Kat reached into her purse. 'It's okay. I've got a condom in my purse. I'm not that stupid.'

'It's not that. I just ...' Finn said as he glanced away from her and sat up on the bed trying to breathe. He was having some kind of panic attack.

'What's wrong?' she asked, but now her tone was verging on annoyance.

'Sorry. It's ... not you. I ... don't know what I'm doing. You know?' Finn stammered. All he knew was that he wanted to be on his own. He wanted to hide under the duvet and lie in the secure darkness of the room. The anxiety was just too much.

Kat moved away. 'I thought we were having a good time?'

'I was. I am ... I just haven't ... before ...,' Finn said, and then instantly regretted it.

'Haven't what?' Kat asked with a look of disbelief on her face. 'You haven't had sex before?'

Her comment hung in the air for a second.

Finn didn't say anything. What was there to say?

'Oh my God! You're a virgin. You can't be!' Kat said with a nervous giggle.

Finn put his head in his hands as his anxiety was replaced with utter rage.

'I want you to go,' he growled.

'It doesn't matter. Honest,' Kat said still giggling. 'I don't mind. Sorry.'

Finn could feel that he was on the verge of exploding. 'I want you to go now, please.'

'I didn't mean to laugh. It's just that it's not like you're fourteen is it?'

Finn stood up and clenched his fists. He wanted to hurt her. Lash out and cause her pain.

'GET OUT!' he thundered.

Kat jumped back on the bed and grabbed her bra and top, utterly terrified. She didn't even bother to put them on, she simply thrust her head in her top, chucked the bra into her bag, and headed for the door. 'Jesus!'

'Just go!'

'You're a fucking weirdo!' Kat shouted at him.

She slammed the door shut.

Finn took a deep breath and closed his eyes, tears running down his sallow cheeks.

CHAPTER 7

IT WAS GETTING LATE by the time Nick and Ruth drove out of Llancastell police station and started to make their way home for the night. Nick clicked on the stereo and *Roll With It* by Oasis was playing. Much to Ruth's annoyance, he turned the sound up. He loved the old Oasis songs.

Ruth rolled her eyes. 'Really?'

Nick pulled a face. 'Oasis? This is great stuff.'

'It sounds like Status Quo!'

'No, it doesn't.'

Ruth turned the volume down a bit. 'If you say so. I never got into the whole Britpop thing.'

'I thought that everyone in London like Blur. And everyone up North liked Oasis?'

'That was a bit of a myth in the media in about 1996. Everyone I knew was into New York house music,' Ruth explained. 'Christ, how old were you in 1996?'

Nick thought for a second. 'Fourteen.'

Ruth laughed. 'Bloody hell. Fourteen. Barely out of nappies.'

'Hey, I lost my virginity when I was fourteen, thank you very much!'

Ruth pulled a face. 'Which is far more information than I required.'

Nick looked over at Ruth and raised an eyebrow with a smirk. 'So, when ...'

Ruth interrupted him. 'I'm not telling you that, so don't even bloody ask.'

Nick smiled to himself as they turned onto the A525 towards Bangor-on-Dee. The road was completely empty, and they sat for a few minutes in a comfortable silence.

Nick watched as Ruth took a cigarette out, lit it, and buzzed down the window. She looked deep in thought. She'd been distracted for the past month or so, but even more so in the past few days.

'You okay?'

Ruth didn't respond for a second and then said, 'Yeah. Fine.'

That wasn't convincing.

'You still haven't brought me up to speed with what happened in London,' Nick said when the silence had got too much for him.

'It's a long story.'

'Okay.'

'I'll tell you about it tomorrow.'

Nick could see how tired she was. 'No problem, boss.'

He also knew how much Sarah's disappearance took out of her. Ruth's tireless quest to find out what had happened to her partner was understandable – but it was also sometimes painful to watch. He didn't know how she did it sometimes. He also wondered what he would have done in the same position.

Catching sight of a blue light in the rear view mirror, Nick was brought back to reality. He slowed the car down and turned to see a uniformed patrol car thundering past them. The car then turned down a narrow country lane.

Ruth shot Nick a look. 'Shall we have a quick look?' she asked.

Nick pressed down on the accelerator. 'Just in case.'

He was hoping that it was nothing serious so he could go home, see Amanda and his baby daughter Megan, and roll into bed. He was knackered. However much everyone had warned him, nothing could have prepared him for the over-whelming tiredness that came with a new baby. Some days he felt like he was wading through thick soup.

Indicating right, Nick followed the route the patrol car had taken. He wasn't sure he had ever been down here before, which was rare in the Llancastell area. The lane was narrow and pitch black. As they went around a tight corner, he could see a row of small cottages set back from the lane. The patrol car's rotating blue lights were strobing across the outside of the first cottage.

Nick parked up and looked over to see what was going on. Officers were already talking to three adults who were all standing on the drive. Whatever had happened, it seemed to have calmed down.

Could be a domestic or a dispute with a neighbour, he thought. He had been to lots of incidents like that when he was in uniform. Often, he felt like a prefect on a school playground as two idiots shouted insults at each other. It was one of the reasons he had made the move to CID. Disputes over the height of a fence or a late-night party didn't do it for him.

'Wanna stop?' Ruth asked.

Maybe we should let the uniformed officers get on with their job?

He knew there was nothing worse for a uniformed officer than some CID detective wading into something they already had in hand and waving around their tackle like Billy Big Bollocks.

Nick peered over at a stocky man, who had registered their arrival, and realised it was an old school friend. 'That's Ben Williams. He was in my class at school. Funny bloke. The roughest prop forward I ever played against.' Except Ben now sported a bushy beard and an extra four stone, but it was definitely him. 'Probably should go and have a word.'

Despite his stocky build, Nick remembered sharing a huge lunchtime spliff with Ben Williams in the sixth form, only for Ben to throw up and pass out for a few seconds in A-level History. He never lived it down and was known as Whitey until they left school.

Nick got out of the car and Ruth followed him down the drive to the small workers' cottage. It was painted white, with a black slate roof.

He could immediately hear raised voices.

Taking out his warrant card, Nick approached the uniformed officer. 'Everything all right, constable?'

The officer came over. 'The father was late bringing the son back home. The stepdad said something and there was some kind of altercation.'

'Thanks,' Nick said, spotting that Ruth had gone over to talk to a woman who he recognised as Natalie, Ben Williams' ex. He had been an usher at their wedding and had been sorry to learn of their divorce a few years ago.

Ben frowned as he approached. 'Nick? Is that you?'

'Hi Ben. You okay?' Nick said quietly. Over on the garden wall, Nick spotted a man sitting in the shadows smoking a cigarette.

'Not really. I was dropping Henry back to Nat when that dickhead had a pop at me. So, I gave him some back. That's all. Then she goes and calls your lot, stupid cow,' Ben growled. He was clearly still very wound up.

'Yeah, well let's calm it down mate, and less of the name calling. What's the issue?' Nick asked.

'I was late back. My phone ran out of charge,' Ben explained. 'I said I was sorry.'

'How late?' Nick asked.

'Two hours. And I'm never late when I have him. And she's got Henry all bloody week so what's the problem?'

'How old is Henry?'

'Six,' Ben said.

'Two hours is a long time, mate. She was probably worried.'

'I know. I apologised. And then that twat waded in,' Ben said, raising his voice again and glaring over at the man perched on the wall. 'It's none of his fucking business.'

Nick put a pacifying arm on his shoulder. 'Hey, that's not gonna help anyone is it? Did you hit him?'

'No, of course not. We pushed each other and he grabbed my jacket. Handbags. It was nothing,' Ben explained. 'But he's hit Henry before and that's not okay.'

'Henry is your son?' Nick asked to clarify. He and Ben had lost touch before Nick knew he had a son.

'Yeah. And my daughter Kat hates the stepdad's guts and calls him a paedo. He's hit her before. When I ask her if he's ever done anything weird like, she says no. But she wants to come and live with me.'

Nick did remember Kat when she was born. He had been over to see her when she was a baby. By that calculation, she had to be eighteen or nineteen.

'Have you brought this up with Nat?' Nick asked.

'Yeah, but she blames the kids. Says they're rude to him.'

'Have you given these officers a statement yet?'

'No ... Look I've apologised. But I don't want that paedo telling my son it's okay to call him 'Dad'. Otherwise, there will be a problem,' Ben said looking over again at the man taking a drag of a cigarette and looking at the ground.

'Don't be making any threats, eh Ben?' Nick turned and gestured. 'Who's the stepdad?'

'Crispin ... Crispin Neal,' Ben said under his breath. 'He's a prick.'

That name rings a bell, Nick thought to himself, but he couldn't place why.

'Listen. Make a statement, go home and let the dust settle, mate. We don't want to be coming back here, okay?' Nick said. 'And you don't want Henry to witness all this stuff, do you? Not at his age.'

Nick had witnessed domestic violence when he was Henry's age. His father had been a nasty drunk. He remembered how terrifying it had been.

'No, I know. Of course not.' Ben nodded a little sheepishly. 'Sorry.'

Ruth approached, gave Nick a nod, as if to ask, 'We all good?' and he followed her back to the car, leaving the uniformed officers to take the statements and put the incident on the PNC (police national computer).

Nick got into the car and then it dawned on him.

Crispin Bell.

'You okay?' Ruth asked.

Nick pointed to the figure who was still sitting on the wall. 'The stepdad over there is a man called Crispin Bell.'

'You know him?'

'I'm ninety-nine percent sure that we nicked him a couple of years ago for having indecent images on his computer. Suspended sentence but he definitely went on the Sex Offenders Register,' Nick said.

CHAPTER 8

BY THE TIME FINN ARRIVED at work the following morning, he had stomach cramps. He was anxious at the thought of seeing Kat and had contemplated phoning in sick. But what was the point? He would have to see her eventually. He couldn't afford to lose a job over it. What would Michael say?

As he was putting his rucksack into his locker, he saw Matty coming towards him. His heart sank.

Oh great. Just what I need.

'Finn-meister!' Matty said in an annoying, joyful bellow. *Please fuck off.*

Finn wasn't in the mood to chat to anyone.

Matty mimed drinking a pint. 'Some of the boys from work are going to The Crown for a few beers and a pool tournament tonight. I said you'd be up for it.'

Finn pulled a face. 'Erm, no. Not really my thing.' He wanted to lock himself away for the next few days.

'Come on. It'll be a right laugh. Unless you've got a better offer?' Matty said, tapping his nose.

'No, it's not that ...'

Matty clapped him on the back. 'Little bird told me you were in The Crown last night with Kat? You're a fast worker, mate. Fair play.'

'I'd better get to work.'

'Did you shag her, then?'

Finn reacted and shoved his arm away. 'Just fuck off, Matty!'

Any more of his shit and I'm gonna deck this fucker!

'Only a bloody joke, mate. Chill.' Matty protested.

'Don't give up your fucking day job, eh?' Finn had to get away before he really lost his temper. If he got angry, he knew from past experiences that he might do something he'd later regret.

Striding past the lockers, he tied the stupid green *BDG DIY Warehouse* apron behind his back.

He gritted his teeth. *I wish everyone would leave me alone,* he thought.

Turning into the paint aisle, he saw Kat pricing up paint brushes. He froze. Had she seen him? She seemed preoccupied. Maybe she hadn't spotted him and he could escape. He turned and began to walk away towards the next aisle.

'Is that it then Finn?' said a voice. 'You just going to ignore me?'

It was Kat. She sounded annoyed.

Shit!

Finn just stopped. His brain was yelling for him to just carry on walking and ignore her. *Just go.* But there was also a part of him that wanted to explain. He didn't want her to think he was some kind of freak. He'd had enough of feeling so alone. He and Kat had made a connection and he had probably ruined that forever. Maybe he could claw something back.

He took a deep breath, turned, and walked slowly towards her.

'Look ... I'm ... really sorry about what happened last night,' he said under his breath.

Kat looked directly at him for a second. 'You made me feel like a right twat.'

'Sorry. I didn't mean to,' he mumbled, hoping the ground would open up and swallow him.

There were a few awkward seconds. Finn noticed some purple bruising around her right eye.

'What happened to your eye?' he asked.

Kat looked away. 'It's nothing.'

'It's not nothing.' Finn knew a black eye when he saw one.

'I walked into a cupboard in the kitchen.'

That's bollocks, if ever I heard it.

'Well, I know that's definitely not true,' he said quietly.

Kat shrugged defensively. 'What do you care?'

'Was it your stepdad?'

'None of your business.'

'Sorry.'

Kat bit her lip and didn't say anything for a few seconds. 'Haven't you got work to do?'

Finn frowned at her. 'He can't do that to you, you know. It's not right.'

'I know. But there's not much I can do about it,' she said defiantly.

I could do something about it, he thought.

Finn gestured behind him, 'I'd better get on, otherwise I'll get on the wrong side of jolly Holly eh?'

Kat gave him a meaningful look. 'Sorry ... I shouldn't have laughed at you.'

Finn didn't know what she was talking about. 'Sorry? I ...'

'Last night ... I shouldn't have laughed at you.'

'Doesn't matter. It's hard for me to explain, that's all.'

'Yeah, well I didn't want us to ignore each other at work,' Kat said with a shrug.

'Yeah. I'd better go,' Finn said, indicating another part of the store.

'Okay. I'll see you around then.' Kat went back to pricing up the brushes.

Finn turned and walked away.

FINN TOOK THE LAST of his chips, stuffed them in his mouth, and chucked the packet in the bin. He stopped and peered into the window of a jewellery shop. He was trying to kill time before he returned to his bedsit. The lights sparkled off the jewels and metals making them look exquisite. He gazed along the row of expensive watches. The Omega Seamaster caught his eye, and then he saw the price tag - £2,999.

Bloody hell! How does anyone ever have so much money that they can pay three grand for a watch? he wondered. *How is it fair that people have that much money?*

He carefully examined the glass, and imagined taking a hammer to it and grabbing everything in the window. Maybe the glass was reinforced to stop people doing that. Finn had known a couple of boys in Ockley Cross who were part of a South London moped gang. They bragged about going into jewellers in upmarket parts of London such as Kensington.

While one of them held up the staff with a handgun, the other would smash the cabinets with a hammer and shove everything into a rucksack. They claimed each raid took them less than five minutes. Then they would jump onto their moped and disappear into London's heavy traffic.

Imagine having the balls to do that, Finn thought.

As he crossed over the road, he saw Kat standing at Llancastell Bus Station further up the pavement completely engrossed in her phone.

Shall I go and say hello? Or is that a bit creepy?

Glancing to his left, Finn got closer. He noticed a bus that was about to arrive at the bus stop, and its enormous black wing mirror at head height.

That's going to hit Kat in the head, he thought.

Moving quickly, he took Kat by the shoulders and dragged her back by a couple of feet.

'What the bloody hell are you doing?' she yelled in shock.

'Sorry.'

Kat was trying to work out what had just happened. 'Finn? What the fuck are you playing at?'

'The bus was going to hit you,' he said, gesturing towards the yellow bus that was now stationary. 'Sorry...'

Kat pulled a face. 'No, it wasn't.'

'The wing mirror. It was going to hit your head. Seriously,' he said, hoping to hell that she believed him.

Kat seemed to realise that he was telling the truth. 'Bloody hell.'

'Yeah. I didn't mean to scare you.'

'Scare me? You saved my bloody life, you nob!' she said, giving him a playful slap on the arm.

'I was more worried about the damage your head would do to the bus,' Finn joked.

'Cheeky bastard.'

The doors of the bus opened, and a couple of passengers stepped on.

'Where are you going?' Finn asked.

Kat fished into her purse for change. 'Home.'

'What about your stepdad?'

She shrugged. 'I'll lock my door.'

'He'd better not hurt you again.'

Kat smiled. 'Why, what are you gonna do about it?'

Finn hesitated – he didn't know what to say. He knew he didn't want anyone to hurt her.

He watched as she stepped onto the bus and showed the driver a ten pound note. 'I've only got this.'

I really like her, Finn thought.

'Sorry. I've got no change,' the driver sneered, rolling his eyes. 'You'll have to go and get some.'

What a dickhead.

'But I'll miss this bus.' Kat looked at Finn. 'Can you lend me some change, Finn, otherwise it's another hour?'

Finn delved into his pocket and then shrugged – he didn't have any.

'Either you give me the right change, or you have to get off the bus,' the driver growled.

He's starting to really piss me off!

Finn glared at him and in a raised voice said, 'She's got the money to pay for it. It's not her fault you haven't got any change.'

'You can't speak to me like that,' the bus driver said pompously.

Kat held up her hand. 'It's all right, Finn. I'll just have to wait for the next one.'

Finn stepped onto the bus. He was getting angry. 'No, it's not all right.'

'I want you two off my bus right now or there'll be trouble!' the bus driver snapped.

Finn fixed the driver in his glare. 'Don't be a dickhead. Just let her on the bus.'

'Right, that's it,' the bus driver said as he opened the driver's door. 'Threatening and insulting behaviour. I don't have to put up with that from people like you. I'm getting the inspector.'

Finn and Kat watched as he stormed off towards the bus station ticket office.

Kat pulled a face and giggled. 'Oh dear, I think you've really pissed him off.'

'Fuck him. I won't let anyone talk to you like that.'

He went over to the vacant driver's cab, leant in, and saw a yellow button marked *Doors*. He pressed it, and with a whoosh of compressed air the doors closed.

Am I really going to do this? he wondered. However, now that the red mist had descended, he wanted to make the bus driver's life a misery.

Kat laughed. 'What the hell are you doing, Finn?'

Finn clicked open the inner door, sat in the driver's seat, and gripped the enormous steering wheel with a grin. 'Fancy a lift home?'

Kat put her hand to her mouth and chuckled. 'Oh my God, Finn. You are totally mental!'

'Woohoo! All aboard Finn's crazy bus!' he yelled. 'Where are we going?'

'What do you mean?'

'I'm taking you home. I'm not joking,' he said as he started the ignition.

'You can't do that!'

'Why not? Where are we going?'

Kat chortled, leant down and pointed. 'Straight down the high street and left at the end.'

Finn was now full of adrenaline – he felt amazing.

I'll show that fucking driver!

He pushed down the accelerator gently and the huge diesel engine reverberated. He could feel the chair shaking with the rhythmic vibrations of the seven-litre engine below him.

Bloody hell! Let's do this!

'Next stop, Kat's house!' he yelled. This was the type of hot-headed behaviour that usually got him into trouble. But right at that moment, he just didn't care.

Kat sat down on the seat nearest to the driver with a broad smile. A female pensioner peered over at her with a frown.

'Does he know what he's doing?' she asked.

Kat shrugged. 'I don't know yet, but we'll soon find out. I'd hold on, if I were you though.'

CHAPTER 9

IT WAS LATE AFTERNOON by the time Ruth and Nick had discovered that Crispin Neal was definitely on the Sex Offenders Register. Nick had suggested that he and Ruth drive out to the address they had visited the night before. They needed to flag up Neal's prior conviction to Natalie.

As they reached the outskirts of Llancastell, Ruth lowered the car window and gazed at the rolling countryside. They were heading east from the town towards the English borders. Throughout the day, the golden rays of brilliant sunshine had created a baking heat. Staring out at the fields, she marvelled at how they had transformed from swathes of rutted mud to rolling fields of every green hue you could imagine. It never ceased to amaze her how the seasons changed the scenery. As she gazed at a distant hill, the countryside looked like a ruffled quilt, as the landscape rose and fell in soft waves.

Taking out a cigarette, she lit it and took a deep drag. *That's better.* She took all this for granted. But she only had to remember the dark, stinking, crack-infested estates of South London to know that her move to North Wales had been a positive one. For a moment, her mind went to Sian and she instantly felt the pain that went with that thought. Taking a deep breath, she knew she needed to bury herself in work and keep occupied.

Opening the file on Crispin Neal, she flicked through the printout Nick had taken from the PNC.

Ruth gestured to the file. 'He got a two-year sentence for the possession of Category B images. He served a year.'

'First offence?'

'He'd got previous for assaulting an ex-partner. She'd had to get a restraining order in 2017. Then GBH for which he got a suspended sentence.'

Nick shook his head. 'What the hell is Nat doing with someone like him?'

'You know the mother well?' Ruth asked. She wasn't aware of how friendly Nick and Ben Williams had been.

'I went to Ben and Nat's wedding. I went out with her sister for a bit when we were kids. Nat has always been a bit mad, but this Crispin Neal sounds vile.'

'You said Ben mentioned his daughter?'

'Yeah, Kat. She's got to be about nineteen now. Lovely girl, from what I can remember. Ben said that she wants to go and live with him because she can't stand Neal.'

'Think there's something to worry about?'

'Possibly. It certainly rang alarm bells, but I checked with social services and they're not on their radar. But that doesn't mean there's nothing going on,' Nick explained as they drew up outside the home.

Ruth and Nick got out of the car and made their way up the drive.

'If this goes how they normally go, she'll back Neal to the hilt,' Ruth said with a slightly weary tone. She was often appalled at how often the mother would believe and support a new partner over the safety and happiness of her own children.

Nick knocked on the door.

After a few seconds, it was opened by Natalie who had a slightly sour look on her face. She was fully made up and her blonde hair was pulled back off her face.

'Hi Nat,' Nick said. 'Can we come in for a chat?'

'Do I have a choice?' she said, as she gestured for them to come in.

Ruth looked at Nick – *this isn't going to go well.*

Natalie led them through to the small living room that was cluttered with washing and toys.

Ruth leant down and moved a pile of washing so she and Nick could sit on the sofa.

'Sorry. I didn't know I was having visitors,' Natalie said as she sat down in the armchair, picked up a menthol cigarette, and lit it.

'Nat, I think you met Detective Inspector Ruth Hunter last night?'

Natalie ignored her. 'I hope you're talking to Ben about what happened here?'

'Mrs Williams, or can I call you Natalie?' Ruth said quietly.

'Nat is fine.'

'We need to speak to you about your partner, Crispin Neal,' Ruth explained.

Natalie immediately went on the defensive. 'Okay, go on then. I've heard it all before though.'

'Are you aware that Crispin is on the Sex Offenders Register?' Ruth asked gently.

Nat took a long drag of her cigarette and looked directly at her. 'Yeah. Of course.'

Slightly defensive, to say the least.

Nick frowned. 'And you're okay with that?'

'He was looking at some pictures of teenage girls. They just looked older than they were. That's it. Easy mistake to make on the Internet these days,' Natalie said, then blew out a stream of smoke towards them.

Well, that's total bullshit for starters.

'Crispin got a two-year sentence, Nat. It wasn't for look-ing at a couple of photos of some teenage girls,' Nick said, clearly trying to get her to see the gravity of the offence.

Natalie just shook her head and gave an audible sigh. 'For fuck's sake.'

She is really starting to annoy me.

'You have two children in this house. One of them is a teenage girl. If we feel that either of them is at risk, then we have to talk to social services and our Police Protection Unit. You do understand that?' Ruth said firmly.

Natalie reacted with a weary shake of her head. 'Why can't you lot just leave us alone, eh? Always bloody interfer-ing.'

Nick glanced at her. 'Ben said that Crispin has hit Henry before?'

'He gave him a clip when he was rude to him. That's it. It's not illegal is it?' Natalie huffed.

Ruth shot her a look. 'Actually, it can be.'

'How does Kat get on with Crispin?' Nick asked.

'Fine. Why?'

'Ben seemed to think there was a problem.'

'She's a teenage girl. You know what they're like. She can be a right bloody madam. If he says anything to her, she goes off like a bottle of pop.'

'Nothing else? Nothing you're worried about?' Nick said with implied meaning.

Natalie stubbed out her cigarette. 'I don't know what you're implying but he's not like that. He's not some paedo.'

Ruth looked over at Nick – *how can she be that naïve?*

Getting up from the sofa, Nick pulled out a contact card and handed it to her. 'If you need anything, give me a ring.'

Natalie sneered at him. 'You know what, I always thought you were a sanctimonious prick, Nick. The only time you were fun was when you'd had a drink.'

'We'll see ourselves out,' Nick said as he and Ruth headed for the front door.

Ruth glanced at Nick as they walked down the driveway. She could see he was deep in thought.

'You okay?' she asked.

'She never used to be like that. She's really changed.' Nick's phone began to ring as they got to the car. 'DS Evans?'

Ruth opened the door and got in.

'Bloody hell!' Nick said as he ended the call.

'What was that?'

'Someone's stolen a bus from the central bus station.'

'What?' Ruth spluttered. He had to be bloody joking.

'Seriously. Some young bloke and his girlfriend had a row with the driver. He went to get the inspector and the bloke drove off in the bus.'

Hitting the blues and twos, Nick turned on the engine, revved it, and they sped away.

FINN GRIPPED ONTO THE bus's steering wheel as they hurtled around a roundabout on the edge of Llancastell. He could feel the back of the bus slide out as he momentarily lost control.

Bloody hell.

There was a scream from a passenger. He tapped the brake slightly as he straightened the bus.

Glancing over at Kat, he could see that she was in fits of uncontrollable laughter.

'This is hilarious!' she yelled.

He knew he was showing off, but it didn't matter.

'I missed the bloody turning to your house!' Finn shouted over at her.

'Doesn't matter. I don't want to go back to that place anyway.'

She won't be going back there if that wanker of a stepdad is going to hurt her. In fact, if he hurts her again, I'll kill him.

Suddenly, Finn saw a flicker of blue light. Glancing in the rear view mirror, he saw that a police car was now chasing him.

'Bollocks, man. Coppers,' he said to Kat, gesturing back with a nod of his head.

As he glanced in his mirror again he saw an elderly woman tottering down the aisle towards him, grabbing each seat along the way to keep her balance. 'Excuse me, we didn't go past my stop and now I'm going to be late for bingo.'

Slowing the bus even more, Finn looked at her with a smile. 'What's your name, love?'

'Brenda. I'm with my friend. We go every week.'

'We'll get you to the bingo, Brenda,' Kat said with a broad smile. 'Won't we Finn?'

Finn grinned. 'Yeah, of course. Where is the bingo, Kat?'

'Back the way we came,' she shouted.

'Right, everyone hold on tight,' Finn said as he floored the accelerator.

I really hope this works, he thought. He hadn't done a handbrake turn since he was a kid and used to TWOC cars with his cousins. His skills might be a bit rusty.

Finn spun the bus's steering wheel as he engaged the handbrake. He felt it beginning the skid.

'HANG ON!' he shouted.

Oh shit! I think we're going to topple over!

There were more screams from passengers.

'Bloody hell, Finn!' Kat screamed as she clung on for dear life.

Feeling the back of the bus swing around but straighten, Finn began to use the foot brake to slow them down.

Bloody hell! I've just handbrake-turned a fucking bus!

Finn whooped with joy and grinned at Kat. 'Now that's a proper piece of driving.'

'You scared the crap out me, you total nutter,' she laughed.

'Let's go to the bingo!' Finn yelled.

He saw Kat's face change. 'Finn!'

As he peered ahead, he saw a blitz of flashing blue lights. Three vehicles were parked across the road, blocking it off. There was a police car, an unmarked Astra, and a police van.

Bollocks.

Finn shrugged at Kat. 'End of the ride.'

Pushing the brakes, he slowly brought the bus to a halt and let out a sigh.

What a mad, bloody rush that was!

He looked over at Kat. 'Get yourself down the bus, Kat.'

'Why? I want to stay with you,' she frowned.

'No. I don't want you to get nicked. Go on, off you go now,' he said sternly, gesturing for her to make herself scarce.

Kat got up, went towards him, and kissed him hard on the mouth.

'You're my fucking hero, you know that?' she whispered in his ear.

Finn felt a surge of pride and excitement as he watched Kat move down the aisle of the bus towards the middle doors.

She's so fit.

He pushed the button for the doors to open.

Within seconds he had been handcuffed and dragged from the bus.

CHAPTER 10

NOW THAT IT WAS EVENING, Ruth had switched from coffee to water. As she unscrewed the bottle top, she went over everything she had gleaned from the new information about Sarah. She had used her contacts in the Foreign Office to find out all she could regarding Sergei Saratov. So far, she had been passed from pillar to post. No one seemed to want to talk to her about Saratov – and this made her suspicious. All she knew was that there was a good possibility that Sarah had been in his company in The Dorchester Hotel in May 2015. She had no idea why. She had contacted The Dorchester to find out if they still held CCTV footage from five years ago. It would be a gross misuse of her power as a police officer, and if anyone got wind that she had done such a thing then she would be reprimanded. However, part of her mind played through the scenario where she got the tapes and saw Sarah walking through The Dorchester on that evening. What an incredible thing that would be!

Ruth's mind had swirled with endless possibilities. Had Sarah become embroiled in some kind of high-class prostitution through Jamie Parsons and the Secret Garden sex parties? Is that why she just disappeared off the face of the earth? But then how did Jurgen Kessler fit into any of this?

Of course, there was part of Ruth that was hugely relieved that Fiona claimed to have seen Sarah in 2015. Ruth had often imagined that Sarah had been taken from that train by some sexual predator, murdered, and buried somewhere. In fact, she often had to admit to herself that that was the most likely thing to have happened. Fiona's testimony was convincing and meant that Ruth's dark theory might be wrong. But it also threw up so many more questions. If Sarah had been planning to disappear on purpose and start a different life under a new identity, how did Ruth not spot that in the weeks leading up to her disappearance? What did it say about her as a partner? What did it say about her as a detective? And why had Sarah felt the need to leave her?

A knock on her open office door broke her train of thought. It was Nick. 'Boss, I tried to get the PNC stuff on this Finn Starling.'

A little startled, Ruth turned to face him in her chair. 'What happened?'

'Classified all over it.'

'You can't see whether or not he has a criminal record?' Ruth asked, thinking that this was very strange.

'I'm sure we've come across this before with one of the teenagers that went up from Mold Magistrates Court to Solace Farm.'

The name *Solace Farm* made Ruth shudder whenever she heard it. It was a place only associated with pain. The horrendous fire, the death of Sian. It threw her for a few seconds as she felt her stomach tighten.

Get it together, Ruth, she thought to herself as she took a deep breath.

'You okay, boss?' Nick could see her reaction. 'We can do this later, if you want?'

'No, no. It was Ketha Langley, wasn't it?' Ruth asked, attempting to get her head back into work mode.

Nick stroked his beard. 'I think so. She was involved in a drug gang up in Manchester, wasn't she? Something about turning in evidence against them and having to go into witness protection. I'm sure that her PNC check had the same kind of classified barriers on it.'

'You think this Finn Starling is in witness protection then?' Ruth asked.

'I don't know. He's downstairs waiting for us to interview him, but I don't suppose he's going to tell us that.'

'Come on then.'

Ruth grabbed her jacket and files and headed out of her office with Nick following.

As they wandered down the corridor to the 6th floor lift, she glanced over at him. 'If you were in a witness protection scheme, wouldn't you keep as low a profile as you could?'

'Yeah. I wouldn't go around stealing buses for starters,' Nick said as they got into the empty lift.

The doors shut.

There were a few seconds of silence and then Nick said, 'You still haven't told me what happened in London.'

'Long story.'

'It's fine if you don't want to talk about it.'

'It's not that. I just don't know where to start or what to do with it.'

'If it helps, you can run it past me,' Nick said with a shrug.

Ruth knew she was very lucky to have that kind of relationship with Nick. They told each other everything – and that was incredibly rare in any police force.

'Fiona Parsons confirmed that she saw Sarah in May 2015 at The Dorchester Hotel.'

Nick's eyes widened in shock. 'Jesus, Ruth! After all this time.'

'I know.'

'Christ! How are you feeling?'

'I don't know. Relieved, angry, upset, confused.'

'I'm not surprised. What was she doing there?'

'She was with a Russian billionaire who was implicated in some sex scandal,' Ruth explained.

'Sergei Saratov?'

Ruth raised her eyebrow. 'You've heard of him?'

'I know you think I'm a parochial Welshman, but sometimes I read newspapers and watch the news,' Nick said dryly.

'Haha ... So, the next step is to do some digging into Saratov.'

The lift arrived at the ground floor and the doors opened.

'Well, let me know if you need me to do anything,' Nick said as they came out of the lift and headed for Interview Room 1.

As she opened the door and entered, Ruth saw that Finn was sitting staring at the floor. Next to him was the duty solicitor, a man in his 60s with a greying beard and glasses.

Ruth sat down opposite Finn and Nick sat in the chair next to her. She waited for a moment before making eye contact with Finn.

'Finn, I'm Detective Inspector Ruth Hunter, and this is Detective Sergeant Nick Evans. We're here to talk to you about what happened earlier today. You have already been read your rights at the time of your arrest, but I need to remind you that you are still under caution. Do you understand what that means?'

Finn nodded. She couldn't tell if he was nervous or angry. He wasn't giving anything away with his face or his body language, which was unusual.

'We're also going to be recording this interview as it may be used as evidence. So, I'm going to press this button. You'll hear a long beep and then I'll start off by naming everyone who is in the room. Okay?'

Finn peered around at the room casually. 'Aye.'

Ruth pressed the button to record and a five-second electronic beep began. 'Interview commencing at nineteen hundred hours. For the purposes of the tape, present are Finn Starling, our duty solicitor John Davies, Detective Sergeant Nick Evans and Detective Inspector Ruth Hunter.'

'Can we just confirm that you are Finn Starling, and that you live at 23a Cresswell Drive, Llancastell?' Nick asked, as he looked down at the paperwork in front of him and clicked his pen open.

'Aye. That's right,' Finn mumbled.

Geordie accent, Ruth thought.

'Have you lived there for long, Finn?' she asked.

'No. Few weeks, that's all,' Finn replied while staring down at his feet.

'Where were you before that?' Nick asked.

'Norfolk. Near Norwich, you know.'

Ruth frowned. 'Norfolk? That's a long way from North Wales, Finn. What brought you here?'

Finn shrugged. 'Dunno. Change of scene. New job.'

Ruth could smell the bullshit from a mile off.

Nick looked at him. 'You don't have family or friends in Llancastell then?'

'No.'

'Do you have any ties to North Wales at all?'

'No.'

Ruth glanced at Nick – *that seems incredibly strange.*

There was a knock at the door.

Detective Constable Dan French poked his head in and looked at Ruth.

'Boss, I need a word,' he whispered, gesturing for her to come outside.

'Is it urgent?' she asked with a frown. It had to be fairly important for French to come and interrupt an interview.

French nodded and Ruth got up from the table.

'For the purposes of the tape, DI Hunter is leaving the interview room,' she said as she went outside into the corridor. 'What's up, Dan?'

'We've just had a phone call from the UKPPS,' Dan explained. The UKPPS, standing for UK Protected Persons Service, was essentially the latest title for the UK's witness protection scheme. It is part of the National Crime Agency and delivered regionally by local police forces. 'The guy in that room isn't Finn Starling but a Finn Mahoney.'

'Where did the call come from?' Ruth asked.

'Northumbria Police.'

'Which explains the Geordie accent.'

'They're sending down the relevant PPS officer now,' Dan said, 'But he can't get here until tomorrow morning.'

'Great. What are we meant to do with Finn until he arrives?' Ruth asked.

'I spoke to DCI Drake. If he's under the UKPPS, we can't hold him here. It's a breach of the terms of his protection arrangements. We have to let him go, and tomorrow he will liaise with his PPS officer,' Dan explained.

You have got to be joking?

Ruth had already feared that might be the case. 'What if he disappears?'

'That's on the PPS, not us. They're meant to be keeping regular tabs on him.'

This is total bullshit, Ruth thought, shaking her head. 'Okay, thanks Dan.' She opened the door to the interview room and said in a withering tone, 'Interview suspended at nineteen fifteen.' She then went over to the table and turned off the recording equipment.

'Everything okay?' Nick asked.

'Not really,' Ruth said as she looked over at Finn who had no idea what was going on. 'Mr Starling, you are now free to go. However, your protected persons officer will be coming from Newcastle to talk to you tomorrow, so please don't leave town.'

'Or steal any more buses,' Nick quipped.

Finn frowned at the duty solicitor. 'I don't understand. Am I free to go?'

The duty solicitor nodded.

AS FINN CAME OUT ONTO the steps of the police station, he buttoned up his coat. He took a long deep breath of cold air and stretched. He couldn't understand why they had let him go and not kept him in a cell overnight. He wasn't going to complain. They were idiots.

Walking down the concrete steps to the pavement, his heart sank a little. He would have to face Michael Bartowski, his protection officer, tomorrow. He was going to go totally mental with him. He had only just arrived in North Wales. He couldn't face the thought of moving on again so soon. And what about Kat? He didn't want to leave her.

'Finn? Finn?' shouted a voice. It was Kat waving to him as she crossed the road.

Brilliant! I can't believe she's waited outside for me!

Before he knew it, Kat had run to him and dived into his arms. For a moment, he swung her around.

They stared at each other.

'What happened?' Kat asked.

Finn was lost for words. How was he going to explain that they let him go because he was in a witness protection scheme? He didn't want her to know what had happened twelve years earlier. Or that he had spent most of the time since in a Young Offender Institution.

'They had to let me out on bail,' he said, thinking on his feet.

Kat grinned. 'Cool.' Reaching up to his face, she pulled him towards her and kissed him hard on the mouth. He responded as he felt his body fizz with excitement. She then pushed her tongue into his mouth. He reacted by copying her, and their tongues intertwined.

Bloody hell, this is incredible.

As they pulled apart to get their breath, he gazed into her eyes. In the amber of the streetlights, they sparkled and gleamed.

She's so beautiful. What is she doing with me?

'I can't believe that you just stole a bus, Finn. Do you know what a legend that makes you?' Kat said shaking her head.

'Does it?' he asked. He couldn't remember anyone ever being this nice to him.

'Fuck yeah. The way you stood up to that driver when he was rude to me. No one's ever done that for me before.'

'Yeah, well I wanted to protect you,' Finn said, trying not to get too carried away with himself. 'No one should speak to you like that.'

'You are my total fucking hero.' Kat grabbed him and led him by the hand. 'Come on, I want to show you something.'

'Where are we going?' he asked. His head was swimming with the events of the day.

Kat laughed. 'You'll just have to wait and see.'

For the next few minutes, they walked hand in hand through the centre of Llancastell. As they strolled over the iron bridge that stretched across the River Dee, Finn watched as Kat stopped, leant over the railings and peered down at the river. The late evening sun glowed in the darkening sky, creating dappled patterns of silvery light across the water's surface.

It looks like a scene from a film, Finn thought.

Kat pointed. 'Look down there.'

Finn gazed down at the river. There were a few ramshackle buildings by the water's edge, then scattered lights as the landscape stretched away to the grey outline of the Snowdonia Mountains on the horizon.

'What am I looking at?' he asked as he moved behind her and wrapped his arms around her waist. He was surprised at how confident he was in her presence.

'What are you up to, cheeky?' she laughed. 'You see there's a tiny white house just before the bend?'

Finn squinted and then he saw it. From where they stood it was really small – like a toy house that wasn't real. 'Yeah, I can see it.'

'I've always wanted to live in that house. This is where I come when I want to be alone or if I'm upset. And I look down the river at that house and think that one day I'll live there. Maybe on my own or with someone I've met,' Kat said in a near whisper.

'It looks perfect. Like from one of those story books.'

'I don't want to go home tonight.' Kat sounded upset.

'You don't have to.' Finn pulled her closer to him.

For a few seconds they just held each other tightly as they looked down the river.

'I don't ever want to go back home again,' Kat murmured softly.

'Is it your stepdad?' Finn asked.

She felt herself tremble a little in his arms. 'He ...'

Finn looked at her. 'It's all right. You don't have to talk about it.'

She shook her head. 'He's so creepy around me ... He tried to kiss me a few weeks ago. And I think he watches me when I have a shower.'

Finn could feel himself getting angry. *How dare he do that?*

'He comes into my bedroom sometimes and sits on the bed. He asks me if I want a massage or anything. I tell him to go away but ...' she started to cry.

He kissed her cheek. 'Have you told your mum?'

'No,' she said with a sniff. 'I don't think she'd believe me anyway.'

Finn put his hands on Kat's shoulders and turned her so that she was facing him. He gazed into her eyes and moved a strand of hair away from her face.

'You know what we should do?' he said.

'What's that?'

'We should run away together.

Kat frowned uncertainly. 'O ... kay.'

'I'm being serious. Start a new life where no one knows us.'

Finn was filled with fear that Kat was going to laugh at his idea and reject him. 'Sorry. That was stupid. I don't know what I'm talking about.'

Running his hands through his hair, he just wanted the ground to open up.

God, I'm such an idiot!

Kat's eyes widened as she smiled. 'No ... Oh my god. That's a brilliant idea Finn!'

CHAPTER 11

PACKING UP HIS STUFF for the day, Nick leant down to turn off the computer. Having done more research on Finn Starling, he had drawn another blank. Whatever the reason Finn had been deemed a protected person, there was no record of it anywhere on the PNC or any other UK police database. Nick's guess was still that Finn had been involved in drugs, maybe a county lines operation. He either got too scared, or got himself arrested and decided to give evidence at trial.

Two figures appeared at the door to CID. One was Detective Chief Inspector Ashley Drake. Next to him was a very attractive dark haired woman in her 20s.

Drake looked over at him. 'DI Hunter around, Nick?'

Nick shook his head. 'You just missed her, boss.'

Drake walked into the CID office. 'DS Nick Evans, this is DC Georgina Wild.'

It wasn't until she came closer that Nick noticed how extraordinarily pretty she was. Chestnut hair, and seamless eyebrows above chocolate eyes. Her cheeks were high and almost cartoonesque in their symmetry. She was dressed in a simple, elegant, coat that made her look older than she really was.

Nick felt his pulse quicken. 'Hi there.'

DC Wild smiled at him. 'Actually, everyone calls me Georgie, boss ...' she said, in a voice that was deeper than her appearance would suggest, '... although some of the older male officers downstairs called me other stuff but I tended to ignore that.'

Drake laughed. '*Me Too* hasn't quite reached all of North Wales yet, I'm afraid.'

Nick watched her flick her hair around her ear and said, 'You get a better class of male police officer up here, don't you boss?'

Drake smiled. 'Of course.'

Georgie made eye contact with Nick. 'I can see that already.'

Bloody hell. Is she flirting with me?

Drake gestured to Nick. 'If you can give Georgie a quick guided tour, Nick?' Nick smiled. 'No problem.'

'You'll meet DI Hunter at the morning briefing,' he said to Georgie as he turned to leave.

For a few seconds, they both watched Drake walk away and out of the CID office.

'Right, Georgie. Where shall we start?'

'Any idea where my desk is going to be? I want to bring some personal things in tomorrow and get settled.'

Nick glanced around CID. Sian's desk was empty and for a moment Nick saw her sitting there in his mind's eye. For a second, he was hit by her loss and took a deep breath.

'Erm ... I'll let DI Hunter sort that out tomorrow.' He wasn't going to put her at Sian's desk – it was too soon.

Georgie looked at him with a serious expression as though she had picked up on what he was thinking. 'I was really sorry to hear about DC Hockney.'

Nick nodded. 'Sian. Yeah, we really miss her. She was a great copper.'

'Big shoes to fill then.'

Nick didn't want to talk about Sian anymore or he might lose it. He gestured to the office. 'You've been up here before when you were in uniform I assume?'

'A few times. It always felt like going to the staff room at school though.'

'Yeah, I remember thinking that.' Nick motioned to the far side of the room. 'Fingerprinting suite is over there. The child protection and family unit officers are based to the right, but they're often downstairs in the interview rooms. Robbery and burglary squad on the left. And then MIT are down here.' MIT stood for Major Incident Team.

Georgie gestured to the MIT area. 'So, this is where all the real action is.'

'Sometimes. And sometimes it's just a lot of paperwork or trawling through hours of CCTV.'

'Forensics and tech are across the road, aren't they?'

Nick grinned. 'Some of the older detectives refer to it as the Nerd House. Obviously not me though.'

Georgie laughed. 'Of course not. I'm sure you're far too professional.'

He smiled. 'Not always.'

'That's all right. I'm incredibly discreet.'

What does she mean by that?

Nick glanced at his watch. 'I tell you what. Most of CID is closed up for the day. There are only two officers on the night shift. Why don't you get yourself home and have an early night? You're better off looking around tomorrow when everything's up and running.'

Georgie shrugged. 'Okay. If you're sure. You're the boss.'

'Yeah. I'm sure your boyfriend will appreciate you getting home at a reasonable time.'

Georgie smiled. 'I don't have a boyfriend.'

'I can't believe that.'

'It's true. Maybe I'm too dedicated to the job to look properly.'

'Well, have a good evening and I'll see you bright and early tomorrow.'

'Thanks, sarge. See you tomorrow.'

Nick watched her walk away. She walked in a straight line, one foot in front of the other, like a dancer.

This is not good.

RUTH WANDERED OUT TO the patio with her cigarette. It was strange how she still felt guilty about smoking in the house. Sian had nagged her to stop smoking and had forbidden her to smoke indoors for most of the time they were together. Now it was just habitual to go outside.

Blowing out a plume of smoke, she gazed up at the sky. The outline of the half moon was dim behind a thin veil of clouds. From somewhere nearby she heard the echoing sound of an owl hooting and then the distant reply of another.

Ruth was plagued by the thought that if she had done something differently, Sian might still be alive. It was a torturous daily belief that seemed to be on some terrible loop.

She walked inside to the kitchen to pour herself a glass a wine, then paused for a few seconds, stunned by the stillness of the room. She gazed around the kitchen. Many things still reminded her of Sian. The brand new olive green oven gloves and tea towel hanging neatly on the oven handle. Sian had bought them only a week before she died. Ruth had made some withering comment about Sian replacing them every time there was the faintest hint of a mark or stain. Of course, Ruth regretted her acerbic comment now. It had been unkind. What did it matter? Sian hadn't even got round to wearing the oven gloves. What would Ruth give for her to be standing there right now cooking them a meal? Anything. Life was so precious, and yet it was sometimes hard to see that until it was gone.

Ruth blinked away a tear. She needed to focus on work as a way of distracting herself from her grief. She poured herself another glass of wine, determined not to dwell on what she had lost. Instead, she turned her thoughts to the young man they had arrested and interviewed that day. She had worked for nearly thirty years as a police officer but had never nicked anyone for stealing a bus. That was what they said about the job when she first joined – *it's never, ever boring.*

She wondered if there had been any further updates. Finn Starling's protection officer would be arriving from Newcastle tomorrow, so she should check her work emails.

It dawned on her as she walked into the living room that she didn't have anything better to do.

I am such a sad bitch. They're going to find me dead one day surrounded by cats.

She put the television on for company, with the volume at a low murmur. As she took out her laptop, she wondered why Finn was in witness protection. If she had to guess, it would be something gang or drug related in Newcastle.

Clicking on her inbox, she immediately saw something she wasn't expecting. An email with an attachment from Brian Stepney, Head of Security at The Dorchester Hotel. He had sent over several files containing the CCTV clips she had requested from Saturday 9th May 2015.

Oh god. That was quick.

She found herself almost gasping as her pulse increased. She had to look through the clips, but the thought of it was making her nervous. What if she actually saw Sarah in The Dorchester on that date? What would that mean? And what if Fiona had been wrong and Sarah hadn't been there? That would be devastating.

Bloody hell, Ruth! Let's get this over with, she thought as she double-clicked the CCTV files and began to trawl through the clips. She soon found the one that was marked *The Bar.* Moving slowly through the footage, she squinted at the various guests coming and going. As the timecode reached *23.45pm,* Ruth began to wonder if Fiona had got the whole thing wrong. She had googled a photo of Sergei Saratov earlier so she could recognise him. However, as the footage played on to *00.55am,* she had seen no one that resembled him, Sarah, or Fiona.

For fuck's sake. Was she mistaken or was she lying to me? What a waste of bloody time.

Sitting back on the sofa, Ruth felt frustrated. And the more worrying thought was that if Sarah hadn't been at The Dorchester in 2015, she now had to revisit the dark theory that she had been taken from the train and murdered.

She closed her eyes. This was exhausting, and it was painful. She bit her lip as tears trickled down her face. How could she have lost the only two women she had ever loved in her life? How was that possibly fair? Why did other people get to find a partner for life and grow old with them?

Looking up at the television, she wondered if she should continue to binge watch *Good Girls* on Netflix as a welcome distraction.

Then she had a thought. *What about the hotel entrance?*

She had checked the guest list for The Dorchester, and Sergei Saratov hadn't been staying there – unless he'd checked in under an alias. If Sarah had come with Saratov and they weren't guests, then they would have had to have come through the main entrance of The Dorchester. They would have been dropped off by cab, or more likely by Saratov's driver.

Clicking through the various files, Ruth eventually found the clip marked *Main Entrance, Park Lane.* She knew it was a long shot. After all, there had been no sight of them in the bar as Fiona had stated.

Ruth watched the pedestrians, and the black cabs and limousines that had dropped off, or picked up, various guests and visitors as the evening progressed. Nothing.

Glass of wine, Good Girls and bed.

She puffed out her cheeks in frustration as she stared at the framed image of The Dorchester's Park Lane entrance. The flat roof that extended over the pavement so that guests would be protected from London's rain. The symmetrical rows of purple flowers above that.

I'll call it a day when the timecode gets to midnight, Ruth promised herself.

She watched as the time ran down, and any hope of finding Sarah was beginning to evaporate. She would be back to square one, with the added pain of having hoped for a few weeks that she was actually still alive.

The timecode reached *23.58pm.*

Nothing.

Then it read *00.00am.*

Nothing. Time to call it quits.

Out of sheer anger, Ruth slammed her fist down on the laptop's touch pad.

For fuck's sake!

The timecode jumped to *00.14am.*

Ruth leant forward to snap her laptop shut.

Then something on the screen caught her eye.

A long, white stretch limousine pulled up outside The Dorchester.

Who the bloody hell is that? Elvis?

The back door opened, and a small group of people got out and huddled together for a moment.

A man in a smart, charcoal grey suit went over to speak to the driver.

It was Sergei Saratov!

Oh my god! That's him.

A blonde woman in a black cocktail dress took him by the hand and laughed.

Ruth focussed her eyes and blinked.

No. It can't be!

But it was.

Sarah.

CHAPTER 12

FINN AND KAT ARRIVED at the DIY warehouse just before their 8am shift started. They had spent the night together at Finn's bedsit and made love in the darkness. Then they had said that they loved each other. Finn never thought he could feel like that. It had been the best night of his life.

Reaching the staff entrance, Finn and Kat stopped holding hands.

'I'll see you later,' Kat said with a beaming smile.

Finn grinned. 'What about a quickie behind Home Furnishings later?'

Kat giggled. 'You're on.'

Finn took her hand and looked at her with a serious expression. 'Did you really mean it? What you said?'

She laughed and gave him a playful slap on the arm. 'A quickie behind Home Furnishings? Yeah, why not?'

'No. I meant about us going away. Starting again?' Finn felt his stomach tighten as he asked the question. What if she said no?

'Yeah. I don't want to stay in this dump of a town for the rest of my life. Do you?'

'Definitely not.'

'Then we'll make a plan. Come on or we'll be late,' she said as she opened the door, and they went in.

As Kat walked away to the female lockers and toilets, Finn turned right.

She loves me. And she wants to run away with me. How could life get any better?

His head was spinning. He felt giddy as the powerful emotions swept through his body. He was so high, so excited, that it was difficult to concentrate or even think clearly.

Finn saw Matty coming towards him with his usual annoying grin.

My bubble is about to be burst.

'Hey, Finn-meister. What have you been up to, eh?' Matty asked, doing a little dance as he approached.

God, the man was annoying. *What's he talking about? Does he know about me and Kat?*

'Nothing much,' Finn said with a casual shrug, but he was now feeling anxious.

'There's some bloke upstairs looking for you. Looks a bit moody. And he's a Geordie like you. Not your dad is it?'

My dad died from a smack overdose eight years ago you prick.

Finn shook his head. 'No.'

'He's in Holly's office. You should probably go and see him before you put your stuff on, mate,' Matty suggested.

Finn gave him a sarcastic smile and wandered out through the double doors and across the store to Holly's office.

As he approached, Finn saw a man he recognised look over at him through the glass from the office.

It was Michael Bartowski, his witness protection officer. He had a different title, but that's what Finn called him anyway.

He went in and closed the door.

Michael looked up from where he was sitting and shook his head.

'What the bloody hell have you been up to, Finn?'

He sounded calm but very disappointed.

Finn sat down and after a few seconds mumbled, 'Not a lot.'

'Stealing a bus? Are you bloody kidding me? You've only been here a few weeks!'

Finn stared down at the floor. He hated feeling that he had let Michael down. Again. 'Sorry ... I ...'

'What happened? I thought this was going to be a new start for you.'

'The driver was being a total dickhead,' Finn said, trying to explain.

'What, so you stole his bus and got chased by the local police? Don't be daft, son!'

It did sound quite mental now Michael had said it out loud.

'Yeah, it's not the brightest idea I've ever had.'

'How am I meant to keep this out of the papers?' Michael growled. 'I've got to go and talk to the local CID and explain who you are and why they can't charge you.'

'I wasn't thinking. I'm sorry ...' Finn mumbled.

'We've talked about this, Finn. If someone finds out who you are, your life will be in serious danger.'

Finn was feeling frustrated. 'I'm just tired of all of it. I can't talk to anyone properly. I can't tell anyone about who I am, where I'm from, what I've done.'

'I know you were very young, but you're responsible for killing two innocent people. What did you think was going to happen?'

'They weren't bloody innocent, and you know it!' Finn snapped angrily.

Michael glanced at him.

Finn had to give it to Michael. He had never judged him for what had happened. Not like some of the screws in Ockley Cross. They'd let him know just what they had thought of him.

You're a fucking cop killer, and one night, when you're least expecting it, we're going to have you, son.

Finn saw Holly walk past. She tapped her watch to show that he needed to get to work.

'But it wasn't for you to take it into your own hands,' Michael said quietly.

Finn sat forward, sighed, and then looked up at Michael. He couldn't keep living like this. It was exhausting. It wasn't living – it was just existing.

'Now what?' Finn asked.

'We have to move you again, I'm afraid.'

Finn shook his head as his heart sank. 'No. I'm not going.' He had found Kat and he wasn't going anywhere without her.

'You don't have a choice. There is no way of us protecting your identity here. And I'm responsible for keeping you safe.'

'I can't do it. I can't move again,' Finn said. He felt on the verge of tears.

'You have to. And there's nothing you or I can do about it. I need you to pack your things up tonight. I'll see if we can get you somewhere to go to by tomorrow night. Okay?'

Finn nodded but he had no intention of going anywhere.

SITTING AT HER COMPUTER in her office, Ruth stared again at the screen. She couldn't help herself. The image of Sarah at The Dorchester Hotel was frozen. It was probably the sixth time Ruth had studied it that morning. She had found it hard to sleep, and even harder to concentrate on getting her paperwork done.

She took a deep breath. Even though the picture was fuzzy, the quality was fairly good. Sarah was wearing more makeup than usual, and her hair was longer. There had been moments when Ruth completely doubted what she had seen. Maybe it was her mind playing tricks on her? So, she went back to the CCTV footage and had to look again. It *was* Sarah. There was no doubting it. There she was, smiling and laughing by a limousine, eighteen months after she had disappeared off the face of the planet.

How dare she? What the bloody hell was she doing? What about her family and friends that had searched for her?

Feeling the anger well up inside, Ruth turned off the screen. She couldn't look at it now, not when she was feeling like this. But she knew it would only be a matter of time before her thoughts returned to it again.

As she sat back and craved a ciggie, Nick appeared at her door. He was holding a folder.

'I've had a meeting with Finn Starling's protection officer. Geordie bloke called Michael Bartowski,' Nick said. 'And Finn Starling wasn't a witness at all.'

Ruth frowned. 'How do you mean?'

'Don't know if you remember a case in Newcastle about twelve years ago? Copper and his pregnant wife died in a house fire. Three local boys had poured petrol through the letterbox and set the house alight.'

Yes. I do remember it now.

Ruth nodded. 'He's one of those boys? Oh my God.'

Nick opened the file. 'Finn Mahoney, alias Starling, did ten years of a twenty-year sentence at Ockley Cross Young Offenders in Kent. He's out on licence, which he has obviously now fucked up. He has a new name, identity, and job.'

'I'm guessing he might get away with a suspended sentence.'

'The PPS seems to think the best thing is to get him out of Llancastell before a journalist, or anyone else, finds out who he actually is. They can bring him back here when he needs to go in front of a magistrate. If he gets a suspended sentence, then he doesn't need to come back here again.'

Ruth shook her head. 'I remember the tabloids at the time. They tore those kids to pieces.'

She recalled the headlines of *Evil little bastards* and *Cop killing kids are freaks of nature.*

'Not surprising. They *were* evil little bastards,' Nick said.

'Were they?' asked Ruth. She'd had this argument before with other police officers. 'Addict parents, dysfunctional, violent homelife ...'

'Don't give me all that. We see plenty of kids with terrible home lives. They don't go around burning down houses with coppers inside.'

'Okay. But I thought it was an accident. Wasn't it in the middle of the day and the kids thought they were out?'

'That's what their defence claimed.'

'Why is a boy like Finn more evil, more despised, for committing a crime like that, than an adult who clearly knows right from wrong. It should be the other way round, shouldn't it?'

'You think he didn't know it was wrong to burn down a house?' Nick snapped.

'No. But his crime isn't worse because he's a child. His view of the world has been created in a house where there was no right or wrong. Where there were no role models.'

Nick shrugged. 'I understand what you're saying, but I'm not going to agree. He killed a copper.'

'Wasn't there something about that copper abusing kids?' Ruth asked.

'That's what the defence team came up with. Catteridge was the copper's name wasn't it? Paul Catteridge. He was a DS, happily married with a baby on the way. You think he was a paedophile? Or just defence lawyers trying to justify what the boys had done?'

'I don't know. Harold Shipman was a happily married father of four, a respected GP, a pillar of the community. He killed over two hundred people.'

Nick let out an exasperated sigh. 'Bloody hell. We could do this all day, boss. Finn Mahoney was found guilty and that's that. Nature or nurture? I don't know.'

'Okay, then we'll agree to differ on this, Nicholas,' Ruth said with a wry smile.

'I'm going to the canteen. Do you want a posh coffee?'

'As long as you don't spit in it,' Ruth quipped.

'What do you mean? I always spit in it,' Nick said, forcing a smile as he headed out of the CID.

FINN WAS WAITING OUTSIDE the female locker room and toilets. He needed to speak to Kat urgently. After his conversation with Michael Bartowski, they needed to leave Llancastell that night. There was no time to waste. The PPS were already putting plans together to transfer him to another town, so he needed to disappear if he and Kat were to be together. And he knew, more than anything else, that he needed to be with her.

Kat glanced over at him as she came out of the toilets. 'Finn, you do know that if you lurk around outside the ladies' loos, everyone will think you're a weirdo.'

'Aye. Most of them bloody think that already,' he said, but he was too preoccupied with what he needed to tell her.

Kat seemed concerned. 'You okay?'

'Not really. I need to talk to you,' he said in a hushed tone.

'What's going on, babe?'

Taking her by the hand, he led her into a doorway along the corridor and glanced about nervously.

Kat frowned. 'Finn? You're scaring me a bit.'

'You want to leave here, don't you? I mean that's what you said this morning, isn't it?' he asked. He was excitable and his words were coming out fast and a little garbled.

'Yeah, I told you that, silly.'

Finn put his hands on her arms to show her that he was being serious. 'Then we need to go today.'

'What? Today? Don't be bloody mental, Finn. I meant sometime in the future.'

Finn's heart sank. She wasn't serious about running away with him. She wasn't going to come with him.

'I can't tell you why yet, but we have to go tonight,' he told her with a growing sense of urgency.

'That's crazy.'

'I'm being serious.'

'Is it to do with stealing the bus?'

'Sort of. Yes.'

Kat looked at him for a few seconds. 'I haven't got any of my stuff.'

'We'll go to your house and you can pack.'

'Where are we going?'

'Maybe Ireland. We'll go to Holyhead and get a ferry to Ireland. You don't even need a bloody passport ... What do you think?'

Kat was smiling at him as if she really was going to run away with him. 'Erm, I don't know. This is all a bit mental.'

'Come on, Kat. We *are* bloody mental, me and you.'

'I haven't got much money.'

'I've sorted that too. You just need to trust me and come with me when I say.'

'Okay. You seem to have thought of everything,' Kat said and gave him a lingering kiss.

'Is that a *yes* then?'

Kat giggled and then shrugged. 'Yes ... It feels really romantic, doesn't it? Running away together?'

'Aye. Now go back out there and act like everything is totally normal. But when I come and grab you, we have to run.'

'Cool. It's like we're in a movie or something.' Kat turned and headed out of the double doors.

Finn waited for about thirty seconds. He had it all planned.

Marching out into the shop, he headed towards Holly's office. Tapping his pocket, he felt the outline and weight of a 16oz steel claw hammer in his orange work apron.

As he came towards the manager's office, there was no sign of Holly.

A voice came from behind him. 'Looking for Adolf, are you?' It was Matty.

'Yeah. Have you seen her about anywhere?'

'Sorry, mate,' Matty said as he waved a plastic wallet that was full of bank notes. 'I'm on the petty cash run.'

This is going to work even better than I thought it was going to.

Finn watched as Matty unlocked the door and went inside. He then glanced around to make sure no one was watching. If he gave Matty about thirty seconds, that would give him enough time to open the safe. His plan had been to threaten Holly and rob the safe.

He took the hammer from his pocket. The texturised rubber handle felt solid in his hand.

Bloody hell. Am I really going to do this?

His heart was thumping. He drew in a deep breath.

Here goes.

Opening the door slowly, he saw that Matty had opened the store's safe. He was exchanging the wallet of bank notes for pre-counted packs of petty cash. Only Matty and Holly had keys to the safe.

Matty saw Finn. 'I can't let you wait for Holly in here mate.'

'Step away from the safe, Matty,' Finn said as he raised up the hammer.

'What the bloody hell are you doing?'

'You need to move away from the safe,' Finn said calmly – but he wasn't feeling calm at all. His pulse was racing.

'I don't think so,' Matty said turning to face him.

'Seriously Matty, now is not the time to be an idiot.'

'What are you going to do. Hit me with the hammer?' Matty snorted.

'Yeah, I am. Or you can sit down on Holly's seat and let me get on with ...'

Before he could finish his sentence, Matty had come towards him and thrown a wild punch.

Finn had spent a decade in Ockley Cross. He knew how to handle himself. Matty was now off balance – and he had left Finn with no choice.

Picking a spot on Matty's right temple, Finn swung the hammer and hit him.

CRACK!

Matty went down in a heap.

Finn hoped he had managed to stun him or knock him unconscious. He remembered his mate Jake Cole, a 15-year-old boy at the Young Offenders Institution, had got into a fight and been hit around the head with a pool cue. He went into a coma for a few weeks but didn't make it.

Putting the hammer back in his pocket, Finn peered inside the safe.

There were packets of money lined up in neat rows. Tens, twenties and fifties. A few thousand pounds at least. Maybe more than that.

Bingo!

Throwing the money into a folded rucksack that he had brought in his apron, Finn looked down at Matty, who started to move and groan.

That's okay. He's not dead.

Something caught his eye on the desk. Car keys. Holly drove a new, metallic blue, Audi A3 Sportsback. That was better than hotwiring an older car, which had been Finn's original plan. When he was a kid in Newcastle, Finn and his mates had hotwired cars on a daily basis. The coppers called it *Twocking* – taking without the owner's consent.

Grabbing the keys, Finn zipped up the rucksack. His stomach was tense with a mixture of excitement and anxiety. He and Kat were going on the run, and they had enough money to make a new start. He couldn't believe that it was actually happening.

Closing the door behind him, Finn breathed deeply.

Nice and steady, Finn. Don't draw attention to yourself.

He passed two male work colleagues who were putting out stock.

'Coming to the pub later, Finn?' one of them asked.

'Yeah, why not,' he answered casually.

'You haven't seen Matty about anywhere?' he asked.

'No, sorry.'

As he turned into the home furnishings aisle, Finn spotted Kat wheeling a trolley towards him. She gave him a look but didn't say anything.

Finn approached, put his hand on her arm and whispered, 'We're going.'

'What?'

'We're going. Now.'

Kat nodded. 'Okay.'

They headed for the staff lockers, went past the canteen and out into the car park.

Finn stopped as the cool spring air blew across his face.

Kat pointed to the rucksack. 'What's in there?'

Finn laughed. 'Money. Lots of money.' The adrenaline was making him giddy.

'Where did you get it?'

'The safe in Holly's office.'

'How much?' Kat asked as her eyes widened with excitement.

'I dunno.'

This is going to be so good.

Waving the car keys at her, Finn beckoned to a car. 'Come on. We need to get going.'

'Whose car are we using?'

Finn broke into a jog and they reached the Audi A3. 'This one. It's Holly's.'

'Does she know?'

Finn pressed the key fob and the doors unlocked. 'No, of course not. We're just borrowing it.'

Kat snorted with laughter. 'Jesus, Finn. You really are a nutter.'

They got in and closed the doors. Looking at each other with wild excitement, Finn grabbed Kat and kissed her long and hard.

'I'm not going without my stuff though,' Kat said.

'Okay. But you have to be quick. I hit Matty with a hammer so they're going to call the bizzies.'

'What? Is he dead?'

'No,' Finn said as he turned on the engine. Music started to play on the stereo – it was Coldplay. 'I'm not listening to this shit!' Finn ejected the CD and tossed it out of the window.

'I love you, Finn, you mad bastard!' Kat shouted loudly.

'I love you too, Kitty Kat!' Finn yelled.

He stamped on the accelerator, the tyres screeched, and they sped out of the car park.

CHAPTER 13

RUTH SAT AND STARED again at the image of Sarah at The Dorchester. She was driving herself crazy with it. She had also started to research anything she could find on Sergei Saratov. What worried her was that every article she could find mentioned Saratov's predilection for high-class escorts and prostitutes.

Nick knocked on the door and glanced over at her monitor before she had time to minimise it.

Oh bollocks. Did he see it?

'I just need you to sign something off for me, boss,' Nick said as he glanced again at the screen.

Yeah, he definitely saw it.

'Do you want to sit down for a second, Nick?'

Nick pulled out a chair and sat down. 'That sounds ominous.'

Ruth pointed to the screen. 'You're wondering what I'm looking at, aren't you?'

Nick smiled and put his hands up defensively. 'No, of course not. I haven't even noticed.'

Ruth raised her eyebrow. 'You're not very good at lying, are you?'

'So I've been told.' He pointed to the screen. 'If I was to make an educated guess, that's the CCTV from outside The Dorchester Hotel in May 2015.'

'Wow, that's brilliant. You should be a detective,' Ruth said dryly.

Nick edged forward and peered at the screen. 'Bloody hell, is that Sarah?'

'Yeah ... I've shown you a photo of her before, haven't I?' Ruth asked.

'Yeah. And this must be Sergei Saratov.'

Ruth sat forward on her chair. She was keen to get Nick's input. 'What if Sarah was working for Saratov?'

'Doing what?' Nick asked.

Ruth pulled a face and shrugged. She didn't want to say it.

Nick ran his hand over his beard as he frowned at her. 'Do you think Sarah was working as an escort?'

'I don't know. She was petite, blonde and attractive. It would explain why she disappeared. It's not exactly a career change you come home and tell your partner, family, and friends about is it?'

'No, I don't suppose it is. But I thought you guys were happy and she liked her job?'

'That's what I thought. But I'm doubting everything I've ever thought now. Maybe she was bored. And maybe five star hotels, limousines, private jets, designer clothes, and travelling the world felt like a better option.'

'But that's not all escorts have to do.'

Ruth looked at Nick. 'I know that. But maybe she thought that was a fair trade off?'

PARKING THE CAR OUTSIDE Kat's house, Finn turned off the ignition. 'Come on, we need to get a move on. It won't take long for the coppers to send a car to check your house.'

Kat smiled as they got out. 'Don't worry. I'll be five minutes. Promise.'

Taking him by the hand, Kat pulled Finn down the pathway to the front door which she then opened. They went inside and Kat ran upstairs to get her things.

Finn took a deep breath as he went into the kitchen which ran into a dining area. It smelled of washing powder and toast.

Keep it together, Finn. Nice and steady.

The house was quiet except for a wooden clock on the wall which ticked loudly. He went over to the fridge and stared at the various photos attached to its door by magnets. A woman, that he assumed was her mother, standing with Kat on the top of Snowdon. Kat holding her brother as a baby. A wedding photograph of her mother and stepdad.

Her stepdad with a beer, a badge on his shirt that read *40th Birthday,* and a banner behind which said *Happy Birthday Crispin!*

It struck Finn that he hadn't been in a family home since he'd left his own on that fateful day in July 2008. Even though he knew that Kat's stepdad was a wanker, Finn envied her for being brought up in a house like this. Neat, clean and tidy. Opening the fridge, he saw that it was well stocked with all the things that should be in a family fridge. He spotted a can of beer on a shelf, grabbed and opened it, and began to gulp it down. It was cold and fizzy.

That's better.

Maybe a beer would take the edge off his nervous, clenched stomach. His pulse was still racing.

He heard a car passing outside. They needed to go.

'Kat?' he called upstairs anxiously.

'One minute!' she yelled back.

Suddenly there was a noise - a door opening and then closing.

Shit! That sounds like someone coming through the front door.

'Kat? You home?' asked a male voice that sounded distinctly unfriendly. 'Whose bloody car is that outside?'

Before Finn could react, a man in paint-splattered clothes came into the kitchen. Finn recognised him from the photographs. It was Kat's stepdad, Crispin. He was short, with a shaved head and tattooed forearms. He glared at Finn for a few seconds.

'Who the fuck are you? And why are you drinking my fucking beer?' he growled.

Finn looked at him with disgust. He knew what kind of man Crispin was. The scum of the earth - a paedo and a bully.

He swigged back the beer defiantly. 'It's not *your* fucking beer anymore.'

'Oh right, funny man are you?' Crispin sneered at him.

Finn finished the beer and dropped the can on the floor by his feet. 'I know what kind of a man you are.'

Crispin moved forward aggressively. 'You can fucking pick that up for starters, you little twat.'

The sound of Kat clomping down the stairs alerted his attention away for a moment. 'Ready to go,' she yelled before appearing at the kitchen door.

Crispin spotted the suitcase she was holding. 'Where the bloody hell do you think you're going?'

Kat glared at him. 'Oh great. What are you doing home?'

'She's coming with me,' Finn said, feeling the anger and fear rise inside him. This is the man who had abused and hurt Kat.

Crispin laughed. 'I don't think so, dickhead.'

'Fuck off, Crispin. You're not telling me what to do anymore,' Kat yelled at him as she turned to go.

In a split second, Crispin moved towards her assertively and shouted in her face, 'Take your fucking stuff upstairs and wait there while I deal with this little prick.'

Glancing at the knife block, Finn grabbed the handle of an eight-inch kitchen knife and walked towards him. 'She's coming with me. And you either get out of our way or I'll kill you.'

Crispin laughed loudly and then fixed his stare on Finn. 'What the hell are you talking about? You're not going to stab me, you little prick. Now be a good boy and put that down, and get out of my house while I deal with this bitch.'

Finn was now about six feet away from him. He was terrified but he wasn't going anywhere without Kat. And he was prepared to kill anyone who stood in his way.

'Last chance. Get out of my way,' he said, holding up the knife.

Crispin rolled his eyes, turned, and grabbed Kat by the neck. He spun her, put her in a headlock, and pulled a screwdriver from his pocket. He pushed it into Kat's throat so that the skin began to stretch.

'Tell your boyfriend to fuck off or this is going to get a whole lot worse.'

Kat had tears in her eyes. 'It's all right, Finn. You'd better go.'

Finn frowned. 'What?'

'Seriously. Just go.'

Crispin pulled Kat's head back. Finn could now see that the screwdriver had drawn blood from where it was pushed into Kat's neck.

'Yeah, *Finn*. Why don't you fuck off like she told you? Run along now.'

Finn glared at him. He didn't know what to do. There was no chance he was going to leave her.

Suddenly, Kat elbowed Crispin in the stomach and pushed him backwards. He crashed into a Welsh dresser and crockery smashed everywhere.

Finn was frozen for a second.

Then he lurched forward, grabbed Kat and pulled her over to where he was standing.

Trying to get his breath, Crispin's face twisted in fury as he came at both of them with the screwdriver. 'You little bitch ...'

As Crispin went to stab them, Finn smashed his arm out of the way and drove the knife into Crispin's body. The flesh was soft, but the blade hit a rib and juddered. He pulled the knife out.

'What the fuck are ...' Crispin spluttered as he clasped his wound with an expression of utter astonishment.

Finn thrust again. He wasn't going to risk Crispin attacking them. The blade went into the flesh of his belly.

Crispin gave a deep moan. 'Jesus ...'

As Finn pulled the knife out, he looked over at Kat. She was petrified and shaking.

Crispin fell in a heap to the floor.

Finn was numb. He couldn't process it. The man at his feet was a vile paedophile and a bully. However, Finn had probably just killed him. If he was honest, he felt as if he was removed from everything. As if he was observing everything from a bubble.

'Is ... he ... dead?' Kat stammered as she came over.

As if on cue, Crispin groaned and moved. He stared at his hand that had been clasped to the wound in his stomach. It was soaked in blood.

'Maybe we should call an ambulance?' Finn said. Wasn't that the right thing to do? He just didn't know.

'I hate him,' Kat said in a virtual whisper.

'We have to call an ambulance otherwise he'll definitely die, and I'll be charged with murder.'

Kat looked at him and then nodded. 'Okay. I'll do it.' She went to the phone, picked it up and dialled 999. Her hand was shaking uncontrollably. 'Ambulance ... I need an ambulance to Rose Cottage, Pickford, Llancastell. A man's been stabbed ... Yes, he's still bleeding ...' She hung up.

Finn put the knife down on the kitchen counter and wiped the blood from his hands onto a nearby Snowdonia tea towel.

There were a few seconds of silence.

Now in shock, Kat froze as her eyes darted around the room.

Finn took her by the hand. 'Come on. We really need to go now.'

Heading into the hallway, Kat followed Finn outside and over to the car.

Still in a daze, she hesitated before putting her suitcase on the back seat. 'Maybe we should wait for the police? It was self defence, wasn't it?'

'I don't trust them. If they don't believe us, then I'll be going to prison for a very long time.'

Finn got into the Audi and started the engine. Kat leaned down and peered at him through the open passenger window.

'Are you getting in?' Finn asked, frightened that she was going to say no.

'I don't know.'

His heart sank.

'It's okay. But I've got to go, Kat. I understand if you want to stay here.'

Looking desperate, she shook her head. 'I don't know what I'm supposed to do, Finn.'

'I can't tell you that. But I have to get going.'

Then she reached out, opened the door and got in.

'I was hoping you were going to do that,' Finn said, feeling a huge sense of relief.

Kat nodded and put her hand on his. 'I'm coming with you. We're in this together now.'

Finn stamped on the accelerator and they raced away out of sight.

CHAPTER 14

IT HAD BEEN THIRTY minutes since Ruth and Nick had arrived at the DIY warehouse. They had quickly established that Finn had assaulted the assistant manager, Matty Freeman, with a hammer, taken money from the safe, and left with his girlfriend and co-worker, Kat. Freeman had been taken to the University Hospital with a suspected fractured skull.

Holly, the store manager, sat on the small sofa drinking tea as Ruth and Nick questioned her.

Nick had his notebook open and his pen poised. 'Can you tell us how much money Finn took from the safe?'

'We carry a float of two thousand pounds,' Holly explained, shaking her head in disbelief.

Ruth shot a look over to Nick – *Bloody hell.*

'And he took the lot?' Ruth asked raising an eyebrow.

Holly nodded. Ruth looked again at Nick – she knew what he was thinking. That kind of money was going to make Finn and his girlfriend's escape a lot easier.

'What about serial numbers for the notes?' Ruth asked.

Holly shrugged. 'I don't know. I would have to ask head office to talk to the bank.'

'What denominations?' Nick asked.

'Mainly tens and twenties. A few fifty pound notes, but we don't really need them.'

'We still don't have a full name for Finn's girlfriend.'

Holly got up and went over to the filing cabinet. 'Sorry. She's only just started.' Thumbing through the files, she pulled one out. 'Here we go. Katherine Williams, but she says she goes by the name of Kat.'

Ruth saw Nick react.

Didn't Natalie have a daughter called Kat?

'Have you got an address?' Nick asked, gesturing to the file.

Holly handed him the file to look at. He glanced over at Ruth. 'Yeah, it's Kat, Ben Williams' daughter. And it's Nat's address.'

'Anyone see how they left, or in which direction?' Ruth asked Holly.

She shook her head.

'CCTV?' Nick asked.

'We do have a camera outside, but I'd have to go and ask the security guard to have a look.'

At that moment, a young man in a green BDG DIY Warehouse overall and baseball cap knocked on the open door and peered in.

'Holly. Did you drive in to work today?' he asked.

Holly frowned at him. 'Yeah, why?'

'I can't see your car anywhere in the car park.'

'Shit!' Holly went over to her desk and searched it frantically. Then she opened the two drawers. 'My car keys have gone.'

'You sure?' Ruth asked.

'Yeah, I always put them here on the desk by my computer.'

'We're going to need the make and registration,' Nick said.

'CK20 VDR. It's an Audi A3.' Nick scribbled in his notepad.

'Colour?' Ruth asked.

'Metallic blue.'

Nick glanced over at Ruth. 'It's a new car so it'll have a GPS tracking device, unless he's smart enough to disable it.'

Ruth's phone rang and she signalled that she had to take it.

'DI Hunter.'

'Boss, where are you?' French asked. He sounded concerned.

'I'm at that robbery and assault at the DIY warehouse. Everything okay?'

'Not really. Call from uniform. Stabbing at an address just outside Llancastell. Might be fatal. They're not sure yet.'

'Any more details?' Ruth asked.

'Car on the driveway is registered to a Crispin Neal.'

Jesus!

Ruth looked at Nick. 'We need to go.'

THUNDERING ACROSS THE Snowdonia countryside, Finn had decided to take a less popular route to Holyhead to avoid detection. The winding roads were narrow, with overhanging trees and small stone walls along their edges. It was hard to get up any speed, but Finn knew that it was far safer than the A5 which was the main route west from Llancastell.

Kat grinned at him as she played around with the car stereo. *Slide Away* by Miley Cyrus was playing, and she turned up the volume. He was glad to see that she had calmed down a little.

Finn peered over at her. 'You okay?'

She pursed her lips. 'Yeah. I'm trying not to think about what happened earlier.'

'Me too ... We're going to have to ditch this car.'

'What? Why? I love this car!'

'As soon as the police interview Holly, they'll have this registration plate, colour, and make of car.'

'Oh yeah. Good point. You think of everything.'

'Might be an idea for us to stop somewhere overnight and let everything settle down a bit,' Finn suggested. His mind was trying to calculate how long it would have taken the police to get to the DIY warehouse and then circulate their descriptions and the car's details. Not that long. Half an hour – maybe even twenty minutes. He knew the police would soon be on to them.

'With all that money we can stay in a five star, can't we?' Kat said with a grin.

Finn shook his head. 'No. Do we look like a couple that can afford a five star hotel?'

Kat shrugged. 'So what? Who cares about that?'

'It's suspicious. And we'd have to pay cash, which would be unusual. We need to make sure that we don't stand out from anyone else. We'll stay in a budget hotel. And it won't be long before the local news will be reporting a young couple on the run and wanted for assault and robbery.'

He saw Kat's disappointed face. He was suddenly struck by how naïve she was. He supposed that his ten years in a Young Offenders Institution had made him a hundred times more streetwise than most people.

A few seconds later, Finn pulled into the large car park of a roadside pub, the Cross Keys. As he looked for a parking space, he scanned the twenty or so cars, hoping that there would be one that was old enough for him to steal. Anything after 2005 was virtually impossible.

'Taking me for a drink?' Kat asked.

'No, we're switching cars, and if you've got your phone, you need to leave it here.'

Kat pulled a face, took the phone from her pocket, and put it on the dashboard. 'How am I meant to ring anybody?'

'You're not going to ring anybody. We're on the run.'

'Can't we stop and at least have a drink?' she asked, pulling a silly face again.

She's starting to irritate me.

'No. We need to keep moving and not take any unnecessary risks.'

'Where's the fun in that?' she groaned.

'Fun? Jesus, Kat! Do you want to go to prison? Do you know what that's like?' Finn thundered at her.

She glared at him and then said, 'No. Why, do you then?'

Finn didn't answer as he reversed the Audi into a parking space at the far end of the car park.

He spotted an old blue Ford Fiesta nearby. It was perfect.

Getting out of the car, he checked around the car park to make sure that no one had spotted them. He went to the back seat of the Audi and pulled out the bag of money and Kat's suitcase.

Finn gestured to the Ford Fiesta. 'Come on. We're taking this one.'

Kat's face fell. 'What? That old heap?'

'I can steal that old heap. Everything else in here has got a built-in immobiliser.'

'I've no idea what that is. Can I go inside for a pee or is that not allowed either?'

Finn could tell she was still annoyed at him for shouting at her.

He nodded. 'Just be quick and don't talk to anyone.'

Kat gave him a mock salute. 'Yes, sir!'

Taking the bags over to the Fiesta, Finn watched Kat run up the concrete stairs to the pub. He felt bad that he had lost his temper with her. She was only young. And the day had been incredibly traumatic.

He peered around to check that the coast was clear. With a sharp bang of his elbow, he smashed a back door window and quickly reached in to open the driver's door. He threw the bags onto the back seat and looked around again. His pulse had quickened. He wanted to be back on the road as soon as possible.

Reaching under the steering column, he grabbed the handful of wires and yanked them free from their connections. He immediately spotted the yellow and white wires that he needed to hotwire the car. He used his nails to peel back the plastic insulation on both so that the metal wires underneath were exposed. Finn had been only nine years old when Kevin Docherty, a kid from his class, showed him how to steal cars. Where they lived, stealing cars was as much a part of growing up as learning to ride a bike. The coppers would chase them until they drove across the local Walker Park or onto the industrial estate, where they abandoned the cars and ran for their lives.

Touching the wires together, Finn heard the engine whirr for a few seconds.

Then nothing.

He tried again. Nothing.

Shit! Why isn't it starting?

Suddenly, he heard the sound of men laughing. Glancing up, he saw three middle-aged men in suits coming down the steps to the car park from the pub.

None of them look like they drive a Ford Fiesta. What if they see the broken window?

Standing up beside the car, with the driver's door wide open, he tried to look as casual as he could.

To his horror, one of the men walked directly towards him.

What the hell does he want?

Holding his breath, Finn gave him his best innocent smile.

'Excuse me, mate,' the man said, with a thick London accent. 'What's the best way to Llancastell from here?'

Bloody hell. This is all I need.

Finn pointed to the exit. 'Right out of here. About forty minutes down the A5 and follow the signs from there.'

'Cheers, pal.' The man gave him a friendly wink and then gestured to the car. 'My first car that was. The old Ford Fiesta.'

'Yeah. Good little runaround.' Finn felt his pulse accelerate.

The man turned and walked over to a large Range Rover. 'Catch you later then.'

Thank God for that!

Taking a deep breath, Finn watched as the men in the Range Rover drove past with a friendly wave.

'Who the bloody hell was that?' came a voice. It was Kat.

'Don't ask,' Finn said, looking at her. She was hiding something behind her back. 'I'm sorry I shouted at you earlier.'

She came over and smiled at him. 'It's okay. I forgive you. And I know I was being a bit annoying.'

Finn raised an eyebrow. 'A bit?'

Kat hit him playfully. 'Oi ... So, to say sorry, I got us this!' She pulled a bottle of champagne from behind her back and waved it triumphantly.

Finn couldn't help but laugh at her. 'So, when I said be quick, don't draw attention to yourself and don't talk to anyone, you took that to mean go and buy champagne?'

She shrugged, then leant forward and kissed him. 'Yeah. Obviously.'

'Where did you get the money from?'

'I stole it out of the bag while you weren't looking,' she said with a twinkle in her eye.

Finn shook his head. 'Cheeky sod.' He then gestured to the car. 'I can't get this bloody thing going though.'

Crouching down, he took the wires again and touched them together. The engine whirred, but then spluttered as it fired and started.

'Yes. Nice one!' he said with a laugh.

Kat popped the cork off the champagne, and it fizzed out of the bottle and overflowed onto the floor. She took a swig and handed it to Finn.

He took the bottle. 'I've never had champagne before.'

Kat giggled. 'Get it down you. The bubbles will go up your nose but it's lovely.'

He took a few gulps and handed the bottle back to her. He wasn't sure that he liked it. They kissed.

'Come on then, Clyde. Let's get on the road,' Kat said in an American accent as she went around the car and got into the passenger side.

'Clyde?' Finn asked as he sat in the driver's seat and revved the engine.

Kat waved the bottle at him. 'You know? Bonnie and Clyde?'

'Oh right, that's who we are is it?' He pulled away at speed.

'Yeah, of course. We're Snowdonia's answer to Bonnie and bloody Clyde.'

BY THE TIME RUTH AND Nick arrived at Crispin Neal's home, the house had been taped off by the uniformed patrols that were now in attendance. A dozen neighbours had congregated on the pavement to find out what was going on.

Ruth approached the young uniformed officer that was holding the scene log, and showed her warrant card. 'Constable. DI Hunter and DS Evans, Llancastell CID. What do we have here?'

The officer nodded. He seemed a little shaken. 'Yes, ma'am. The victim's partner found him in the kitchen just before the paramedics arrived. She said he was still alive. The paramedics did all they could, but they said the victim had lost too much blood. He died about twenty minutes ago.'

'Where is Natalie Williams now?' Nick asked.

'She's sitting in the dining room with Constable Hegarty, sir.'

'Any idea about what happened?'

'He was stabbed.'

'Any sign of a weapon?' Ruth asked.

'Yes. Large knife on the kitchen counter. Someone's given it a wipe but there's blood on the handle.'

'Thank you, constable. Can you make sure that SOCOs get down here as soon as possible? And let's make sure that everything is being done in here to secure the crime scene. I don't want anyone wandering through it by accident.'

'Yes, ma'am.'

Ruth and Nick ducked under the police tape and headed down the drive towards the cottage. Another uniformed officer was stationed at the open front door.

'You think Ben Williams has anything to do with this?' Ruth asked Nick.

'After the other night, I don't know. What about Kat Williams?'

'You think she could have done this?'

'I don't know. I doubt it, but she was with Finn Starling.'

'It fits with the timing of the attack and theft at the DIY warehouse,' Ruth said thinking out loud.

'Why would they come here? If you half kill someone and steal a load of money, surely you'd get as far away as you could?'

'Unless they're planning on going away forever. Kat wants to get her stuff before they go.'

'Taking a big risk.'

'She's a teenage girl. They think differently to other humans,' Ruth explained.

'So, they rob the warehouse. Come back here to grab Kat's stuff. Crispin Neal interrupts them. There's a fight and one of them stabs Crispin.'

'Sounds feasible. Although after the other night, Ben Williams has to be our prime suspect. I wonder when we'll get something from the ANPR on that Audi?'

ANPR, Automatic Number Plate Recognition, referred to a network of cameras that could alert the police to a specific number plate on a car.

Nick gestured to the door. 'We should have a word with Nat.' He opened it and Ruth followed him inside.

The dining room was tiny. There was a round table with six chairs and little space for much else. The dining table itself was strewn with paperwork and a laptop. The walls had been painted in a pale blue and there was a series of framed landscapes in a neat row across the back wall.

Natalie looked up at them. Her face was smeared with makeup from where she had been crying. A female police officer stood up as they entered.

'Thank you, constable,' Ruth said with a nod, and the officer exited the room quietly.

Nick went over and sat down. 'I'm so sorry, Nat.'

Natalie shook her head. 'No, you're not. I know what you thought of him.'

Ruth spotted Natalie's blood-smeared hands from when she had found Crispin on the floor.

'I'm very sorry for your loss ... Can you tell us exactly what happened when you got home please,' Ruth asked gently.

Natalie seemed lost. 'I got home. I came through the front door. I came into the kitchen and ...' She began to cry again.

'I know this is very difficult, but was Crispin alive when you found him?' Ruth asked.

'Yeah ... I tried to help him but ...'

Her hand was shaking as she wiped another tear from her face. Ruth took a tissue from her pocket and handed it to her.

'Here you go.'

'Thanks.' Natalie glanced at Nick. 'Have you arrested him then?'

Ruth knew that she meant Ben Williams, her ex-husband.

'Have we arrested who?' Nick asked.

As police officers, it wasn't for them to put words into Natalie's mouth.

Natalie twisted her mouth with anger. 'Him. Ben. Have you arrested him yet?'

'You think that your ex-husband attacked Crispin?' Ruth asked.

'Oh my God! Are you thick or something? Who else is going to come in here and stab him?' she growled. 'They had a fight out there the other night. You were here for God's sake!'

'Nat, we will be questioning Ben. But we would also like to talk to Kat,' Nick explained.

Natalie glared at him. 'Kat? What's she got to do with this? She's at work anyway.'

'We're not sure yet. We believe that she might have been involved in an assault and a robbery at her place of work,' Ruth said.

Natalie scowled at them. 'What? What the bloody hell are you talking about?'

'We believe that her boyfriend, Finn Starling, seriously assaulted the assistant manager and stole money. Kat was seen leaving with Finn in a stolen car. We need to speak to her,' Nick explained.

'She hasn't got a boyfriend and she tells me everything.'

Ruth looked at her. 'We have several eye-witnesses.'

Natalie shook her head. 'No, Kat wouldn't do that. And what the bloody hell has this got to do with what happened to Crispin anyway?'

'We're not sure yet. But we do need to talk to Kat,' Ruth said.

'Nat, can you do me a favour. Can you go up to Kat's bedroom and see if anything's missing? Clothes, bag, make-up,' Nick asked.

Natalie pulled a face. 'Why? You think she's run away or something?

'Please. Just go and check.'

Natalie got up from the table. Ruth and Nick followed her out of the room into the hallway. SOCO officers, dressed in white forensic suits, were beginning to tape off the kitchen and lay down metal stepping plates.

Ruth peered inside the kitchen. She saw Crispin Neal's body lying on the floor in a huge pool of blood.

A SOCO approached with an evidence bag. Inside was a yellow and black screwdriver. 'We found this on the floor by the victim, ma'am.'

'I'd like the forensics on it as soon as possible.'

Moving out of the kitchen to let the SOCOs continue their work, Ruth looked at Nick who was standing in the hallway. 'What do you think?'

'I'm not sure. I guess we need to see if Ben Williams has an alibi for this afternoon.

'I still can't see that Kat's involvement in the assault and robbery, and then this at her home, all in the space of an hour, aren't linked. Otherwise, it's a huge coincidence.'

Nick gave her a meaningful look. 'And we don't believe in coincidences.'

Natalie appeared on the stairs. 'Kat's taken all her stuff. Clothes, makeup, everything. And her suitcase is gone.'

CHAPTER 15

THE SUPERMARKET'S DISPLAY of sunglasses spun as Finn searched for a pair of cheap Ray Ban Aviator copies. He grabbed the circular rack to stop it spinning anymore.

Kat appeared from the other side. She was grinning and wearing a pair of lime green, Wayfarer-style sunglasses. 'What do you think?'

Finn rolled his eyes. 'Belter.'

'They're like the ones Billie Eilish wears.'

'Okay.'

Kat took them off with mock indignation. 'What's wrong with them?'

Finn smiled and pointed to the basket he was carrying. 'Pop them in there, then.'

'Thanks, pet,' Kat said, poking fun at him.

They were in a supermarket on the outskirts of Bala, on the eastern edge of Snowdonia. Finn knew they needed to change their appearance as well as buy provisions.

Glancing down into his basket, he could see hair clippers, two hoodies, and an assortment of booze and snacks. It wouldn't be long before Llancastell police had circulated their descriptions to the whole of the North Wales force, and possibly the media too.

Kat danced over to a shelf that was full of shampoos and hair products. Finn watched her with a smile – he loved her so much. He would do anything to keep her safe. However, he was beginning to worry that she had barely mentioned what had happened at her home the day before. He had stabbed her stepfather in front of her and probably killed him. But Kat was acting as if nothing had happened. It was making him feel uneasy.

Kat pointed to the various boxes and bottles of hair dye. 'Here we go! Shall I get some of this?'

'Unless you want to wear a wig.'

'God, no. That'd be really uncomfortable,' she said as she scanned the shelves.

Putting the heavy basket down on the floor, Finn glanced around. Kat's loud voice and lively antics were going to catch someone's attention in a minute. There was a CCTV camera high on a wall nearby.

Finn then spotted something on a fingernail of his right hand. He thought it was fluff but it wasn't. Even though he had washed at the petrol station toilets, somehow there was still a fleck of what he assumed was Crispin's blood on him. It made him shudder.

He thought about the moment when he had driven the knife into Crispin's stomach. The look of utter astonishment on his face which then twisted with the agony of the wound. He had probably killed a man. He could try to justify it in his head. Crispin was physically and sexually abusing Kat. He was trying to kill them both. He deserved to die, didn't he? Finn felt the anxiety of what he had done sweep through him in a surge of panic.

'Electric Blue or Smoky Rose?' Kat asked loudly as she waved two different boxes of hair dye at him.

Jesus! She's really starting to annoy me.

'Are you an idiot? We're trying not to get noticed and you want to dye your hair blue or pink? Bloody hell, Kat! Get dark brown or black, would you?' Finn snapped at her.

Kat looked hurt. 'Don't call me an idiot!'

Finn put his finger to his lips and glowered at her. 'Keep it down!' He grabbed the basket and pushed past her. 'I'll see you at the till. You've got two minutes.'

Trying to get his breath and think clearly, he marched to the end of the aisle and headed for the nearest empty till.

HAVING DROPPED RUTH back at Llancastell CID, Nick pulled up outside Bisset & Sons Estate Agents in the middle of town. The frontage and lettering were in dark red and brown, befitting an old-fashioned estate agents that had been there since the 1950s.

As Nick turned off the ignition, he stared over at the Red Lion pub opposite. Even though it had only just gone midday, two men were standing outside nursing pints and smoking. From their animated conversation and slight swaying motion, he could tell they were drunk. As a recovering alcoholic, Nick could spot a drunk at a hundred yards. He remembered long, boozy Saturday afternoons in there, playing pool with his mates, watching sport, and placing the odd bet at the bookies next door which was now a tanning salon. For a moment, he wished that he could relive those days.

Wouldn't it be nice to meet up with my old mates, have a few pints, play pool, and watch the rugby?

And just as quickly as that crazy thought had entered his head, the counter thought came thundering in. Buying a bottle of vodka on the way home. Waking up in a bed full of vomit and urine. Then the overwhelming desire to consume more alcohol to get rid of the hangover. And so it would go on until he was drinking twenty-four seven. That was the beauty of having a 12-step programme. He had very slowly reprogrammed his mind to play forward what an 'innocent' afternoon in the pub would actually lead to. And that stopped him from picking up that first drink.

No thanks. That's a really stupid idea, Nick, he thought.

Getting out of the car, he glanced up at the clear blue sky. He took a deep breath, arched his back, and stretched.

God, that feels good.

He needed to remember what a gift it was to wake up and go to bed sober every day.

He strode over to the glass door of Bisset & Sons, pushed it open, and went in. There were various people sitting at desks, most were on the phone.

'Can I help?' asked a young woman with a forced smile, who was sitting closest to the door.

'I'm looking for Ben Williams,' Nick answered. If this was Ben's place of work, it wasn't the time to be waving around his warrant card.

The young woman got up from her desk. 'I'll go and find him. Who shall I say it is?'

'Nick Evans. I'm an old friend.'

Shoving his hands in his pocket, Nick glanced around. There were many drawbacks to being a detective. However, the job was never boring, and he knew he couldn't have coped with the monotony of being in an office like this every day.

Ben came out and gestured behind him. 'Nick, come through.'

Nick followed him to a back office where Ben worked as a mortgage advisor. He took a seat as Ben closed the door.

'Everything all right?' Ben asked nervously.

'Don't worry. Nothing's happened to the kids,' Nick said immediately. He knew that would be Ben's instant thought.

He could see that Ben's whole demeanour relaxed. 'Sorry. You coming here. It just scared me for a second.'

'Sorry. I just need to check your whereabouts this morning between ten and midday.'

Ben shrugged and pointed to his desk. 'In here. I'm always in here unless I pop out for lunch.'

'But you didn't pop out anywhere this morning?'

Ben shook his head and gestured to the rest of the office. 'No. You can ask anyone out there. What's going on?'

'Crispin Neal has been murdered.'

'What? Jesus!' Ben sat back in his chair, aghast. 'How?'

He looks bloody shocked to me, Nick thought.

'He was attacked at his home this morning.'

Ben seemed nervous. 'Oh my god. What about Kat and Henry?'

'They're fine, don't worry. And Nat is fine too.'

'God, that's horrible ...'

Nick looked at him. 'You were here all morning, Ben?'

'Yeah. Wait ... you don't think I could have done it?'

'After what we saw the other night we have to check where you were at the time of the attack.'

'Yeah, of course. I was here ... Nat and the kids weren't there were they?'

'No, they weren't there,' Nick said, even though now he strongly suspected that Finn and Kat may well have been at the house and attacked Crispin.

'I've got a couple of missed calls from Nat. I thought she was just ringing to have a pop at me. I can't believe it,' Ben said, shaking his head. 'I didn't like him, but bloody hell.'

'There is something else.'

'What's that?'

'We think that Kat and her boyfriend were involved in an assault and robbery where she works.'

Ben shook his head. 'Kat? No way. She'd never get involved in anything like that.'

'She has a boyfriend apparently. Finn Starling?'

Ben shifted awkwardly in his chair. 'No. No idea. She doesn't tell me stuff like that. Have you arrested her or something?'

'That's the thing. She's packed her stuff up from home and gone. We think she might be on the run with this Finn. So, if she gets in contact, you need to let us know.'

Ben closed his eyes. 'Jesus, Nick. How the hell has all this happened?

Nick's phone buzzed. It was Ruth.

'Sorry, I've got to take this. One sec ...,' Nick said to Ben as he answered the call.

'Nick. We've found the stolen car that Finn and Kat were in. Pub car park on the A527. You okay to come and pick me up?' she asked.

'Yes, boss. I'll be ten minutes.' Nick ended the call and then glanced over at Ben. 'I've got to go. Let me know if Kat tries to contact you.'

CHAPTER 16

WITH THE WINDOW WOUND down, Finn let the cool air blow into his face as they drove west into Snowdonia, with the enormous Bala lake to their left. It was four miles long and a mile wide, making it by far the largest lake in Wales. It had been formed at the end of the last ice age in a glacial valley that ran along the Tal-y-Llyn to Bala fault line. The lake was edged by blue, green, and pink algal blooms, and held vast numbers of pike, perch and trout.

Finn gazed at the immense stretch of water. It seemed to have a reassuring calmness at its core as the tiny ripples on its surface danced and swirled gracefully in the blue reflection of the sky. He spotted a couple of orange canoes gliding along the water on the far side.

How nice would it be to sit out there in a canoe without a care in the world? he thought.

Kat glanced over at him, swigged from a bottle of vodka, and smiled. With her blonde hair swirling in the wind, her nose-ring and lime green sunglasses, she looked like a pop-star.

'It's beautiful isn't it?'

'Yeah. You can hardly see the other side,' Finn said.

Kat gestured to the enormous lake that dominated the view. 'You know there's a monster in there, don't you?'

Finn rolled his eyes. He wasn't falling for that. 'Okay, yeah.'

Kat sat up in her seat. 'Seriously. I'm not joking. The Welsh version of the Loch Ness Monster. Teggie.'

Finn laughed. 'Teggie? Now I know you're making it up.'

'Oh my God. It's meant to be this huge crocodile thing. Some Japanese film crew came over and made a film about it.'

'Did they find it?'

'Well, no. But that's not the point. This lake is called Lyn Tegid. So, they called the monster Teggie. My taid told me about it,' Kat explained.

What's she talking about?

'Taid? What the hell is taid?' Finn asked.

'It's Welsh for grandad you moron.'

'They didn't teach us much Welsh at school in Newcastle.'

'You've never really told me why you're in North Wales anyway.'

Finn wasn't in the mood to start this type of conversation. He wanted to concentrate on getting away and not being arrested. Every time he saw that a car had appeared behind them, he felt the sudden grip of anxiety in case it was the police. He hadn't shared his worry with Kat. There was little point in both of them being scared. Anyway, she was tipsy from the vodka and seemed in a good mood.

'It's a long story,' Finn said, hoping that would be enough.

'I didn't know we were pressed for time.'

'I'll tell you the next time we stop.'

'Running away from something, were you?'

'Something like that.' Finn hoped that would bring an end to it.

'Man of mystery, that's what you are, Finn Starling, you know that?'

'In Newcastle we'd say you were a pure belter, Kat Williams.'

'Oh yeah. They say that on *Geordie Shore*, don't they?'

The music from the radio stopped, and the hourly news began.

'*BBC News, it's six o'clock. Police in North Wales have confirmed that they are looking for a 22-year-old male and a 19-year-old female in connection with the murder of an un-named 40-year-old man on the outskirts of Llancastell. The pair are believed to be travelling together in the North Wales area. Police stress they are keen to talk to the young couple, who have not yet been named, as part of their ongoing enquiries. Anyone with any information should contact the North Wales Police helpline.*'

Kat reached over and snapped off the radio.

'I was listening to that,' Finn grumbled. He wanted to know if there was any more information.

Kat was staring into space as though hearing the news had suddenly made what they had done become very, very real.

HAVING ARRIVED AT THE Cross Keys pub, Ruth and Nick were standing in the car park with a uniformed officer beside the Audi that Finn and Kat had stolen.

'Have you looked inside, constable?' Ruth asked.

'Only through the window, ma'am. I didn't want to touch anything until you guys got here.'

'That's fine. Thank you, constable,' Nick said.

Ruth and Nick pulled on their forensic gloves. Ruth headed to the driver's door while Nick went to the passenger side.

Opening the door, Ruth glanced at the steering wheel and spotted a small smear of blood.

She pointed to it. 'I've got blood on the steering wheel.'

Nick crouched down and then went into the back of the car. 'Plastic wrappers in the back. Must have been carrying the banknotes.'

As Nick and Ruth reconvened by the car boot, she clicked her radio. 'Three six to Dispatch, three six to Dispatch, over.'

'Three six from Dispatch, receiving.'

'We're at the Cross Keys pub. I'm going to need SOCOs down here immediately to look over a stolen car. I'm also going to need a patrol unit to come and take witness statements from staff and customers, over.'

'Three six, received. Will advise on ETA, over, out.'

The constable approached. 'My sergeant is over there taking a statement from the manager, ma'am.'

'Okay. I want witness statements from everyone inside. No one leaves until they've spoken to us. And see if they've got CCTV for the car park.'

'Yes, ma'am,' he said, and made his way towards the pub.

Nick frowned at Ruth.

'What's up?' she asked.

'How did they get away?'

'Sorry?'

'They dumped the Audi here but we're in the middle of nowhere. How are they travelling now?'

It was a very good point.

'They don't strike me as being organised enough to have had another car here. Maybe someone came to pick them up?' Ruth suggested.

The uniformed sergeant came over holding his notepad. 'Ma'am, I've just taken a statement from the landlord. A Keith Fletcher.'

'Anything interesting, sergeant?' Nick asked.

'About an hour ago, a girl bought a very expensive bottle of champagne from the bar. A hundred and twenty pounds. She paid in cash and apparently pulled out a thick wad of notes from her trouser pocket.'

'Didn't they ID her?' Ruth asked.

The sergeant raised his eyebrow. 'Apparently not, ma'am.'

'Did they give you a description?'

'Late teens. Blonde hair. Nose-ring.'

Ruth looked at Nick – *sounds like Kat Williams.*

'Anything else, sergeant?' Nick asked.

'Yes, sir. A barman, Will Nelson, went out to the car park about ten minutes ago when he noticed his car has been stolen. He's just phoned it in to Bala Police Station.'

Ruth exchanged a look with Nick – *now we know how they left the car park.*

HAVING FOUND A SMALL, budget hotel, Finn and Kat were now in their hotel room. It was neat, clean, and functional. The television was blaring, and Kat was sitting against some pillows drinking. She had said very little since they'd heard the BBC news an hour earlier.

Finn went back to the mirror. He had taken the electric clippers to his hair and now he had a grade 1 buzz cut all over. He rubbed his scalp over the sink. The last few tiny fragments of hair dropped from his head.

Looking at his reflection, Finn liked what he had done. More importantly, it had changed his whole appearance so that he no longer fitted the description that the police would have. He hadn't had a haircut this short since his first few years at Ockley Cross. Having a shaved head in the Institution often signalled that you thought you could handle yourself, and attracted the wrong sort of attention. He had kept it long ever since.

Putting on his Aviator-style sunglasses, he made his appearance from the bathroom and grinned at Kat.

'Hey, what do you think?' he asked.

Kat gave him a cursory glance and then went back to watching the television. 'Yeah, it looks good.'

Not the reaction I was looking for.

Finn frowned. It seemed that the events of the day were starting to sink in and Kat looked pale and frightened.

'I think I look like a hitman, don't you?' Finn said, swaggering around and attempting to get her attention and make her laugh. 'Proper hard.'

There was no reaction from Kat, which annoyed him. She wasn't the only one who was worried, for God's sake!

'Why've you got a face on?'

'What?' Kat snapped at him.

'Is there a problem? You haven't been the same since we heard that thing on the news.'

'Is there a problem? Are you bloody kidding me?' she growled. 'I watched you murder my stepdad. How do you expect me to be, Finn?'

'Hey, he was trying to kill us! I'm not having you try and put all the blame on me,' he said forcefully, feeling himself tensing with anger.

'That's not what I mean. I just mean he's dead. We did that,' Kat said as a tear rolled down her face and she sniffed.

Finn took off the sunglasses and sat down next to her on the bed. She hugged her knees and looked so young that it was hard to stay angry with her. 'You know what type of a man he was. He was a bloody creep. He was trying to abuse you Kat. He would have killed us if I hadn't stabbed him.'

Kat broke down in floods of tears. 'I know. Sorry. I'm just so bloody confused. He was a bastard. He hurt Henry. He hurt mum. He made me feel fucking sick to my stomach.'

Finn put his hand on her head and stroked her hair. 'Hey. The man had it coming to him. What were we supposed to do?'

Kat sat up, moved her hair from her tear-streaked face and sniffed. 'I know. I feel so guilty about getting you involved in all this.'

Finn wiped a tear from her cheek. 'You don't need to be. I was protecting you. I won't let anyone hurt you ever again.'

Kat looked at him with a growing smile. 'Thank you. What did I ever do to deserve someone like you?'

'We're in this together, okay? You don't need to worry about a thing.'

Kat moved closer and pulled Finn to her. She kissed him on the lips and then put her arms around him.

'Promise me something,' she whispered.

'Anything. What is it?'

'Promise you'll never hurt me, Finn.'

He moved away from her and took both her hands in his. 'I promise. I could never hurt you. Never.'

She smiled.

Finn bounced off the bed and went to a shopping bag. He pulled out two boxes of hair dye and waved them at her with a smile. He wanted to cheer her up a little. 'Come on. Your turn. We've got 'deeply wicked black' or 'bitter sweet chocolate.'

Kat laughed. 'Deeply wicked black!'

CHAPTER 17

IT WAS 10PM AND DARK outside. Ruth was sitting in IR1, Incident Room 1, which had now been transformed with scene boards, files, and everything else that went with a murder case. CID only moved across to IR1 when there was a major crime.

Ruth sifted through some of the reports and emails. Traffic and ANPR had made no progress in finding the Ford Fiesta that Finn and Kat had stolen from the Cross Keys pub.

There was a knock at the open door. It was the new DC, Georgie Wild. Ruth felt guilty that she hadn't had the time to sit down and have a welcoming chat yet. That was the thing with a murder case. There was no time for anything else.

'Georgie?'

Georgie smiled and looked at the printout in her hand. 'Boss. A few sightings of our suspects. One in Cardiff and one in Cumbria. I don't think either of them is a solid lead though.'

'Why's that?'

'I spoke to both callers and they were incredibly vague. The one in Cardiff thought there might have been kids in the back of the car.'

'Okay, thanks Georgie. How are you settling in?'

'Fine. Good actually ... boss.' She smiled. 'It's going to take me a bit of time to get used to calling you boss and not ma'am though.'

Ruth nodded. 'Yeah, I remember that. When this investigation is over, we'll have a proper sit down and a chat, eh?'

'Yeah, I'd like that. At the risk of jumping the gun, I already have my eye on getting my sergeant's exams done,' Georgie said.

Ruth shrugged. 'Nothing wrong with that. I want ambitious officers in CID.'

Georgie looked suitably encouraged as she turned and left.

She's impressive, I'll give her that, Ruth thought.

Getting up from her desk, she grabbed her lukewarm coffee and wandered over to the scene boards that DC Jim Garrow and DC Dan French had assembled that afternoon.

Ruth saw Garrow coming down the corridor and entering IR1. He was tall and wiry, and he had recently grown a beard. Although she knew beards were fashionable, she wondered if he subconsciously looked up to Nick and tried to copy his style.

'What have we got Jim?' she asked him as he made his way over to her.

'I did some digging around into Crispin Neal's prior convictions. The restraining order he received in 2017 was a Section 12. It was issued after an allegation that Neal had made inappropriate advances to the fourteen-year-old daughter of the woman he was living with. When she threw him out of the house they lived in, Neal made persistent attempts to make contact until North Wales Police were contacted,' Garrow explained.

Ruth liked Garrow. Even though he was young, he had a good instinct for police investigations.

'What about the GBH?' Ruth asked.

'Same MO. Neal had been living with a woman up in Rhyl. He made several advances towards the woman's thirteen-year-old daughter. When the girl's father found out, he confronted Neal, who then hit him with a brick and put him in hospital.'

'So, this is a pattern of behaviour going back years,' Ruth said, thinking out loud.

'Looks like it, boss. If he had tried something like that with Kat Williams, then it would explain why an argument could have developed with her and Finn Starling.'

'Thanks, Jim. Great work,' Ruth said. She could see that her praise had given Garrow a lift, even though he tried to be uber professional.

'Thanks, boss.'

As Garrow wandered back to his desk, Ruth went over to the scene boards. Looking at the photograph of Crispin Neal, she wondered what made a man repeat that pattern of predatory behaviour. If she had been Kat Williams, and confronted by a man like Neal, would she have stabbed him?

HAVING JUST BATHED his daughter Megan, Nick wrapped her in a towel and carried her through to her bedroom. She laughed at nothing in particular. Nick and Megan rubbed noses before he put her in a nappy and her pink pyjamas. The room was warm and smelled of talc and baby lotion. In moments like this, Nick felt an overwhelming sense of how lucky he was. Lucky to have found someone like Amanda, and lucky to have a beautiful daughter.

He tickled Megan and was carrying her over to her cot bed as Amanda appeared at the door.

'Fish cakes or fish pie?' she asked.

'Erm, steak,' Nick grinned.

'We don't have any steak. And I thought we were going pescatarian.'

'You choose. Honestly. I don't mind.'

Amanda disappeared downstairs to start cooking dinner. Nick knew that a few years ago he would have scoffed at this scene of domestic bliss, and thought it dull and boring. Instead, he thought that the endless nights of drinking to blackout, urine-soaked beds, sweats and shakes, were the rock'n'roll lifestyle he was destined for.

Once he had read Megan a bedtime story, he went downstairs where Amanda had set the table. She had dimmed the lights, lit candles, and soft music was playing.

What's going on? Nick wondered as he sat down.

'Here we go, sir,' she said with a smile as she brought the plates through.

Nick raised an eyebrow. 'Erm, everything all right?'

Amanda sat down. 'What do you mean?'

'All this. Candles, music. You do know that I'm happy to have sex with you whenever you want? You don't need to seduce me.'

'Oh, that's nice. I just thought it would be romantic.'

'Have you done something? Or bought something you shouldn't have?'

Amanda rolled her eyes. 'You don't have to be a dickhead all the time.'

'You say that, but I do find it a bit of a struggle.'

Amanda nodded. 'That's true. You really do ... How's the new DC shaping up?'

'She's all right. Very young but she'll be okay.'

'She? You didn't say the DC was a woman.'

Nick grinned. 'Didn't I? Well, the DC is a woman.'

'Ha, ha. Is she a replacement for Sian?'

'No one is going to say it, but I suppose she is.'

'That's going to be hard for her. And hard for Ruth having a new female officer.'

'I suppose so. I looked at Sian's empty desk today. It really got to me.'

Amanda reached over and touched his hand. 'Of course. You two were close.'

There was silence.

Nick was keen to change the subject. 'So, why are we having a candlelit dinner?'

'Okay. I lied. There is something I want to talk about.'

'That sounds ominous,' Nick said. 'Do you want a new kitchen?'

Amanda gave him a playful hit on the arm. 'Why do you say stupid things like that?'

'Because I'm emotionally stunted and find serious conversations very awkward and uncomfortable. I use humour as my defence,' he quipped.

Amanda stared at him for a second. 'Well, I'm pregnant so make a joke out of that.'

Wow! I did not see that coming.

'What? How did that happen?'

'How the bloody hell do you think it happened, you twit.'

'Oh yeah ... Brilliant. That's great,' Nick said, feeling shocked.

CHAPTER 18

RUTH HAD ARRIVED AT work early. She had always been lucky that she could survive on five or six hours of sleep a night and still function. She remembered reading that Margaret Thatcher had only slept for four hours a night when she was Prime Minister. Ruth was amazed at this fact until she read a recent report that described how Thatcher had slept in her official car between meetings. In fact, the Prime Minister's security team were so worried that she would be injured while asleep in the back of her Daimler that they fitted special headrests to protect her. Thatcher's boastful claim about her lack of sleep had also now been proved to be foolhardy. Such sleeping patterns are thought to be a major cause of dementia, a disease from which Margaret Thatcher died in 2013.

Sitting back in the chair, Ruth looked down. Her stomach strained a little at the waist of her trousers. She knew she had put on weight since Sian's death. It was a mixture of too much booze and comfort eating. She also couldn't remember the last time she had been running. It had been part of her daily routine in her 40s in London, and when she had first arrived in North Wales. She had told everyone that it was going to be one of the great benefits of moving to Snowdonia. A daily run in the stunning countryside. It sounded romantic and empowering. But, like every other resolution she had ever made, it had petered out and eventually stopped.

After another hour of tedious paperwork, Ruth walked along the corridor and headed downstairs to get a coffee. She didn't have time to go outside for a ciggie as well, however much she was craving one. She had no idea how heavy smokers ever managed to quit. She had tried nicotine patches and gum. Her daughter Ella had even suggested hypnotherapy, but Ruth thought that sounded like money for old rope.

As she waited in a short queue in the canteen, her mind turned to the case. They were still waiting for a decent lead on where Finn and Kat were hiding out. And with the stolen £2,000, they would be at an advantage in their ability to stay undetected.

She glanced at her watch. It was 6.50am. As she took her coffee over to the till, she became aware of someone approaching. It was DCI Drake, her boss. He was an imposing figure. Black, shaved head, goatee, and handsome. It had taken her three years to stop thinking of him as 'Guvnor' after decades in the Met.

Ruth gestured to the till. 'Do you want anything, boss?'

'No, I'm fine thanks. I'm on my second coffee of the day already.'

'Caffeine addiction. One of the many perks of the job.'

Ruth paid for the coffee with her police smart card, stirred in some sugar, and put on the plastic lid that was now required by Health and Safety for all hot drinks being carried in the building. What was the world coming to?

Drake gestured to the door. 'You heading back to CID?'

'Yes, boss. I've got morning briefing in ten minutes, so I'd better get my skates on.'

'I'll walk with you then,' he said as he rubbed his hand over his goatee. It was something Ruth had noticed that he did when he was deep in thought.

As they reached the door, they manoeuvred around three uniformed officers entering the canteen and laughing loudly. It reminded Ruth of her more carefree days as a PC on the beat. In those days, it was walking the beat or riding in a patrol car. Bit of paperwork and that was that. Ruth was now responsible for over a dozen CID detectives and was the SIO, Senior Investigating Officer, on every major crime in Llancastell and the surrounding area. Even though she had come to North Wales Police for a quieter life, she now enjoyed the challenge of running her own team. She'd never had the chance in the Met. There were just too many ambitious coppers willing to screw over anyone and everyone in their way.

Drake held open the door for her and then asked, 'What have we got on the victim?'

'Crispin Neal. Forty. Stabbed at his home and died at the scene,' Ruth explained as they walked along the corridor and headed for the lift to the sixth floor.

'Possible suspects?'

'Nick and I attended a domestic dispute two nights ago between Crispin Neal and his wife's ex-husband Ben Williams. Some argument about Williams' children who live with their mother, Natalie, and now with her new husband Neal,' Ruth said as they stopped to wait at the lift.

Drake reached over, pushed the button, and the lift doors opened with a metallic clunk. 'Was it serious?'

'Don't think so. Just a bit of shoving. But Nick remembered that Neal had previous for possession of indecent images. Two years suspended and he's now on the Sex Offenders Register.'

The lift doors closed. Ruth felt the rickety lift lurch as it headed up to the sixth floor.

'Do you think that's relevant to his murder?'

'We're not sure if there's a connection. He has previous for inappropriate behaviour around the teenage daughters of his ex-partners.'

'Does this Ben Williams have an alibi?' Drake asked.

The lift jolted to a halt and the doors opened. They both stepped out and turned left towards the CID offices.

'Yes. He's a mortgage advisor at an estate agents in town. According to five people in the office, Williams was there all morning and didn't leave. In fact, he had a meeting at the time of the attack.'

'That sounds pretty conclusive ... Did the wife know Neal was on the register?'

'Yeah. Although Nick and I went there to check that she was aware of his record as there are children living there.'

'What did she say?'

Ruth shrugged. 'She wasn't concerned at all about his record. She said it was all a big mistake. She couldn't see that having a man with that type of conviction, who was on the Sex Offenders Register, in a house with two children was a problem.'

Drake shook his head and said sarcastically, 'Of course, not. Does the wife have an alibi?'

'No. But she discovered the body. When we interviewed her earlier, she was in a complete state. We can't rule her out, but my instinct is that she had nothing to do with it.'

Ruth glanced into IR1. Her CID team were sitting, chatting, and waiting for the morning briefing to begin. 'I'd better go, boss.'

Drake gestured to the room. 'Mind if I sit in?'

Ruth opened the door and motioned for Drake to go in. 'Of course not. Be my guest.'

Once in a while, Drake would sit in on briefings, particularly if there had been a serious crime such as a murder. He didn't need to ask, but that was his style of man management. Respect.

As Drake sat discreetly at the back of the room, Ruth marched through IR1 and took her position by the scene boards. 'Thanks everyone. If we can settle down now, please. DCI Drake will be joining us this morning.'

Even though Drake was an excellent and approachable DCI, his presence in a briefing always changed the atmosphere. Everyone was on their toes, and the ambitious officers were keen to impress.

Ruth pointed to the photograph of Crispin Neal. 'As you are now aware this is our victim, Crispin Neal. Our initial prime suspect was Natalie's ex-husband, Ben Williams, but he has a watertight alibi. We do, however, have a strong line of enquiry. Nick?'

Nick got up from where he was sitting, approached the boards, and pointed to a photograph. 'This is Finn Starling, age twenty-two. He is the young man who decided to borrow one of the town's buses two days ago.'

French shook his head. 'How could we forget?'

There was muted laughter from some of the detectives.

Nick pointed to another photograph. 'His girlfriend is Kat Williams. Nineteen. She lives with her mother and stepfather Crispin Neal. Ben Williams, her father, implied to me that she had a very difficult relationship with Neal and that his behaviour around her was creepy. Yesterday morning, Starling attacked an employee at the BDG DIY Warehouse where he and Kat Williams both work. He then took £2,000 from the safe and stole the manager's car. He and Kat fled the scene together.'

Georgie looked over from her desk. 'How does that tie in with Crispin Neal's murder, Sarge?'

'Natalie Williams confirmed that her daughter had packed and taken a suitcase with all her possessions. Our hypothesis is that Finn and Kat left the scene of the crime and made their way to Kat's home to collect her belongings. Crispin Neal was either there already or returned home. There was some kind of confrontation and Neal was stabbed by one of them. They fled, and Natalie Williams returned home to find him still breathing. He died shortly after the paramedics arrived.'

Ruth motioned towards Garrow. 'Jim did some digging last night.'

Garrow glanced up from where he was sitting. 'Neal has previous for inappropriate behaviour around the teenage daughters of his partners. That has led to a charge of GBH with one of the girl's fathers and a restraining order from another ex-partner.'

Nick nodded. 'That fits in with what Ben Williams told me. He claimed that Kat described Neal as a creep, and she wanted to leave the house and live with her father.'

Drake sat forward on his seat. 'If Neal made inappropriate advances or even abused Kat, that gives us a motive for his murder.'

Ruth went over to a map of North Wales and pointed to a red pin. 'This is the Cross Keys pub where they abandoned a stolen Audi, and where Finn and Kat stole a Ford Fiesta. That means they were heading west away from Llancastell and into Snowdonia.'

'Any leads to where they might be going?' Drake asked.

Ruth picked up her bottle of water and had a swig. 'Finn's family are in Newcastle, but he hasn't seen them for over a decade.'

'Why's that, boss?' Garrow asked.

Ruth glanced over at Nick. 'Finn is in witness protection. At the moment, that's all you need to know.'

She spotted Garrow frowning and looking over at French. She knew that CID officers were never happy investigating a case where information was being withheld. However, she wasn't about to divulge the details of why Finn had been taken into the PPS.

Time to move this on.

'I'm waiting for Natalie Williams to give us the name of anyone that Kat might know in the area. Friends or family. She couldn't think straight at the time, but she'll let me know if someone springs to mind.'

Georgie marched over. 'Boss, we've got a report of a young couple staying in the Lakeview Hotel in Betws-y-Co-ed. Their car's plate matches the stolen car from the Cross Keys pub.'

Bloody hell.

Ruth felt a surge of adrenaline. 'Thanks, Georgie. Right, let's get going. Nick, you drive, and I'll smoke. Someone call the local plod and seal off the hotel.'

CHAPTER 19

FINN TURNED OVER IN the bed. The sheets were crisp and cold on his face. His sleep had been restless as he had been dreaming about his brother Steven. They were playing football in Walker Park but had become distracted by a dead wood pigeon that Steven had found lying in the goal. Steven was crying because he thought that the bird's death had been his fault.

As Finn blinked in the light of the morning, he started to piece together everything that had happened the day before, and his stomach began to tense with nerves. He sat up in bed and spotted Kat sitting by the window drinking tea.

'Why didn't you wake me up?' he asked, rubbing his head before remembering that all his hair had gone.

Kat smiled at him. 'After yesterday, I thought you could do with a lie in. You were talking in your sleep. It was really cute.'

Finn squinted at the sunshine coming in through the window. 'What time is it?'

Kat put down the tea and glanced up at the television which was on but silent. 'Nearly nine.'

Finn launched himself out of the bed. 'Bloody hell! We need to get going.'

'But no one knows we're here.'

'The longer we're in one place, the more chance of someone seeing the car or hearing the news,' Finn explained as he got dressed. He had hoped to leave at first light and assumed that he would have woken up early.

Kat came over and put her arms around him. 'Hey, it's all right. We'll just pack up our stuff, get in the car, and go. We'll get breakfast on the way.'

Finn felt himself relax in the pressure of her arms. She was right. He was over-reacting. They kissed.

'Yeah. Sorry. It's fine.'

Kat went to the kettle and clicked it on. 'I'll make you a quick brew before we go.' She then glanced out of the window. 'Shit! Finn!'

That doesn't sound good.

His heart sank.

He went over to see what she was looking at. 'What is it?'

A police patrol car had blocked the exit from the hotel car park.

There were a couple of uniformed officers walking around slowly and checking each car as they went. Two other figures were heading for the main entrance and reception. He recognised them. They were the two detectives that had interviewed him at Llancastell Police Station.

Shit!

The blood had drained from Kat's face. 'What are we going to do?'

Finn was trying to concentrate but his head was whirling in a total panic. 'We can't go out the front or anywhere near the car ... Grab your stuff and I'll bring the money.'

Kat quickly threw her makeup and hair dryer into her small, pink suitcase and zipped it shut.

Finn's heart was thudding hard against his chest. He went to the door and listened. Nothing.

'Where are we going to go, Finn?' Kat sounded terrified.

'It's going to be fine. I've got an idea.'

He opened the room door slowly and peered along the corridor. At the far end, there was a housekeeping trolley piled high with white towels and sheets.

No sign of coppers yet. Time to move.

They crept cautiously into the corridor.

Spotting a fire alarm on the wall, Finn walked over and gave it a sharp jab with his elbow. The glass smashed and a second later the loud alarm began to wail. It was deafening.

Doors along the corridor began to open.

He reached back and took Kat by the hand, then they walked calmly down the corridor towards the doors marked *Fire Exit*.

Several confused residents had now come out of their rooms, asking each other if there really was a fire, or if it was a drill.

Finn glanced at Kat and whispered, 'Don't stop and don't make eye contact with anyone.' His pulse was racing and his breathing shallow.

They reached the fire doors and pushed them open. In front of them was another, darker, corridor. At the end were two fire exit doors with emergency release bars. Finn let go of Kat's hand and strode towards them. He hit the bars, and the doors swung open with a bang.

Looking around and squinting in the daylight outside, Finn realised that they were at the back of the hotel where deliveries were made. Across from the loading area were a series of industrial bins and a six-foot wire fence. Beyond that, fields stretched away and down to a dense wooded area.

'Come on,' Finn said, aware that some of the hotel employees were now outside due to the alarm.

'Where are we going now?' Kat asked.

'This way. Quickly.'

They headed past the bins and followed the line of the fence for a minute. Finn glanced back. No one was following them, or seemed particularly interested in where they were going.

Spotting a fence pole, Finn stopped and looked at Kat. 'This will do.'

'We're going over that?' she asked.

'Yep.' Finn tossed the bag of money and Kat's suitcase over the fence and then cupped his hands so he could give Kat a boost to help her get over.

She put a foot onto his hands, and he lifted her up. She swung her leg over the top of the fence and then dropped down the other side.

Finn grabbed the wire mesh, pulled himself to the top, and slid down to the ground.

He retrieved the bag and case. 'Haven't done that for a while.'

Kat stared at the fields and woods ahead of them and then down at her flimsy pumps. 'I'm going to ruin my shoes.'

Finn patted the bag of money. 'It's okay. I think we can afford to buy you some more.'

HAVING ESTABLISHED that there was no fire in the hotel, the alarm had been turned off. Guests were sent back to their rooms and told to wait until they had spoken to the police. Although they knew from the CCTV that Finn and Kat had checked in and stayed the night in Room 17, Ruth wanted every room thoroughly searched. The staff on reception hadn't seen a young couple leaving the hotel that morning and were fairly sure they would have noticed if they had.

Ruth and Nick cautiously approached Room 17. The anxious-looking Duty Manager had an electronic master key in his hand. Behind them, two uniformed police officers stood ready for the arrest.

Nick banged on the door. 'Police! Open up!'

They waited for a few seconds. Ruth listened carefully but there was no sound of movement from inside.

Nick banged again. 'Police! Open the door!'

There was still no answer, so Ruth gave the Duty Manager a nod and he used his master key to open the door.

When they entered, it was clear within a few seconds that Finn and Kat had gone. Nick inspected the bathroom and pulled back the shower curtain. 'Nothing, boss.'

'Shit! They can't have got very far if they don't have a vehicle,' Ruth said, thinking aloud.

'Unless they've stolen another one. How did no one see them leave?'

Ruth looked at the Duty Manager. 'Do you have CCTV on all the exits to the hotel?'

He shook his head. 'There's CCTV on the main entrance, the guest car park, and around the side. Coverage to the rear of the hotel is minimal as we don't tend to need it there.'

'Thank you. We're going to need to look at all your CCTV from this morning.'

The Duty Manager nodded, his eyes blinking nervously. 'I'll get straight onto that now.'

Nick came out of the bathroom with a small, aluminium bin. 'Boss, you need to take a look at this.'

Peering inside, she could see clumps of brown hair. There was also an empty box of black hair dye. 'They've changed their appearance, which is pretty smart.'

Nick gestured to the bin. 'I guess they didn't count on us finding this.'

Ruth glanced over at the two uniformed officers. 'Take witness statements from everyone in the hotel. Get their names and contact details. I want to know if they saw a young couple anywhere in the hotel this morning, particularly when the fire alarm was going off. The man has shaved or very short hair, the girl has black hair.'

The constables went out of the room.

Ruth held the door and motioned to Nick to come outside. 'When they left the room, they must have come down this corridor.' Glancing left, she saw the small red Fire Alarm. The glass front had been broken. 'They set off the fire alarm here.'

Nick gestured to the *Fire Exit* sign further down the corridor. 'And in all the confusion, they headed out there.'

Ruth and Nick strode down the corridor, went out through the fire exit, and soon found the double fire doors wide open.

'Bollocks,' Ruth said as they came out of the fire doors at the back of the hotel. She was certain that Finn and Kat had escaped this way.

'Explains why no one on reception saw them leave this morning,' Nick groaned.

'Where did they go from here?'

Nick motioned to their left. 'That way would have led them to the main car park and reception. Which leaves that way.'

Ruth stared at the fence and then at the fields that stretched away. 'You think they're going cross country?'

'I can't see where else they could have gone.'

'Let's get the helicopter to have a look, shall we?'

Ruth glanced at Nick as she clicked her radio.

CHAPTER 20

FINN AND KAT WERE TRAMPING uphill through the dense trees of Gwydir Forest Park to the west of Betws-y-Co-ed. The park covered thirty square miles, most of which was woodland. It was divided by various enormous valleys and rivers. The majority of the forest was coniferous – everything from the Scots pine to the Norway spruce. The trees were particularly suited to the poor, shallow soil. Further to the west, the dark mountain ranges of the Glyderau, the Carneddau and even Snowdon rose into the sky.

As he stopped to take a breath, Finn looked down at Kat's slip on, ballet-pump shoes that were covered in mud. 'Your feet okay?'

She pulled a face as she wiped sweat from her face. 'I would kill for some walking boots.'

'First chance we get, we'll buy whatever you want.'

'You could give me a piggyback?'

He snorted. 'I don't think so. Not up this hill.'

Kat hit him playfully. 'Hey. What are you trying to say? I'm not that fat thanks very much.'

Finn put down the bag of money and the suitcase. He stretched out his aching arms and shoulders, and gazed up at the forest ahead. It seemed like a different country. Sweden or Denmark, was it? He thought he had seen forests like this on TV.

Kat came over and put her arms around his waist. 'We're going to get out of this okay, aren't we?'

'Of course.' He leant in and gave her a kiss.

She screwed up her face. 'Eww. You're all sweaty.'

'I thought I was your prince?'

'A bloody sweaty, smelly prince.' Kat laughed.

Finn hauled the bag of money back up onto his shoulder, which was now sore, and grabbed Kat's case. 'Come on. We need to keep moving.'

Glancing up, he could see that even though the sun was bright, its light was blocked by the interwoven branches of the pine trees high above them that formed a dark canopy. The forest was dank, but the air was clean and pure. The pines had a citrus-like smell, like a lemon.

Being out of the sun and hidden away in the forest was exactly what they needed as they escaped, Finn thought.

As they trudged on, Kat glanced over at him. 'You keep saying that we're going to Ireland. And that we're going on the ferry from Holyhead. But you haven't said where we're going in Ireland once we get there.'

'I've got a friend there. Sean. He lives in Tipperary, which is down in the south. He says it's beautiful. He told me to look him up if I was ever there.' Finn didn't divulge that he and Sean Brennan had shared a cell for two years at Ockley Cross. Sean had been sent there after he stabbed and nearly killed a drug dealer in Liverpool when he was only thirteen.

'How do you know Sean then?' Kat asked.

'You know. Round and about.'

'Did you meet him when you were in prison?'

What did she just say?

Finn stopped in his tracks and glared at her. '*What*?'

'I'm not stupid, Finn. You said it the other day. You said "do you know what it's like in prison?" You could only say that if you had been inside.'

I do not want to talk about this now!

Finn started to feel defensive and angry. 'Don't be daft. That's not what I meant.'

'I don't care if you have. But if we're in this together, you have to tell me everything or what's the point?'

He looked at her for a second. Her expression was soft and caring.

Maybe she isn't going to judge me after all? Maybe she really does love me despite what I've done?

Finn mumbled, 'Okay ...'

'Okay? Is that okay you've been to prison?'

'Yes, I went to prison. Well, a young offenders institution. Sorry.'

'Why are you sorry?'

'I should have told you before ... but I was embarrassed.'

Kat went over to him and put her hand to his face. 'Why would you be embarrassed with me? We're soulmates.'

She paused for a moment then said, 'You didn't kill anybody did you?'

Finn felt sick as his stomach lurched.

That's exactly what I did. It was an accident, but I killed two people and an unborn child.

He shook his head. 'No, no. It was arson. Someone got hurt but it was an accident. I didn't know they were going to be there.'

Kat shrugged. 'Right, so now I know.'

Finn turned and continued to walk. He took a deep breath of the forest air. Even though he hadn't told her the whole truth, it still felt good to have told her some of it. It was one less lie to carry around.

'What was it like?' Kat asked.

'The young offenders place?'

'Yeah.'

'Horrible. You just live on your nerves the whole time in case someone wants to attack you.'

'Is that how you got those scars on your back?'

'Yeah. Some nutter with a Stanley knife. All I did was laugh when he tripped over in the canteen. Two hours later he cornered me in the tool shed and cut me to pieces. I lost so much blood I nearly died.'

Kat reached out and took his hand. 'Hey, you've got me to look after you now.'

Finn felt a rush of emotion as their palms touched. He squeezed her small and delicate hand in his. 'I thought it was my job to look after you.'

'Works both ways.'

In a clearing up ahead they saw a large, white farmhouse. Finn noticed that there were clothes hanging up on the line. He could also smell a wood fire burning somewhere nearby. Someone was definitely inside.

They heard a crunch to the right, and out of the trees a car appeared driving along a track. It was heading for the farmhouse.

Finn ducked and pulled Kat down into the under-growth. He couldn't tell if the driver had spotted them or not.

Bloody hell!

Kat whispered, 'Shit. Do you think they saw us?'

He put his finger to his lips as he moved very slowly to take a look.

The car was now parked outside the farmhouse.

As Finn slowly moved some leaves out of his view, he saw that the driver was now making his way down the slope to where they were hiding.

IT WAS MID-EVENING by the time Ruth had assembled the CID team in IR1. Drake had agreed that they now needed to use the media to track Finn and Kat down, so Ruth was to hold a press conference early the following morning.

Striding from her office, Ruth could tell that the team was now running on adrenaline. It was always like that with a murder case. It's what many officers joined CID to do. The big, glamorous cases. It was also the thing that got up uniformed officers' noses who were sometimes treated as second rate by younger detectives who didn't know better.

Ruth walked over to the large map of North Wales and pointed to an area close to Betws-y-Coed that had been circled. A red pin had been placed to indicate the hotel from where Finn and Kat had escaped. 'After much begging on my part, we got the helicopter to do a sweep over this area here. Unfortunately, there was no sign of Finn and Kat. It's dense woodland so visibility is difficult. There are lots of isolated farms, houses and small hamlets all around here and we have no idea where the couple were going.'

Garrow leaned forward on his chair. 'They won't want to spend the night outside though. It will be a bit cold up there.'

'They could be hiding out in a barn,' French suggested.

Ruth leaned against the table to take the weight off her feet for a second. 'I think our use of the media is going to be vital. A young couple on foot like that would stand out in those places.'

'We know that Finn can hotwire cars. They might be back on the road already,' Nick pointed out.

Ruth nodded with a frustrated wrinkle of her nose. 'That's another possibility. Whoever is on the night shift needs to liaise with the switchboard about any calls coming in reporting stolen cars.'

Georgie met Ruth's eye with a trace of uncertainty before she said, 'And they've got all that money. Which means they can get petrol, food, and a change of clothes whenever they want. They might even find someone who will sell them an old car for cash.'

Ruth gave Georgie a subtle but encouraging smile. 'Good point, Georgie.'

Nick looked over at Ruth. 'There is even the possibility that they've taken someone hostage so they can use their house to rest overnight.'

Ruth thought about this for a second before frowning. 'It's possible.'

'You don't seem convinced, boss?'

'I'm not sure that these two are like that.'

Nick furrowed his brow. 'I know that Kat's not. But Finn probably killed Crispin Neal in cold blood.'

Ruth could see that Nick had already made his mind up about Finn.

'Did he? Crispin Neal had a history of attempting to abuse the teenage daughters of his partners. It wouldn't be a stretch to assume that he had tried to abuse Kat, or even succeeded. She might have stabbed him in self defence. We don't know what happened.'

'Finn's not exactly a choir boy. He hit someone with a hammer and stole two grand.'

Ruth knew that what Nick was saying was true. But her instincts told her that Finn and Kat were not two lawless criminals on the run. Wondering where they had got to, and what they were doing now, Ruth was also getting an increasingly uneasy feeling about what they might do next.

She looked out at her CID team and said with a sense of urgency, 'Whatever you think, they are a young couple who are getting increasingly out of their depth. I want them found as soon as ever possible before they do something really stupid and ruin their lives, or someone else's.'

CHAPTER 21

FINN SHIFTED HIS CHAIR away from the long wooden table and got up. He looked around the farmhouse kitchen as he went over to the elderly woman who was carrying over two serving bowls of food.

We've really landed on our feet here, he thought cheerfully.

The air smelled of food and the wood that was burning in the log burner at the other end of the room.

Finn and Kat had been invited into the farmhouse two hours earlier when Bill had spotted them from his car and come down to ask them if they were lost. Finn told him they had been staying in Betsw-y-Coed, then headed into Gwydir Forest hoping to find a guesthouse further down the A5, but had become lost.

'Let me help you with that, Gwen,' Finn said as he took the bowls from her and carried them to the table where Kat sat with the woman's husband.

Gwen chuckled as she peered over at Kat. 'You've got him well trained haven't you love?'

Kat laughed as she ran her hand through her long dark hair. 'Sometimes, Gwen. Other times I have to crack the whip to keep him in line.'

They all laughed.

Finn gave Kat a wink as he put the blue and white china bowls down on the placemats.

Gwen was short with greying hair and glasses. Bill had a shock of swept-back white hair and bushy, unkempt eyebrows.

Bill gestured to the food as Gwen and Finn sat down. 'Tuck in, you two. No need to stand on ceremony here.'

Finn and Kat helped themselves to stew, potatoes, and mixed vegetables.

'Thanks. This is so kind of you,' Kat said.

'Just a few days away is it?' Gwen asked.

Finn finished a mouthful of stew. 'Yeah. Just a change of scene, that's all.'

'You're a long way from the A5 here lad,' Bill said, before glancing at Gwen. 'They must have taken the wrong track at Cae'n y Coed and ended up here.'

Kat smiled and pointed her fork at Finn. 'It's a bit embarrassing. But I'm blaming him as it was his idea to come away walking.'

Finn shrugged with a smile. 'Guilty as charged.'

'You're not from around here are you lad?' Bill asked.

'No. I'm not.'

'That's a Tyneside accent if I'm not mistaken.'

'Spot on. I was born in Newcastle. It's Kat's fault I'm in North Wales now.'

Gwen looked at them approvingly. 'Doesn't matter where you are as long as you're together.'

Kat gave Finn a smile as she moved the food around the plate. He was getting a thrill from playing the happy couple at the dinner table. It felt warm and reassuring.

Bill glanced down at his watch and sat forward. 'I tell you what. It's getting late. Why don't you two stop here with us tonight? Get a decent night's sleep and I'll drop you down to that guesthouse, or wherever you want to go, in the morning.'

Finn looked over at Kat. It wasn't the worst idea to spend the night in a farmhouse in the middle of nowhere.

Kat smiled at them. 'That's very kind but we couldn't.'

But we could.

Finn shook his head. 'No, no. We can't do that.'

'There's a lovely spare room upstairs that our son uses when he comes to stay with us. Clean sheets. We won't take no for an answer,' Gwen said, looking at them.

Nice one.

Finn shrugged. 'If you're sure?'

Bill nodded. 'Aye lad. No problem. I've got a bottle of Scotch in the cabinet. We'll go and sit by the fire while these two do the washing up, eh?'

Gwen gave Bill a playful slap on the arm. 'You've got a bloody cheek, William Tomlinson.'

Finn grinned and sat back in his chair. 'Sounds good to me, Bill.'

Kat raised an eyebrow. 'Don't even think about it. You're doing the washing up with me.'

They all laughed.

IT WAS LATE. THE NIGHT air was cool as Nick made his way into the car park to drive home. He was still getting his head around Amanda being pregnant. It hadn't been planned. If he was honest, Nick had hoped to have two or three years before they had another child. In fact, they hadn't even discussed having another baby yet. Even though he loved Megan to bits, their lives had become chaotic and tiring since her birth. He wanted to get back to some sort of normality and routine before more nappies and sleepless nights.

Buttoning up his jacket, he suddenly heard the sound of a car door opening. He turned and spotted Georgie getting out of her car and looking down at something.

Looks like she needs some help, Nick thought.

He strolled over with a little flicker of excitement in each step. He couldn't help it. Georgie was very attractive. And it wasn't as if anything was going to happen.

'Everything all right?'

'Not really.' Georgie pointed to the front tyre on the driver's side. It was completely flat.

'Right. Bit of a pain. Where's your spare?' Nick asked.

Georgie indicated the thinner rear tyre on the same side. 'That's my space saver.'

Nick rubbed his beard. 'Which means that you haven't got a spare?'

'No. I've been meaning to go and get it repaired. But with this new job ...'

He grinned and shrugged. 'Oh well. Looks like you're here for the night. See you tomorrow.'

Georgie laughed. 'Hey.'

'You'll be all right. In fact, DCI Drake has a very comfy sofa in his office that you could sleep on. There's a blanket underneath it.'

'How do you know that?'

'No comment.'

Georgie smirked. 'No comment? I know what that means.'

'Yeah, well that was in my bad old days. I haven't slept there in a while.'

'You can't seriously leave me stranded here. What happened to the art of chivalry?'

Is she flirting with me?

'Sorry? You said something? Chivalry? No idea what you're talking about.'

Georgie gave him a sarcastic smile and then glanced at her watch. 'I could drag my brother out of bed to come and get me.'

'Or I could give you a lift to the bus stop?'

Stop flirting back, you idiot!

'Ha. There aren't any buses at this time. And you're being horrible.'

They made eye contact for a second.

'I'll give you a lift home. But only if it's on the way,' Nick said, pointing to his car.

Georgie smirked. 'You can give me a lift home even if it's not on your way, Sergeant Evans.'

'Oh, it's like that is it?'

'Yes. Come on. It's getting late.'

FOLDING DOWN THE OLD-fashioned, bottle-green, bedspread in the spare room in the farmhouse, Finn caught sight of himself in a small, Deco-style mirror that hung from the wall. For a split second he was taken aback by his appearance. He had forgotten that he had shaved all his hair off, and it was as though a stranger was looking back at him.

Sitting on the edge of the bed, he gazed out at the night sky and took stock of the evening. He found it hard to believe what lovely, generous people Bill and Gwen were. Part of him felt guilty for lying to them.

For the first twelve years of his life, he had been surrounded by violence, shouting, chaos, and substance abuse. When he had sought solace in the apparent safety of the local football team, he had found himself subjected to sexual abuse. After the fire, there had been ten years at Ockley Cross and a year in Norfolk. It was hard to fathom that there were 'normal' people out there who were caring and kind with no hidden agenda. He wondered what his life would have been like if he had grown up with parents like Gwen and Bill. It would have been completely different. It was hard not to feel a degree of self pity and anger at that thought.

A figure appeared from the bathroom in a towel. It was Kat. Her wet hair was tied back. She looked stunning.

She motioned to the bathroom. 'It's all yours, sir.'

'I thought you were going to wait for me to come in the shower with you?'

Kat pulled a snooty face. 'Sometimes a lady needs to shower on her own.'

'That's great for ladies, but what about you?' Finn quipped.

'You cheeky bastard!' Kat took two steps forward and dived on top of him, pushing him back onto the bed.

She began to kiss him hard and passionately. Her wet hair fell onto his face. It smelled clean and citrusy.

Finn put his finger to his lips. 'Shh. We don't want them to hear.'

Kat laughed. 'They're probably at it themselves.'

'Eww. Don't be sick,' he groaned, pulling a face.

'Old people still have sex!'

'Really. Well, I don't want to think about that.'

Kat put her hand to his face and smiled. 'Oh, so that means you won't want to have sex with me when we're seventy. Charming!'

'That's different.' Finn kissed her. 'If I closed my eyes now, I'd be asleep in two seconds. I'm so tired.'

There was a beep from Finn's pay-as-you-go phone on the bedside table. The only person he had contacted since they had gone on the run was Sean.

Moving Kat to one side, he crawled across the bed to the phone. 'Just a sec. This might be Sean.'

Finn started to read the text out.

Mate, be grand to see you. Plenty of room here, no bother. Can't wait to meet the missus. Stay as long as you want. I inherited me nan's house last year. Just me here at the moment. Here's the address fella ...

Kat grinned at him. 'That's brilliant.'

Finn felt an overwhelming sense of relief that they now had somewhere to go where they could hide out. 'Looks like we're definitely going to Ireland then.'

NOW ON THE OUTSKIRTS of Llancastell, Nick drove towards the small suburb where Georgie lived. He was starting to feel guilty. He knew that technically there was nothing wrong with him taking home a colleague who was stuck at work. In fact, Amanda would have been horrified if he hadn't offered Georgie a lift home. What concerned him was that he was incredibly attracted to her.

He was aware that he was a bit of a fantasist. Was it just human nature for him to be attracted to someone else when he had a pregnant wife and baby at home? He didn't know. Was it okay to have a bit of a crush on someone if you didn't act on it? He should probably talk to his sponsor.

Georgie pointed. 'It's about a mile up here and then on the right.'

Nick switched his headlights to full beam as the streetlights began to disappear. 'I haven't been out this way for ages.'

'Do you live in town?'

'No. Out in the sticks. Dinas Padog.'

'Oh yeah. I used to go out with a boy from Ysgol Dinas Padog.'

'What was his name?'

'Darren Williams.'

'Don't remember him, but then again I left that school a long time ago.'

'You can't be that old.'

Do I lie about my age?

'Really? Well, I left the sixth form there nearly twenty years ago,' Nick explained. He felt a little unnerved saying the number out loud. It was a scary thought.

Georgie glanced over at him and raised an eyebrow. 'I don't believe that. I thought you were about thirty.'

Thirty? Nice one.

'Must be the beard. Hides all the lines and wrinkles,' Nick quipped.

'Oh, I like men with beards. I actually like older men.'

Her comment hung in the air.

What the bloody hell do I say to that?

'Right ...'

Georgie giggled. 'Oh god, Nick. I didn't mean it like that. I wasn't making a pass at you.'

I feel sort of relieved but also sort of disappointed.

'No, I know that. It's fine ... How long were you in uniform before you came to CID?'

'Thanks for changing the subject. Erm, four years altogether, if you include my probation.'

Nick calculated that Georgie must have a degree, or a similar qualification, and done the two-year probation period.

'You're a fast tracker then?'

She shrugged. 'Why not? CID is where all the fun is, isn't it?'

'That's what they tell me.'

She then pointed. 'Right here please.'

Nick turned into a cul-de-sac of small, newly-built houses.

'This is nice.'

'It's my little sanctuary ... I'm just here,' Georgie said leaning forward and gesturing to the last house in a row of four.

'Thanks Nick. Sorry ... Sarge. You're a life saver.' She smiled at him as she took off her seatbelt. 'Do you want to come in for a coffee? I'll show you around.'

What does she mean by that?

He shook his head. 'I've got to get home. Another time.'

She glanced over at his left hand and frowned. 'Oh, are you married or something?'

Bloody hell! She's already checked out my wedding finger!

'No, not married.'

'But you live with someone?'

'Yeah. And we've got a baby daughter so I should get back,' Nick explained, not really knowing why they were having this particular conversation. 'Do you need a lift in the morning?'

Georgie got out of the car and then pulled a face. 'Do you mind?'

'Of course not. And I know someone who will come and fix that tyre while you're at work.'

'If you're sure, that would be great.'

For a moment, their eyes locked for longer than was customary.

'We're on an early one I'm afraid. I'll pick you up at six.'

She rolled her eyes. 'Better get in and get my beauty sleep then.'

Nick smiled at her. 'I wouldn't worry about that.'

Georgie gave him a cheeky grin. 'Charmer.'

She closed the door and Nick watched her walk to her front door.

He spun the car around and started to drive home.

CHAPTER 22

IT WAS SIX-THIRTY IN the morning and the bleary-eyed detectives of CID had assembled in IR1. As Ruth grabbed her notes, she was hit by the smell of bacon and coffee. Why was it that whenever they had an early start, half the officers in Llancastell CID went and bought bacon sandwiches? In fact, it had been the same at the Met. And in the early days, male police officers seemed to eat bacon every morning, early briefing or not. Combined with heavy smoking and drinking, it did explain why a lot of them seemed to drop dead in their 60s, just after they had retired.

It's a good thing that the canteen opens at six, she thought.

'Morning everyone. Lovely to see your beautiful faces here bright and early,' Ruth said as she strode into the middle of the room. 'Nothing much more to report since our briefing yesterday. Jim, you were on the nightshift. Anything crop up that we should know about?'

Garrow shook his head. 'Nothing, boss. Except an old lady in Glasgow who said she had seen Finn and Kat in a McDonald's in the city centre.'

'You sure there was nothing in it?' Ruth asked.

'By the time I'd got her to go through her story again, she had realised that the girl had purple hair and the young man she was sitting with was probably Indian.'

There was laughter in the room.

'God bless the great British public,' Nick said sardonically.

'Okay. The press office at St Asaph is releasing a more detailed statement from North Wales Police. Then I'm doing
a full press conference at nine. I'm hoping that the combi-
nation of these will jog someone's memory in this region.'
Ruth pointed to a marked area of the map on the case board.
'Until we hear otherwise, we're assuming that they are still in
here somewhere. So, I want you all out in this locality knock-
ing on doors.'

French looked over. 'We've had no reports of a stolen car
yet. If they're on foot, they haven't gone very far, boss.'

Georgie glanced up from where she was sitting. 'They
would have needed to eat at some point. And there's only
about half a dozen shops in that area where they could have
bought food.'

'You've got yourself a job, Georgie.' Ruth then spotted
Garrow on the phone. There was something about the expression on his face as he scribbled notes and then hung up.

'Boss!' Garrow said looking over.

'What's going on?'

Garrow read his notes as he headed for the map. 'Phone
call redirected to our switchboard from a Mr Tomlinson. He
and his wife live in an old farmhouse in Llugwy.' Garrow
went over to the map and pointed. 'It's a tiny hamlet close to
the Gwydir Forest.'

Ruth walked over. 'What did he say?'

Garrow's eyes widened. 'He said that the young couple
that the police are looking for are asleep in his house.'

'What?' Ruth said, incredulous. She had only been expecting a sighting.

'He said they claimed to be on a walking holiday and got lost. Mr and Mrs Tomlinson gave them some food and put them up for the night. He said he thought they were a lovely young couple. But then he saw the BBC Wales news this morning.'

Ruth's mind started to whirr. 'Jesus. I'm going to need to speak to him right now and see if he can keep them there without any bloody heroics.'

'I don't think there will be any heroics. He sounded pretty old,' Garrow said.

That doesn't sound good.

'Great ... Nick, can you liaise with the local plod and see if they can get a patrol car over there immediately? Dan, see if you can get all the roads from there sealed off. Georgie, it might a bit early, but I'd like to see if we can get a canine unit up there in case they decide to do a runner into the forest again.' Ruth looked at Garrow for a second. 'And he was sure it was them?'

'Yes, boss. He said the young man had shaved hair and a Newcastle accent.'

Ruth felt a surge of adrenaline. It was the first breakthrough they'd had in the investigation. 'Right, give me the phone number. Everyone else, let's go and bring them in.'

WITH A GROWING SENSE of unease, Finn turned over in bed. He had been dreaming that someone had been shouting at him. His eyes flickered open and he saw Kat's black hair draped over the pillow.

'Get up!' a voice barked.

Finn froze. *Who the hell is that?*

Shifting around, he saw Bill standing at the other end of the bed. His face was contorted with anger and he was pointing a shotgun directly at him.

Shit! He knows who we are.

Kat gave a soft groan as she turned over and woke up.

'Get up, the both of you!' Bill shouted.

Kat sat up, blinked, and tried to focus her eyes. 'What's going on?'

Bill's hands shook as he moved around the bed. 'I've seen the news. I know who you two are.'

Finn put his hands up as he moved slowly out of the bed. Bill seemed very shaky and Finn didn't want to do anything to startle him given that his finger was on the shotgun's trigger. The blast would kill them both.

'Okay. I'm going to get dressed, Bill. So, take it nice and easy, eh?'

'Can't believe we've been so bloody stupid,' Bill snarled.

A figure appeared at the door. It was Gwen. 'Bill, be careful. I told you we should leave them until the police arrive.'

'Get downstairs woman!' Bill thundered.

Without taking his eyes off Bill or the shotgun, Finn pulled on his jeans.

'Police?' Kat said as she got dressed.

'Aye. I've rung the police. They're on their way, don't you worry about that.'

How are we going to get out of this? Finn wondered. He wasn't about to let him and Kat spend the next twenty years in prison without a fight.

'It's not what you think,' Kat said, as she pulled on her hoodie and then grabbed her suitcase. Finn could see she was getting upset.

Bill shrugged. 'I'm not interested. You killed a man. That's all there is to it.'

Kat exploded in a fit of frustrated rage. 'No. That's not all there is to it. That disgusting man was my stepfather. He was trying to sexually abuse me. He terrorised my little brother. He had a screwdriver, and he was going to kill me and Finn. So that's *not all there is to it* you stupid old man!'

Finn watched as Bill blinked and tried to take this in. Kat's outburst had certainly rattled him. 'Aye, well you can tell all that to the police when they get there. They can sort it out.'

'But they won't, will they? They'll say that we murdered him!' Kat yelled as she picked up an empty glass from the bedside table. 'Is that what you want? For me and him to be in prison for stopping a man like that?'

Kat looked as if she was going to throw the glass at Bill.

You're going to get us shot.

'Kat?' Finn said gently.

Bill gestured with the shotgun. 'Put the glass down, will you?'

Kat moved forward a step. Finn could see that she was full of rage. 'Or what, Bill? What are you going to do? Shoot me in the chest? Is that what you're going to do? Because none of this is fair. And we're not going to prison for a man like that!'

Kat stared wildly around the room and then hurled the glass in utter frustration. It hit the wall behind Bill and smashed loudly.

In that moment, Finn saw that Bill was distracted. He launched himself forward, grabbing both barrels of the gun and pushing them up towards the ceiling. He hit Bill with his shoulder and sent him flying across the room and sprawling to the floor.

Finn turned the gun around. Moving swiftly over to where Bill was groaning on the carpet, he pointed the gun down at him.

Bill put his hands up defensively and shook like a leaf.

'Stay down there! And if you try to follow us, I will shoot you!' Finn bellowed.

Glancing over at Kat, he motioned towards the door. 'Come on.'

Holding the shotgun to his chest, Finn dashed down the wooden stairs. Kat followed behind.

Darting into the kitchen, he saw Gwen flinch and cower.

He pointed the gun at her. 'I'm not going to hurt you. But I need your car keys and a mobile phone.'

As his heart pounded, he watched Gwen shuffle over to a table, unplug a phone from its charge lead, and take some keys from a bowl.

Kat strode over and held out her hand to take them. 'I'm sorry, Gwen. You were really kind to us. But we're not murderers.'

Gwen seemed to be shaking all over as she handed Kat the keys and phone.

Finn motioned to the back door. Rushing over and opening it, Kat peered outside. 'The car's just over here.'

Finn gave Gwen a final glance, turned, and ran outside. Across the yard was an old, muddy, Volvo V70 Estate. He ran over, opened the boot, and placed the shotgun carefully inside.

Kat put her case on the back seat.

Sitting in the driver's seat, Kat put the keys in the ignition and took a deep breath. Finn got in and sat beside her.

'The money?' Kat said, turning to him in a total panic.

'Shit!' Finn said, his stomach twisting anxiously.

'Where is it?'

'It's in the wardrobe in that bedroom upstairs.'

Finn quickly opened the car door and got out. There was no choice. He would have to get the gun and go back inside to retrieve the bag.

'Don't worry. I'll go and get it,' he shouted as he opened the boot and put one hand on the shotgun.

Then he froze.

The sound of a police siren.

It was getting closer.

He looked at the shotgun and then over at the house.

Have I got time to go inside, get the money, and escape?

Kat got out of the car. She had heard the siren too. 'Get in the car.'

'What about the money?'

This is a total disaster.

'It doesn't matter. Come on. It's not worth the risk, Finn.'

'Fuck!' He slammed the boot shut in utter frustration and got back into the car. He glanced over at her. 'Sorry.'

'It's not your fault. We just need to get out of here right now,' Kat said as she motioned to the track. 'We'll sort it out.'

As they sped away down the bumpy road, Finn knew that being on the run had just got a million times more difficult.

CHAPTER 23

MAKING HER WAY ALONG the ground floor of Llancastell Police Station, Ruth felt a little apprehensive about holding the morning press conference. Public speaking had never been her forte, and even though she had done over a dozen press conferences since arriving in North Wales, they just didn't get any easier.

As she turned the corner, French came jogging towards her. 'Boss! Finn Starling and Kat Williams escaped from the farmhouse just before the uniformed patrol got there.'

'Shit! How did they get away?' she asked angrily.

'Finn wrestled the shotgun from Mr Tomlinson. They stole their car and phone.'

'What about the shotgun?' Ruth asked nervously.

French gritted his teeth. 'Yeah, they took it with them.'

Ruth shook her head in frustration. 'Bloody hell! This is not good.'

Finn and Kat were now armed. It took the hunt for them to a whole new level of danger for everyone.

'But there is something else, boss.'

Oh god, how could this get worse?

'Go on,' Ruth said, reluctantly.

'A bag full of bank notes was discovered in the bedroom where Finn and Kat had been sleeping. I'm guessing it's the money he stole from the warehouse.'

Ruth processed this for a second. 'Having no money will slow them down and reduce their options. But it will also make them desperate. And now they've got a firearm, that's a major concern.'

'Yes, boss. We've got the plate and make of the car they've stolen so I'll get onto Traffic straight away.'

'Make sure that we have some ARVs on standby now.' ARV stood for Armed Response Vehicles.

'They are already, boss.' French gestured to the Media Conference Room door. 'I'll speak to you in a bit then.'

'Thanks, Dan. Good work.'

Opening the door, Ruth went inside and made her way to the table at the front. The room was already buzzing with journalists. She sat down and took a sip of water. There were a few minutes before the briefing was due to start and she wanted to run through what she was going to say. However, she was distracted by thoughts of what she had just learned. The idea that Finn and Kat were now out there with no money and a shotgun made her feel very uncomfortable.

Glancing out at the packed room, she was aware that the search for Finn and Kat was now national news. The tabloids were already making comparisons between them and Bonnie and Clyde with puerile headlines. Giving the story a romantic twist certainly didn't make the police's job any easier. A journalist had also discovered that not only was Crispin Neal on the Sex Offenders Register, but he also had previous convictions for targeting young teenage girls. Even though the newspapers and social media weren't yet saying that he deserved to be murdered, they were painting an increasingly sympathetic portrait of the fugitives. She had no reason to think the leak about Neal's past had come from Llancastell CID. It could have been anyone who had worked on his previous convictions.

Ruth's phone buzzed and she looked at her most recent update.

BBC Wales @ BBC Wales Breaking News
Sources claim that murder victim Neal was a sex pest and a paedophile.

She had to admit that a social media explosion was probably going to help them catch Finn and Kat. Although she knew that they had changed their appearance, the latest press release mentioned his hair had been shaved and hers dyed black. In the sparsely populated region of Snowdonia, they would be fairly recognisable. However, she worried how they might react to being confronted, especially as they now had a firearm.

Checking her watch, Ruth stared out at the assembled journalists. A figure marched up the side of the room towards her. It was Kerry, the Chief Corporate Communications Officer for North Wales Police, who had come across from the main press office in Colwyn Bay. Ruth had met her on various occasions over the last three years and found her arrogant and irritating.

Kerry sat down next to her. 'Morning, Ruth.'

Ruth gritted her teeth. 'Good morning, Kerry. Get here all right?'

Let's get the pleasantries out of the way.

'Yes, fine. I've got a hybrid car which runs like a dream. Trying to do my bit for the environment.'

God, you're such a self-righteous bitch. I wish I could afford a hybrid car.

Ruth and Kerry had never seen eye to eye on how to handle the press. Kerry seemed to believe they needed to be manipulated with careful control of when and how information about a case was released. In contrast, Ruth believed that they should keep them fully informed and up-to-date. They stood a better chance of catching criminals if they used the media to appeal for witnesses and kept local communities fully in the loop.

Glancing down at the microphones and tape recorders, Ruth realised it was time to start. *Let's get on with this,* she thought.

'Good morning, I'm Detective Inspector Ruth Hunter and I am the Senior Investigating Officer for the investigation into the murder of Crispin Neal. This press conference is to update you on the case and to appeal to the public for any information regarding his death. We are currently looking for a young couple, Finn Starling and Kat Williams, in connection with Mr Neal's murder. If you have any information about their whereabouts, please contact us on the North Wales Police helpline. Mr Neal was killed at his home two days ago. We are looking for anyone who was in the area at the time, or saw anything suspicious, to come forward. At this stage of the investigation, our main focus is to find the young couple who we believe were in the house at the time of Mr Neal's murder ... Now, I do have some time to take questions, if there are any.'

A reporter peered up at her from the front row. 'James Peake, Mirror Group. Can you confirm that Crispin Neal was on the Sex Offenders Register and had prior convictions for assault and harassment?'

Bloody great! I don't want to have to talk about this now.

'I'm not prepared to discuss Mr Neal's criminal record. He is the victim of a brutal, senseless crime that has devastated his friends and family. I think we need to remember that,' Ruth said firmly.

A television journalist made a gesture from the back of the room and Ruth nodded.

'Sophie Pemberton, BBC News. Detective Inspector, are you therefore ruling out any possible connection between Crispin Neal's criminal past and his murder?'

'Although I'm not at liberty to discuss the case in detail, obviously we cannot rule out any line of enquiry. But I want to reiterate what I've already told you. As far as we are concerned, Mr Neal was an innocent man who was attacked and killed in his own home. My main concern is to find and interview Finn Starling and Kat Williams. Right, thank you, everyone. No more questions.'

Ruth was feeling a little flustered as she stood and gathered up her files. She noticed Kerry giving her an all-too-familiar supercilious look.

Kerry got up and blew out her cheeks. 'It looked like you found that a bit tricky, Ruth?'

Please fuck off.

Ruth shrugged. 'Nothing that I haven't handled before.'

Kerry moved closer and lowered her voice to a virtual whisper. 'The trick is not to show them that they've got to you, Ruth. It's your press conference and you're in control.'

Ruth wanted to punch her in the face, but instead gave her a forced smile. 'Thanks, Kerry. I'll bear that in mind.'

Spinning on her heels, she walked out of the conference room and headed outside for a ciggie to calm herself down.

FINN COULD STILL FEEL that his whole body was tense and anxious following their escape from the farmhouse and forgetting the money. What were they going to do? How were they going to survive? He felt physically sick.

As Kat turned right, he glanced over at the dashboard. 'How much petrol have we got left?'

'Thirty miles.'

Finn let out an audible sigh. 'Jesus. What's the point?'

Kat frowned. 'What does that mean?'

He felt like he was starting to lose it. 'We're fucked. We are totally fucked. How are we going to get petrol? How are we going to eat? How are we going to get to Ireland?'

'Calm down, Finn. It's going to be all right.'

'How is it going to be all right?'

'It just is. Trust me.'

Finn shook his head and then closed his eyes. He was exhausted and he felt like crying. 'I can't do this,' he whispered.

Kat seemed to have gone from a vulnerable girl to a confident woman in a matter of hours. 'Listen to me. We've come this far and we're not going back. I'm not going to prison and neither are you.'

'What are we going to do? Hold up a petrol station?'

Kat shrugged. 'It's not a bad idea.'

Finn couldn't think clearly. His head was a whirling mess.

'I'm too tired for this,' he groaned.

'Get in the back.'

'What?'

'I'm serious. Get in the back and have a sleep. You look tired. I've got this,' Kat said with a half smile.

'Really?'

Kat motioned with her head. 'Go on. Shift.'

Finn shrugged, climbed onto the back seat, and laid down. He gazed out of the window. The altocumulus clouds lay like a crocheted cloth across the sky. As the sun began to slip down behind the plum-coloured ridge of mountains, it had started to stain the clouds with a touch of orange. It was beautiful.

Finn felt his eyelids become heavy. He gave up fighting the inevitable sleep and closed them.

CHAPTER 24

THE GROUND FLOOR MEETING room was cold from the air conditioning and smelled of coffee. Ruth sat forward and looked at Michael Bartowski, Finn's witness protection officer from Northumbria Police.

He doesn't have the manner of a copper, Ruth thought.

His eyes were dark green. His hair had started to turn silver at the temples, his lips were thick, and his dark stubble appeared almost blue in the light. His manner was gentle, considered, even soft.

He rubbed his hand over his chin. 'And there's been no sign of them since then?'

Ruth had just relayed Finn and Kat's escape from the farmhouse to Michael.

She shook her head. 'We've got the make and plate of the car they stole. And without the money, I don't think they'll get far.'

Michael took a breath, sighed, and sat back. 'It's a shame. He's a good lad at heart.'

Ruth frowned. 'He stole a bus, hit someone with a hammer, and might have murdered somebody.'

'I know that. And don't get me wrong, I'm not condoning any of that. But I've been working with Finn for three years now. And I've worked with some very unpleasant, vicious, young men in the past. He's not one of them.' Michael looked at her. 'He was dealt a really shitty hand.'

As a copper, Ruth had never judged criminals in the simplistic shades of black and white that some of her colleagues did. It wasn't unusual in the Met to hear the phrase *'He's a wrong 'un. You can tell.'* Some criminals had childhoods and traumas that had made her stomach turn. However, she wasn't a bleeding heart liberal who believed that bad parenting, poverty or even abuse legitimised crime.

She raised an eyebrow. 'Plenty of kids are dealt a shitty hand, Michael. They don't all burn down a house with a copper and his pregnant woman inside.'

'I've seen the files on Paul Catteridge. There's no doubt in my mind that he was sexually abusing boys at Walker Park Rovers. No one wanted to know. He was a copper. He targeted the kids from broken homes or where the parents were addicts. You've got to remember that the whole scandal around sexual abuse at football clubs didn't come out until 2016. No one had ever heard of it back then. And no one wanted to believe that it could have happened.'

Ruth remembered her shock at the case. Coaches at some of Britain's top football clubs had abused young boys for decades and no one knew. Once the floodgates opened, hundreds of men came forward to report sexual abuse. By 2018, nearly a thousand victims had been recorded.

'I recall. It was sickening. But we need to remember that three people died in that fire.'

'Yes. And that's a terrible tragedy. But Finn claims that Catteridge first abused him in 2005 when he was seven. When Finn told his parents, his dad punched him in the face and told him to stop causing trouble. The local police had information at the time that Alan Mahoney, the father, was selling smack from their house. He was never caught but he didn't want the police snooping around, especially as Catteridge was a copper. Finn claimed that Catteridge abused him until he was nine, along with his friend Declan Keane. A year later, Catteridge started to abuse his younger brother Steven. When Finn told his parents of this, his father told him to stop making up lies and beat him. A few months later, the three of them went to burn down Catteridge's house because he had abused all of them and no one would listen.'

Ruth took a breath as she thought about what Finn Mahoney, and the other boys, had been through. It was horrific, and no child should have to suffer that. Did that excuse what had happened, or what Finn had done?

'I didn't know any of that. It's horrendous. Why did none of this come out at trial?' Ruth asked.

'Young, inexperienced, defence barrister. All the claims against Catteridge were hearsay and not admissible in court. When Alan Mahoney was cross-examined he denied that Finn had ever told him about the abuse that he and his brother had suffered. He also said that Finn was prone to lying and making up stories.'

Ruth shook her head at the idea of a father testifying against his own ten-year-old son in court. 'Do you think that's true?'

Michael shook his head sadly. 'No. Tyneside Police now have seventeen reports of historic abuse by Paul Catteridge at that football club. And I think that's just the tip of the iceberg.'

Ruth nodded despondently. 'And there's all those young men out there having to live with what happened to them.'

'The damage is unbelievable. Of the men that came forward to report Catteridge, two have since committed suicide. There's a couple who are heroin addicts and most of them drink heavily. It's a mess.'

There were a few seconds of bleak silence.

Michael finished his tea and put the mug down on the table. 'Do you think Finn murdered this Crispin Neal? Or could it have been his stepdaughter?'

'To be honest, I don't know for sure. Neal was on the register. He had a history of inappropriate behaviour towards the teenage daughters of his partners. His murder might have been through self defence,' Ruth explained. 'A screwdriver was found close to his body. Until we find the two of them, we won't know what happened. Or their version of what happened.'

'I'm praying that they don't do anything stupid.'

Ruth thought of the mobile phone that had been reported stolen from the farmhouse. 'If I could contact Finn, would you talk to him?'

'Of course. Finn trusts me more than anyone else he knows. So, I'll do whatever you need me to do.'

Ruth felt that contact with Michael might just work. 'Good. Maybe you can persuade him to give himself up. I've got a horrible feeling that with a firearm and no money, we're running out of time before something catastrophic happens.'

WAKING SLOWLY FROM a deep sleep, Finn could feel something hard digging into his back. As he shifted, he reached behind and realised it was the clip to a seatbelt. He flickered open his eyes and saw that they had just stopped in a remote petrol station.

Kat smiled as she turned off the engine. 'Are you okay, sleepy head?'

Finn sat up, ran his hand over his head and yawned. 'Yeah. Better now I've had a sleep.'

'You were talking in your sleep. And shouting. What were you dreaming about?'

'No, idea. I can't remember.' Finn stared out at the petrol station. A van pulled out of the exit and they were now the only car on the forecourt. 'How much petrol have we got left?'

'Couple of miles.'

'What are we going to do?'

Kat opened the driver's door. 'Leave it to me. But I'm going to need your help.'

What is she talking about?

Opening the back door, Finn got out with a slight groan and stretched his legs. He watched Kat go to the back of the car, open the tailgate and take out the shotgun.

What's going on?

Finn frowned. 'Kat? What are you doing?'

She slammed the tailgate shut and walked around to where he was standing. 'We're getting some petrol.'

He motioned to the shotgun.

'Right. Maybe I should take that though?' he said, holding out his hand.

Kat gave him a half smile. 'Don't be a sexist dickhead. I know how to handle a shotgun, Finn. I used to go shooting with my taid. Hold on. Wait a minute. Don't we need a disguise or a mask, or something?'

Finn rolled his eyes and pointed to the car. 'Kat, they know we stole that car. It's not going to take a genius to work out it's us getting out of it, mask or no mask.'

Kat laughed. 'Oh yeah. Good point. Well come on then.'

She seems very cheery.

Finn shrugged and followed her towards the entrance. Even though he was anxious, he knew they needed petrol, money, and food. What other option was there?

As he followed Kat inside, he spotted a bearded man behind the till and a middle-aged woman stacking shelves beside the coffee machine.

Oh God. Here goes.

Kat lifted up the shotgun, aimed it at the bearded man behind the till and yelled, 'Okay, everyone. This is a robbery.' She turned and aimed the gun at the woman stacking the shelf who had now dropped half a dozen packets of biscuits onto the floor in shock. 'If you could get down on the floor, that would be great.'

That was very polite.

The woman nodded as she got down onto her knees. 'You're not going to shoot us, are you?'

'Not if you do everything we say.' Kat moved forward and swung the gun back at the bearded man. 'I'm going to need you to open the till and put all the money into a carrier bag, then hand it to my lovely boyfriend here.'

Finn moved the last few yards to the till.

The bearded man's eyes widened as he stared at Finn. 'You're that couple that are on the run, aren't you? The Welsh Bonnie and Clyde, the papers said.' But he didn't sound scared. If anything he was excited, as if they were famous pop stars.

This is very weird.

Finn nodded. 'Just put the money in the bag.'

The woman, who was now prostrate on the floor, looked up at them. 'Oh, yeah. I read about that in the papers. They said that bloke you killed was some kind of paedophile. I think they should give you two a bloody medal rather than arresting you.'

Kat shrugged. 'Thanks. He was a horrible bastard if I'm honest.'

Finn glanced back at Kat. 'We're going to need some food.'

The woman motioned to the door. 'Baskets are by the door, dear. We're not going to stop you, so take what you want.'

The bearded man smiled at Finn and pointed at some big bars of chocolate. 'Dark chocolate is two for one at the moment.' Then the man stopped and thought for a second. 'Except you're stealing stuff, so it doesn't really matter does it?'

Finn raised an ironic eyebrow. 'Not really. Chuck in a bottle of vodka and a bottle of Scotch, would you?'

The bearded man smiled again. 'I'll put in the good stuff. Obviously.'

Finn glanced over at Kat who was carrying the shotgun in one hand and had now filled the basket with sandwiches, crisps, and biscuits. 'We should probably get going.'

Kat pointed at the basket. 'You take the basket and go and fill up the car. I'll stay here to make sure Mr Beard over there puts the pump on and doesn't ring the feds.'

Finn snorted. 'The feds? Bloody hell, Kat! Just because you've got a gun and you've robbed a petrol station, it doesn't make you a gangster.'

Kat was offended. 'I think it does.'

Finn took the basket from her. 'Okay, I'll go and fill up the car.'

'Good luck!' the woman called as he went to the door.

Finn glanced back at her, lying on the floor and waving. 'Erm, thanks.'

Kat took the gun with both hands and smiled. 'You two are going to have one hell of a story to tell your friends and family later.'

The woman chortled. 'That's true. I've never been held up at gunpoint before.'

This is completely surreal, Finn thought as he went outside.

Strolling across the empty forecourt, he put the basket into the back of the car, went to the pump, and started to fill the car.

Glancing up at Kat through the petrol station window, he saw her grin and wave as if she was having the most fun of her life.

CHAPTER 25

RUTH, NICK, AND MICHAEL Bartowski were busily setting themselves up in a small office on the sixth floor, close to IR1. They now had the number of the mobile phone that Finn and Kat had stolen from the farmhouse. A technical operator, from the Digital Forensics Team, was sitting beside some recording and tracking equipment that would allow everyone to hear the phone call. Ruth was also hoping that if Finn or Kat stayed on the phone for long enough, they would be able to triangulate the phone's signal and get their location.

As Ruth sipped her coffee, she thought of everything that Michael had told her about Finn and his childhood. When she combined that with what she suspected had happened to Kat, she couldn't help but think that they were two young people who had been terribly let down and damaged by the adults around them and the system that was meant to protect them. Ruth had her own daughter, Ella, who was in her early 20s. Even though Ruth had made many mistakes as a parent, Ella always knew that she was loved, that she was safe, and that she could trust those around her. It was hard for Ruth not to imagine what kind of lives Finn and Kat might be leading right now if they hadn't faced those challenges.

A knock at the door broke Ruth's train of thought.

Georgie opened the door and stuck her head in. 'Ma'am ...'

Ruth corrected her. 'Boss ...'

'Sorry. Boss.' Georgie glanced up and made eye contact with Nick. Ruth could see that he had returned her fleeting look. *What the hell was that about?* She didn't like what she had just seen or what her instinct was telling her.

Ruth gave her a half smile. 'How can I help, Georgie?'

'We've got a report of an armed robbery at a petrol station close to Bethesda. Descriptions match our suspects.'

Ruth's heart sank. 'Anyone hurt?'

'No, boss. They stole money, food, and a tank of petrol. No force used but the girl was holding a shotgun.'

Ruth raised an eyebrow. She was surprised to learn that it had been Kat brandishing the gun.

Nick's eyes widened. 'Kat had the shotgun?'

Georgie shrugged. 'That's what they said, sarge.'

Nick shook his head in disbelief. 'Bloody hell.'

'Thanks, Georgie.' Ruth watched her go. She would talk to Nick later about their 'little look'. Nick was a terrible liar, especially now he was in recovery. Any hint of something going on between them, and Ruth would be putting in a transfer request for DC Georgie Wild straight away.

Michael came over. He seemed anxious. 'This is exactly what we thought was going to happen.'

Ruth nodded uneasily. 'Better make this call before they make it any worse for themselves.'

Standing up from the table of electronics and recording equipment, Nick held up a cordless phone. 'Michael ... boss ... we're ready to go now.'

There was a soft electronic hum from the speaker through which they would be able to hear the phone call.

Michael took a long breath before taking the phone from Nick. 'Here goes.' He dialled the number from the piece of paper in his hand.

Ruth sat back in her chair. She could do with a ciggie. There was a chance that the mobile phone they had stolen had been turned off, run out of battery, or was not within range for them to get a signal. They were travelling through Snowdonia where a phone signal was intermittent at best.

Suddenly the speaker burst into life with the sound of a phone ringing.

Well, that's a start.

The atmosphere in the room was tense.

Ruth looked at Nick and then at Michael. They needed this to work.

Come on. Come on. Pick up.

The ringing continued.

Then it stopped as an automated answerphone kicked in.

'Bollocks!' Nick said under his breath.

Michael shrugged as he took the phone away from his ear. 'Now what?'

'Try again. They might be debating whether or not to answer it,' Ruth insisted.

Michael clearly agreed with Ruth's suggestion. He dialled again.

There was the sound of the phone ringing.

Just pick up the bloody phone.

Then more ringing.

Great. It's going to ring out again.

'Hello?' said a voice as the ringing stopped. It was Finn.

Thank god. Keep him talking.

'Finn? It's Michael.'

There were a few tense seconds of silence.

Michael looked over at Ruth. 'Finn? Are you there?'

'Yeah.'

'I just wanted to see how you and Kat are doing?'

'How did you get this number?'

'It doesn't matter. I just need to know if you and Kat are okay?'

The line went quiet again. Ruth feared Finn was just going to hang up.

'I don't know. I guess we're okay.'

'I've heard that you're getting yourself into a bit of trouble out there?' Michael's tone was paternal and calm. It was exactly what was needed to get Finn to open up.

'Yeah. A little bit. We're not going to hurt anyone, but we needed petrol and money and stuff, you know?'

'Yeah, I understand that. I'm just worried that if you're waving around a shotgun, things are going to get serious.'

'I'm not going to shoot anyone,' Finn snapped.

'Finn. *I* know you're not going to shoot anyone. But the police don't know that, do they?'

Another long silence.

'No. But we're not handing ourselves in.'

Michael pulled a face. 'Okay ... But things are only going to get worse while you're out there.'

'They're saying that we're wanted for murder. I ... I didn't murder him. That's not what happened.' Finn was beginning to sound emotional.

'Well, why don't you tell me what happened, Finn.'

Finn's anxiety was getting the better of him. 'He ... he had a screwdriver. He was ... going to kill us, so I had to ... stop him. That's not murder, is it?'

'No, it's not. But the longer you're running away and hiding, the more guilty it makes you look. Can you understand that?'

'Yeah. But no one's going to believe me after what I've done. I killed a copper, Michael. Didn't I? They're not going to believe a bloody word I say. They all hate me.'

'That's not true. If you were protecting Kat because you thought she was in danger, then what you did was manslaughter.'

Ruth shot Michael a look. He was starting to tread a fine line. They already had Finn confessing to the attack on Crispin Neal from the phone call. She didn't want his defence team accusing Michael of being coercive in any way and having the trial thrown out of court.

Finn sounded desperate but defiant. 'Yeah. But no one's going to believe me. And you're not going to find us.'

'You've got a plan then Finn?' Michael asked.

'I didn't say that. I said you're not going to find us.' Finn sounded agitated.

Ruth mouthed to Michael for him to keep Finn talking. The longer he was on the stolen mobile, the more chance they had of triangulating the call and getting their location.

'So, what are you planning to do, Finn? You can't run forever, can you?'

There were a few seconds of silence.

'You've been really good to me, Michael. But I've got to go now.'

'Wait a second, Finn. I ...'

The line went dead.

Ruth gave an audible sigh. Although she hadn't expected Finn to agree to hand himself in, it was clear that what had happened back in Newcastle meant that he would never trust the police. And that meant that they would have to use force to stop him.

'Thanks, Michael. At least we know they're okay and what he's thinking.'

Michael shrugged. 'Sorry. I tried to keep him on the line for as long as I could.'

Ruth gave him a half smile. 'You did a great job. He obviously completely trusts you.'

Nick shifted in his chair. 'Sounds like Finn is going to claim self defence.'

Michael frowned. 'You don't believe him?'

Nick shrugged. 'No, I don't. He's been in the system for so long that lying is just second nature to him.'

Michael shook his head. 'Finn doesn't have it in him to kill someone in cold blood. He's not like that.'

'Except for a policeman and his pregnant wife,' Nick muttered under his breath.

Ruth saw Michael bristle and she shot Nick a look. It wasn't a helpful comment. 'Anything from forensics on that screwdriver, Nick?' The results might confirm what Finn had told them.

'I'll chase it up, boss,' he replied.

The technical operator stood up. 'Boss, I've got a partial hit on the phone. If you give me fifteen minutes, I should get a proper fix on their location and tell you where they are and where they're going.'

Ruth nodded. Even though it would be good news to have their location, she worried that Finn and Kat might not give themselves up without some kind of a fight. And because they were now armed, she would have no choice but to use armed firearm officers in their arrest. It all made her feel very uneasy.

FINN STOOD BY THE CAR still trying to process the phone conversation he'd just had with Michael. Looking up, he saw Kat, now wearing a red Porsche baseball cap they had found in the car, heading his way. He was still holding the mobile phone. Ten minutes earlier Kat had needed a pee, and they had pulled into a layby where there was a portaloo.

She seemed anxious. 'Everything all right?' he asked.

'Bloke in the burger van gave me a funny look. We should probably get out of here.' She gestured to the phone. 'Calling someone?'

Finn frowned. 'No, someone called me.'

'Really? Who was it?'

'Michael. He used to be my probation officer.'

'Eh? Isn't that really weird? How did he get the number?'

Finn shrugged. 'The police must have given it to him.'

'What did he want?'

'He wanted us to give ourselves up. He said we were making things worse for us.'

'What did you say?'

'I told him we weren't going to do that.'

Kat smiled. 'Good ... Come on, we need to go.'

'Hold on a second.' Finn walked a few yards over to an open-backed lorry full of building materials. The driver was sitting in his cab smoking a cigarette, drinking tea, and reading a newspaper. 'Excuse me, where are you going, mate?'

The man frowned. 'Chester. You two need a lift?'

Finn shook his head. 'No thanks. I just thought I recognised the lorry, that's all.'

The driver buzzed up the window and went back to his paper.

I bloody hope he's not reading about us, Finn thought.

Turning back, he gently lobbed the mobile phone onto some bags of sand that were in the back of the lorry and then strolled over to Kat.

She looked utterly confused. 'What did you do that for?'

'They're going to trace the mobile signal from that phone. And they think we've still got it. Instead, it's going all the way back to Chester.'

Kat laughed. 'Brilliant. What made you think of that?'

'Think I saw it in an episode of Vera once.'

Kat snorted. 'Vera? Are you kidding?'

'Why? I love that programme. It's set all around where I come from,' Finn said, giving her a very gentle and playful shove.

The lorry's engine started and they stood and watched it drive away, heading east towards England.

Finn gave Kat a wink. 'That should keep the coppers off our tale for a bit.'

She grabbed his hand and pulled him towards the car with a sense of urgency. 'Come on, Finn. I'm really worried that the burger guy is going to phone the police.'

'Okay. You map read and I'll drive then.'

'Shouldn't we switch cars soon too?' she asked.

'Yeah. We should.'

A black Porsche 718 Cayman drove into the layby. Finn could see the driver, in his designer sunglasses, was talking into a mobile phone that he had to his ear.

What a wanker!

Kat watched the car come in. 'Nice car. Probably some rich English twat on the way to his holiday home in Abersoch.'

Finn already had a plan. He went to the boot of the Volvo to retrieve the shotgun, and a thick roll of black gaffer tape that he had seen earlier. As he walked back to where Kat was standing, he grinned. 'What do you think?'

Kat shrugged. 'Why not? It's a lot nicer than this dirty old Volvo thing.'

Finn tossed her the roll of gaffer tape. 'Yeah. That's what I thought. I might need some help, though.'

Marching over to where the Porsche was parked, Finn hid the shotgun out of view as he tapped on the driver's window.

The driver, probably in his forties, appeared rich and full of himself. He looked up as he lowered his sunglasses and buzzed down the window. 'Can I help?'

Definitely English. Definitely posh.

Finn smiled. 'Actually, I think I can help you.'

The driver seemed confused. 'Erm, okay.'

Finn pointed over to the Volvo. 'You see that Volvo over there?'

'Yes.'

Finn dangled the keys and smiled. 'I was wondering if you fancied doing a swap?'

The driver smiled as though this was a big joke, and pushed his sunglasses back up the bridge of his nose. 'Yeah, okay. Very funny, mate.'

In a flash, Finn pulled the shotgun up and pointed it in the driver's face. 'Actually, I'm not joking, *mate*. Get out of the car.'

The driver put his hands up. 'Oh God! Please don't shoot me.'

'Get out of the car, now,' Finn growled.

The door opened and the driver got out with his hands up. He looked very shaky. 'The keys are in there. And so is my phone and wallet. Just don't shoot me.'

Finn gestured for the driver to walk towards the Volvo. 'That's very kind of you.' He looked over at Kat. 'Can you do us a favour? Gaffer tape this nice man's hands behind his back and tape his mouth.'

Finn could see the driver physically shake as Kat wrapped the tape around his wrists. She then tore a strip off and smiled. 'Sorry, but we just need a faster car.' She applied the tape over his mouth and then smoothed it down onto his skin. 'There you go.'

Finn opened the back door of the car and gestured for the man to get in. His eyes were wide with fear as he lowered himself slowly inside. Kat grabbed her suitcase and the bags of money and food they had stolen from the garage.

Standing back, she slammed the back door shut. The driver glared at them from inside. Kat gave him a little wave. 'Bless. What if he gets cold?'

Finn rolled his eyes. 'He'll be all right.'

Kat locked the car, then launched the keys into a nearby hedgerow.

'Come on then, babe,' she said, pointing at the Porsche.

Putting the shotgun, cash, food and suitcase into the boot, Finn got into the driver's seat and closed the door. He pushed the automatic ignition and the deep rumble of the V6 4.0-litre engine kicked in. It sounded like a racing car.

Bloody hell. This is mint.

Kat turned on the stereo and a song by U2 was playing. 'For God's sake, every time,' she laughed, as she ejected the CD and tossed it out of the window.

Finn turned to Kat and they kissed.

'Let's see what this baby can do!' he yelled as he floored the accelerator.

CHAPTER 26

NICK AND RUTH WERE heading across Snowdonia at speed. The tech team, as they were known, had managed to triangulate the mobile phone signal and then trace its location. Finn and Kat seemed to be heading back east towards England but had stopped for a while at a service station along the A5.

Grabbing a cigarette from her jacket pocket, Ruth lit it and took a deep drag as she buzzed down the window. Her mind wandered away to Sarah and what she had discovered in recent days. Was Sarah really working as a high-class escort for Saratov? She knew that Sarah had slept with men in the past. Plus, there had been the Secret Garden sex parties and the affair with Jamie Parsons. It was so utterly confusing. None of this seemed to tally with what Ruth knew of Sarah. How could she have got it so wrong? How could she have built a life with someone and yet known so little about their inner thoughts and desires? She was meant to be a good copper and yet at no point had she ever suspected a thing.

'I've got some good news, boss,' Nick said as they slowed at the traffic lights.

'I could do with some good news at the moment,' Ruth replied gloomily. She was finding it hard to be optimistic about very much.

'Amanda's pregnant.'

Ruth glanced over at Nick and saw that he had a half smile.

She nodded at him. 'Congratulations.'

'Thanks.'

Ruth frowned at him as they pulled away from the lights. 'If it *is* congratulations?'

Nick shrugged unconvincingly. 'Yes ... of course. Not planned, but we wanted more kids. Or at least one more.'

'But not now?'

Her comment hung in the air for a second or two.

'Not now, no. But that doesn't make it a bad thing.'

Ruth shook her head. 'Jesus, Nick. You couldn't sound less excited or convincing if you tried.'

'Sorry. I'm just trying to process it and take it in.'

'And what's going on with DC Georgie Wild?' Ruth asked as she tapped ash from her cigarette out of the window and watched it fly away.

Nick pulled a face. 'Georgie? What are you talking about?'

'I just saw a look between you two today that made me feel very uncomfortable.'

Nick scratched his beard as they indicated to join the main road. 'No ... Seriously, boss. There's nothing going on.'

'She's a very attractive young lady.'

'What am I meant to say to that?'

'Nothing. But I take my responsibilities as godmother to your daughter very seriously. And if you do anything to jeopardise her or Amanda's happiness, I will seriously hurt you.' Ruth smiled over at him. Even though she was joking, there was enough substance for it to be a gentle warning.

'Yeah, all right, Don Corleone,' Nick quipped.

Looking up, Ruth saw that they had arrived at the service station.

As they stopped, Nick gestured to a patrol car that had joined them in the car park. 'Plod are here, boss.'

Ruth could feel her pulse quicken as she scoured the car park. 'Any sign of that Volvo?'

Turning off the ignition, Nick jumped out of the car. 'Can't see it.'

As Ruth climbed out, she saw that there couldn't have been more than fifteen cars in the service station and the Volvo that Finn and Kat had stolen was nowhere to be seen.

Shit! Where is it?

Nick was using his phone which was now linked to the GPS tracker back at Llancastell.

'How accurate is that thing?' Ruth asked as her eyes roamed the area.

Where are they?

Nick looked around. 'I don't get it. The phone is in this car park, but I can't tell you which vehicle.'

'Oh, well that's useful,' she said in frustration.

Motioning to the service station itself, Ruth marched over to the main entrance. 'Come on! We'll have a snoop around and see if anyone has seen them.'

As Ruth and Nick made their way from the car park, Ruth's phone rang.

'DI Hunter?'

'Boss?' It was Georgie. 'We've found the stolen Volvo. But no sign of our suspects with it unfortunately.'

Ruth frowned, turning this way and that, scouring the car park. 'What? Where?'

'A layby near Tregarth, boss. Uniformed patrol car found it.'

How can it be in Tregarth?

Nick shot her a look.

'Are they sure it's the right car?' Ruth asked, now confused.

'Yes. There was a man taped up in the back of the car. Finn and Kat held him up at gunpoint, put him in the back of the Volvo and then stole his Porsche.'

'Bloody hell!' Ruth growled in annoyance and then looked at Nick. 'I think we've been bloody conned.'

HAVING JUST FILLED up the Porsche with petrol, Finn sat preoccupied in the driver's seat trying to use the mobile phone the driver had left behind. The phone call from Michael had thrown him. Even though he had told Kat that there was no chance of them giving themselves up, he wondered if it was an option. Would it be better for Kat? Would she be put on a less serious charge if they just handed themselves over to the police right now?

Kat put her hand on his arm and broke his train of thought. 'Is Tipperary close to the Blarney Stone?'

Finn shrugged. They needed to get safely to Ireland before they worried about that. 'No idea. We'll look it up later.' He was aware that he had snapped a little.

'We did a project on Ireland in primary school. I did a whole thing on the Blarney Stone. If you kiss it, you become very clever and witty.'

Finn tried to shake himself out of his disconsolate mood. 'Aye. The gift of the Blarney. Where I grew up in Newcastle, everyone was originally from Ireland. My dad said our family came from County Cork,' Finn explained, but then felt awkward at the mention of his father and his family.

'You don't ever talk about your family, do you?'

'Not really.'

Kat smiled and put on her best Irish accent. 'I love you, Finn Starling.'

He laughed. 'You're going to fit right in in Tipperary.'

Kat's eyes widened as she glanced out of the window. 'Finn?'

Looking up to see what she was staring at, Finn saw that a black Toyota Hilux pickup truck had parked in front of them. It looked like it had been done deliberately to block them in. In the back of the truck, there were two German Shepherd dogs barking and pacing around.

A man in a camouflaged jacket and baseball cap got out and walked over determinedly.

'What's he doing?' Kat asked in an anxious voice.

'No idea. But he looks like a redneck.'

The man stopped about ten yards from them, pointed aggressively and yelled, 'I know who you two are. I've called the police. You're going nowhere 'til they get here.'

Finn gasped. 'Shit!'

Now what?

Opening the car door, Finn felt Kat's hand on his arm. 'Be careful. Don't do anything stupid.'

'It's all right,' Finn assured her as he climbed out.

A white van pulled into the garage and parked beside the petrol pumps behind them.

The man in the baseball cap gestured to the old man as he got out, then pointed to the Porsche and shouted, 'Mate! It's that couple that are on the run. The ones from the papers. I've boxed them in and called the police. Just keep your van there so they can't get out, eh?'

The old man nodded anxiously, 'Erm ... Right you are.'

Finn spun and looked at him for a second. The old man seemed scared and scuttled back inside his van and locked the doors.

'What are we going to do?' Kat yelled nervously from inside.

'Just stay there, Kat.'

Opening the boot, Finn grasped the shotgun with both hands, put the butt into his shoulder and aimed at the man in front. 'Move the truck.'

The man shook his head and glared at him. 'No chance.'

Finn stepped forward two paces, aiming the shotgun directly at him. The German Shepherds started to bark and strain at their leashes.

'Move the fucking truck, or I'll shoot you,' Finn growled.

'You're not going to shoot me,' the man snorted. 'You haven't got the bottle.'

Finn raised an eyebrow. 'The last bloke who said that to me is now dead.'

He saw a flicker of uncertainty in the man's face, but he didn't look like he was going anywhere.

'Finn? Don't do anything stupid,' Kat called from the car.

Finn wasn't about to shoot the man. He couldn't. But it didn't look like being threatened with a shotgun was going to work.

Shit! Now what? We're not going to sit here and just wait for the police.

Glancing at where the truck was parked and then back at the white van, he could see they really were boxed in. There was no room to manoeuvre.

Chucking the shotgun into the boot, Finn got back inside the car and slammed the door in frustration.

'Bollocks!'

'What are we going to do?' Kat asked, sounding scared.

Finn snapped at her. 'I don't know, do I?'

There were a few seconds of tension as Finn thought it through. He had an idea.

He glanced across at her, turned on the engine, and revved the accelerator. 'Hold on tight.'

'What are you doing?'

'Watch and learn.'

Slamming it into reverse, the Porsche hit the van behind and stopped. Finn pushed down hard on the accelerator. The huge engine strained but after a moment the van began to move backwards slowly. First a yard, and then two. The air was full of the smell of burnt rubber.

It was just enough to allow Finn to pull out of the space they had been boxed into.

Pulling forwards, Finn saw the Toyota driver run towards them. With a sharp flick of his hand, Finn hit the central locking.

The man appeared at Kat's door and pulled the handle. She screamed.

'For fuck's sake!' Finn shouted.

Kat shrieked at the man through the window. 'Just fuck off! Leave us alone!'

The man, his face twisted in fury, continued to yank at Kat's door even though it was locked. Then he punched the glass.

'Get us out of here, Finn!'

'I'm trying to. I'm also trying not to kill that twat in the process.'

Finn pulled forward until the nose of the Porsche was touching the pickup truck. The man had now resorted to kicking the side of the car in anger and shouting at them.

'Fuck this!' Finn snarled as he glanced behind. He had just about enough room.

Here we go!

Crunching the Porsche back into reverse, they sped backwards.

As they raced back past the white van, the garage forecourt opened up a bit.

Finn yanked the handbrake up.

He spun the steering wheel.

The back of the car skidded around with a loud squeal, clipping the garage wall but not stopping.

Bingo!

He slammed the brakes on and the car juddered to a halt.

They were now facing forwards.

'How the hell did you do that?' Kat laughed with a huge sigh of relief.

Finn grinned. 'I used to do it on a daily basis when I was about ten.'

With another stamp on the pedal, Finn accelerated out of the entrance and onto the main road.

'Bloody hell, that was close!' Finn gasped.

'What a dickhead!'

Leaning back into the driver's seat, Finn allowed himself to relax. He blew out his cheeks and then hollered, 'Woo hoo!'

'Never mind bloody woo hoo,' Kat said. She was looking in the wing mirror.

With a glance in his rearview mirror, Finn saw the blue flashing lights of a patrol car that was now directly behind them.

Are you bloody kidding me?

Changing down gears, he pushed the accelerator and the 4.0-litre engine roared. He gripped the steering wheel as they screeched around the bend.

'What are we going to do?' Kat shrieked.

'Outrun them.'

80 mph.

Kat glanced back. 'They're still there.'

90 mph.

Finn felt the back tyres losing their grip and sliding as they cornered a bend at 100 mph. He glanced again in the rearview mirror. The police car was slipping further and further behind.

Finn looked over at Kat. 'You've gone white, babe.'

'I'm scared we're going to crash.'

'No chance.'

110 mph.

Finn went hammering up the hill, and over the crest. He pulled out to overtake a car towing a caravan, and went past in a blur.

125 mph.

Checking his mirror once more, Finn saw the police car was now a small dot behind them.

'Fuck you!' he yelled, full of adrenaline.

Kat glanced back nervously. 'Have they gone?'

Then the police car seemed to have stopped and soon disappeared out of sight.

Finn grinned at her. 'They have now.'

Kat punched the air. 'Yes. You are a total ledge!'

She leaned over to the stereo and put on the radio. *Levitating* by Dua Lipa was playing. She cranked up the volume and began to sing at the top of her voice as they sped away.

CHAPTER 27

HAVING CALLED AN AFTERNOON briefing of the CID team in IR1, Ruth sensed a strange atmosphere in the room that she couldn't put her finger on. The press was beginning to treat Finn and Kat as glamorous, romantic young runaways who had killed a paedophile and didn't deserve to be hunted down. It was something that was being hotly debated across the country on social media, television, radio talk shows, and in every workplace.

'Afternoon everyone. If we can get started on this.' Ruth walked over to the scene boards. 'Just to bring you up to speed, our suspects ditched their stolen Volvo and took a Porsche from a driver at gunpoint, leaving him taped and gagged.' She then went to the large map of North Wales that was now dotted with pins to indicate the locations where Finn and Kat had been spotted. 'My question is, what is Finn and Kat's plan? Where are they going? Or are they driving around until they work out their next move?'

Garrow looked up from where he was sitting. 'Boss, I spoke to Natalie Williams. The only relative that Kat has any contact with is an Aunt. Sadie Williams, Ben Williams' sister. She lives in Aberystwyth and works at the University there.'

Ruth inspected the map. Aberystwyth was on the western coast of Wales but a long way south of where Finn and

Kat had been spotted. 'It doesn't look like they're going south. How far are they from Aberystwyth now?'

French sat forward in his chair. 'Eighty miles. Maybe more.'

'That's only two hours in a Porsche,' Georgie pointed out.

Nick stood and went over to the map. 'If we plot where they've been seen so far, then they are definitely heading north west.'

Ruth peered at her team and asked in a slightly frustrated tone, 'Well? Come on. Any ideas?'

Georgie glanced up from her desk. 'Boss, maybe they just don't have a plan?'

Ruth shrugged. 'Maybe. But if you were on the run and in this area, where would you go?'

'They're only an hour or two from Holyhead and that's north west,' French said.

'Ferry to Ireland?' Ruth asked.

'You don't need a passport to go from Holyhead to Dublin,' Garrow pointed out.

Ruth studied the map. 'Okay. If they're making for Holyhead, then they are going to travel on the A5, unless they keep to the back routes. What they do have to do is cross either the Menai Bridge or the Britannia Bridge to get onto Anglesey. Right, Dan and Jim, liaise with Anglesey police and position patrol cars near both bridges in case we need to close them off.'

A phone rang at the back of IR1 and Georgie went over to answer it.

Nick sat back and leaned against the edge of a table. 'Any progress on the Porsche's GPS signal?'

Garrow tapped at his computer. 'Still waiting for the Porsche dealer to send us the code that allows the tech boys to track it.'

'Any idea how long that might take?' Ruth asked.

'They promised by first thing tomorrow.'

Ruth sighed audibly. 'Tomorrow? Jesus, they might be out of the bloody country by then!'

FINN AND KAT SAT TOGETHER in the car, looking over Llyn Padarn, a huge, glacially formed lake to the north of Llanberis, in the heart of Snowdonia. It was over two miles long and a hundred feet deep, covering an area of two hundred and forty acres. At its south-eastern end, it was linked to the Llyn Peris reservoir which served the local Dinorwig power station. Padarn Country Park lay to the north, with its ancient sessile oak woodland.

From where Finn and Kat sat, the mountains rose to the right and were covered in dark pine trees. Behind them, the setting sun tinted the sky with colour. Clouds stretched like cotton wool, with tendrils forming a sea of shimming orange and pink.

Kat took Finn's hand in hers and clasped it gently. 'It's beautiful, isn't it?'

'Yeah. I've never seen anywhere that looks like this, Kat.'

'That's why I wanted to bring you ... My dad brought me here when my mum was in hospital with Henry. He wasn't well for a few weeks, so me and my dad came up here for a night away. He took me canoeing on that lake. I can remember it so clearly.'

'Do you miss not living with him?' Finn asked.

'Yeah. Loads ... I wish I'd gone to live with him, but my mum always got so upset when I mentioned it. None of this would have happened if I had been living with him, would it?' Her voice sounded a little choked.

'You don't know that. And we can't do anything about what's happened now.' Finn smiled at her and they kissed. 'But I will look after you and make sure you're safe no matter what.'

They both gazed out at the sky and clouds, which were now awash with hues of pink, crimson, plum, magenta and burnt orange. Black silhouettes of birds rose from the trees.

'Why don't you ever go back to see your family? Don't you miss them?' Kat asked.

Finn stopped himself from concocting another lie. He needed to tell her everything and get it off his chest.

'Yeah, I miss my brother, Steven.'

'So, why don't you go back?'

'I'm not allowed to go back to Newcastle.'

Kat pulled a face. 'What? Why not?'

Finn composed himself. He wasn't really sure where to start with his story.

Kat gave him a reassuring look. 'It's all right. Whatever you tell me, it's all right.'

Finn nodded, but recalling what had happened to him and his brother, who he hadn't now seen in years, was painful. 'I was abused ... sexually abused.'

Kat just looked at him. 'What? Oh my God.'

'Lots of us were abused.' Finn blinked as a tear came into his eye. 'Sorry ... I ...'

Kat reached to his face as the tear rolled down his cheek. 'It's all right ... I'm so sorry.'

Finn drew in a deep breath and then blew out his cheeks. This was going to be difficult.

'There was a football coach at our local team. Paul Catteridge. He took the under 8s. He was a copper, so everyone trusted him. My parents never came to the games or training, so I had to walk home on my own. One night, this Catteridge ... he offered to give me a lift home because it was pouring with rain. And we stopped on the way home by this old church and he ....' Finn tried not to let himself become overwhelmed by what he was telling her.

Kat took his shaking hand and squeezed it. 'It's all right. You don't have to say it or explain.'

His eyes were now full of tears. He sniffed and rubbed his face with the cuff of his jacket. 'And ... then it happened every week for the next few months until the end of the season.'

'Did you tell anyone?' Kat asked in a whisper.

'I tried to tell my mum and dad. He just slapped me and told me to stop causing trouble. I knew my dad was selling drugs and fiddling benefits. He didn't want the police anywhere near us.'

'That's so awful. Poor you. Did it stop after that?' Kat asked.

Finn looked at her. 'Not for another year. I found out he had done the same to my friend Declan. He tried to tell his teacher, but she didn't seem very interested. When I was ten, he started to abuse my brother Steven, same as he had me. I knew it had happened because Steven cried at night and then wet the bed. I told mum and dad to do something and my dad punched me in the face and told me to stop making stuff up and lying.'

'Oh my god, that's horrible.'

They held hands and stared out over the lake for a minute.

'So ... we decided to get him back ... for what he had done to us. I went to his house with Declan and Steven. We poured petrol through his letterbox and threw a match inside.'

'Right. That was the arson you told me about.'

Finn blew out his cheeks again as more tears came. 'They were meant to be out, you see?'

Kat frowned. 'Who was meant to be out?'

Finn rubbed his face again. He had never told anyone his story before. 'Catteridge ... and his wife. It was the middle of the day. That's why we did it then. They were meant to be at work.'

Kat asked in a virtual whisper, 'They were inside?'

Finn nodded. It made him sick to think of what he had done. It didn't matter that it had been an accident. 'Yeah. And she was pregnant.'

Kat's eyes widened. 'And they died?'

Finn was shaking. He couldn't look at her. 'I'm so sorry. I should ... I should have told you.'

There were a few agonising seconds of silence. Finn was bracing himself for Kat to scream at him or attack him for what he had done, or for not telling her.

She put her hand gently to his face and shook her head. 'It was an accident.'

'I know. But ...' Finn sobbed. 'I'm sorry ...'

'No one had listened to you. I can't believe you went through all that. How could they put you in prison after everything you'd been through?'

Finn looked at her for a second. He couldn't believe that she had reacted with such understanding. He feared that she would judge him and reject him. 'I don't know ... No one believed that he had done those things to us. They said it was an excuse. And there was no evidence. My dad stood up in court and told them I was a liar and made up stories all the time. They gave me and Declan a twenty-year sentence.'

'Oh my God. That's disgusting.'

Finn furrowed his brow. 'I ... I thought you'd be so angry at me?'

'Why? You were sexually abused from when you were seven, Finn.'

Finn nodded and looked down. This was so hard.

Kat put her hand gently on his arm. 'How could I be angry with you?'

Finn looked up and met her gaze. 'I should have told you before.'

She shook her head. 'No. You had to tell me when you were ready. And that is now.'

Finn was choked. 'I love you so much.'

Kat moved forward so that their foreheads touched and said under her breath, 'I love you too, and we're going to get through this. We're going to have an amazing life together. You deserve to be loved and to be happy.'

CHAPTER 28

KICKING OFF HIS SHOES, Nick sat back on the sofa and sipped his tea. Amanda had waited up for him, but had dozed off almost as soon as she'd sat down. He wasn't surprised. Being pregnant with Megan had made her incredibly tired and fatigued. This second pregnancy would probably be the same.

He watched as her chest moved up and down slowly. Her breathing was close to snoring, but quiet enough to be cute. He remembered the first time he had met her for a coffee. Her big brown eyes had bewitched him instantly. As had been pointed out by his Auntie Pat, Amanda knew how to handle Nick, which wasn't always an easy thing.

He smiled to himself. He knew how bloody lucky he was. There were many who would give anything for a beautiful wife and daughter, decent job, roof over their head, and money for food and bills. And that should have been more than enough. His sponsor, Dundee Bill, always said "A grateful alcoholic won't drink." The longer Nick was sober, the more he knew that it would be dangerous to take that stuff for granted.

Amanda caught her breath and opened her eyes as if surprised. 'Was I sleeping?'

Nick grinned. 'Oh yes. And snoring.'

'No, I wasn't. I don't snore,' she protested as she got up out of the armchair.

'How can you possibly know that? You were asleep!' Nick laughed. 'It's a cute snore. You know. Like a baby rhino.'

Amanda hit him playfully, but hard enough to make him wince. 'You're such a dickhead.'

Nick took her hand and kissed the back of it. 'I'm *your* dickhead and don't you forget that.'

'Lucky old me, eh?' she said as she leaned over and kissed him.

'You going to bed?'

Amanda went to the door. 'I'm knackered.'

'I love you,' Nick called after her.

'If you love me, will you please stop getting me pregnant,' she joked.

'I think you'll find that you were involved in the process.'

'That's what you say,' she said with a smirk before disappearing towards the stairs.

Nick stretched back on the sofa, finished his tea, and put down the mug. He channel-surfed but nothing caught his attention. What he should do is ring his sponsor for a catch up. It had been months. Either that or maybe read something related to his recovery.

His phone buzzed with a text. It was from Georgie.

Up to much?

He felt his pulse quicken a tiny bit. *Why is she texting me? What's that about?*

Although he knew the sensible thing to do was to ignore the text and not reply, he also knew there was just no way he was going to do that. Where was the harm? She was a work colleague. Wasn't he allowed to have female friends from work?

He texted her back.

No. Nothing. Telly and tea. My rock'n'roll lifestyle.

Then he waited with slightly bated breath. Was she going to reply? And what would she say? He felt a pang of guilt when he thought of Amanda upstairs.

His phone buzzed again.

Ha ha! When the case is over, we'll all have to go out for a rock'n'roll night in town. Bet I could drink you under the table!

Nick looked at the message with a slight pang of disappointment. His ability to go and have a 'rock'n'roll night out in town' had vanished in his early 20s. His head still managed to tell him that it would be such a great night out. But the recovery side of his brain countered with wet beds, shakes, vodka for breakfast, and the overwhelming desire for continuous alcohol that would never stop.

He typed a reply.

I don't drink, so you would definitely drink me under the table!

There was no point lying about it. Maybe he should just turn his phone off and go to bed.

Another message came through.

Recovery?

He wondered how she knew? It wasn't something that your average person would ask. He typed back,

Yeah. A few years now.

Good for you. My Uncle is a recovering alcoholic, so I know how horrible it is. Hey, and being in recovery is VERY rock'n'roll these days!

Nick smiled and laughed to himself at her text. It wasn't what he was expecting. Before he had time to reply, Georgie had sent another message.

Happy to go for a coffee, if you fancy?

Nick found himself texting back before he had really thought it through.

Yeah, that would be nice. I'm off to bed now. Night.

A few seconds later, Georgie's text came back.

Night xx

CHAPTER 29

HAVING TAKEN THE EARLY morning CID briefing, Ruth had been asked to go across the road with Nick to the North Wales Police Forensics Laboratory. As they entered the new building, Ruth wondered what forensics had discovered.

'Amanda okay?' she asked, as they hurried through the myriad of corridors.

'Knackered,' Nick replied.

'She was like that with Megan, wasn't she?'

'Yeah. Could be worse. She's not suffered any morning sickness, at least not so far.'

'Lucky sod. I was sick as a dog with Ella.' Ruth raised an eyebrow. 'Must be nice to be a man. Your contribution to a pregnancy lasts a whole two minutes.'

Nick grinned. 'Bloody hell. How many times do you think we did it?'

Ruth laughed as they entered the main forensics lab. Katy Simpson, who was the new Senior Forensics Officer for North Wales Police, smiled and came over. She had cropped red hair, freckles, and a thick Glaswegian accent. After a few of the looks and comments that she had made in previous meetings, Ruth was pretty sure that Simpson was gay.

'Morning, morning. How are things across the road?' Simpson asked.

Nick grinned. 'Horrible. Place is full of coppers.'

She laughed. 'Sounds horrendous. I've got something for you on the Crispin Neal murder case.'

She gestured for them to follow her over to a computer where she sat down. 'I was going to send over these further results, but I wanted to show you.'

'Are these the forensics on the screwdriver?' Ruth asked.

Simpson tapped the keyboard until she brought the data up onto the screen. 'Yes. Here we go.'

'The blood definitely matches Katherine Williams' DNA?' Ruth asked, wanting to confirm the results that she'd already been sent.

'Yes. And Crispin Neal's prints are the only thing we could find on the handle. As far as I can see, no one else has held that screwdriver,' Simpson explained. 'But what really interested me was the stuff that I found on the tip, along with Katherine Williams' blood.'

Ruth peered at the screen, but the data made no sense to her. 'Which was what?'

'A mixture of iron oxide and bismuth oxychloride.'

Nick shrugged. 'And what's that?'

'It's the chemicals you would find in a woman's foundation makeup. The bismuth oxychloride is the stuff that gives you that shimmering glow.'

Ruth rolled her eyes. 'I wish I had some kind of shimmering glow.'

Simpson laughed and then pointed to the screen again. 'And something else which I couldn't work out for a while. Benzoyl peroxide. A little bit of digging reveals that benzoyl peroxide is used in the treatment of acne.'

Ruth raised an eyebrow. 'Kat Williams?'

Simpson nodded. 'I cross-checked the benzoyl peroxide and foundation with evidence that was taken from Katherine Williams' bedroom.'

Nick looked at Simpson. 'And?'

'They are a direct match. There are tiny fragments of her skin within the tip of that screwdriver.'

Ruth processed the information. Then she saw the relevance. 'We can show that Crispin Neal was the only person to have held the screwdriver. If it has Kat's blood, and skin with makeup and acne treatment in its tip, it shows us that Neal pushed the screwdriver into her neck or face hard enough to draw blood.'

'And that would be very strong evidence that Crispin Neal was killed in self defence.'

HAVING SLEPT THE NIGHT in the Porsche, Finn and Kat had stopped at a retail park just as it opened. Finn was sure that the driver of the Porsche, as well as the redneck from the garage, would have given the police detailed descriptions of them both. They needed to change their appearance again – and the car. Having found *The Party Shop*, Kat bought herself a silver-grey wig while Finn picked up a white Adidas baseball cap from a nearby sports shop.

It was seven o'clock and they were eating a breakfast in the car in the corner of a fast food restaurant car park.

Kat swished her head so the wig moved. 'I can't get used to it. It's really heavy.'

Finn gave her a wink. 'I think it suits you babe.'

'Oi, kinky!' Kat laughed and then waved a hash brown. 'I only ever have hash browns when I get breakfast from Maccies.'

'We used to have hash browns every Friday at Ockley,' Finn said as he pushed food into his mouth.

'What was the place called?'

'Ockley Cross Young Offenders Institution.'

'Sounds like it was horrible.'

'You get used to it,' Finn said with a shrug. He picked up a new pay-as-you-go mobile phone they had bought earlier. They had ditched the phone from the Porsche so that they wouldn't be traced.

'What are you looking at?'

Finn showed her the screen. 'Ferry times for Holyhead to Dublin.'

'Ooh, which one are we getting?'

Finn screwed up the fast food wrapper. 'There's one at three but I don't think we'll get there in time. Next one is nine o'clock tonight.'

'How long does the ferry take?'

'Just over three hours.'

Kat smiled. 'It's exciting, isn't it?'

Finn nodded. She looked so young when she smiled like that. 'Yeah. We need to ditch the car though.'

Kat pulled a face. 'Oh, really? I like Ferraris.'

'Yeah, well it's a Porsche, you doughnut. And I'm worried that it stands out too much. It also might have a GPS tracker on it and I've no idea how to turn it off. What we really need is a car that no one is going to miss or report to the police.'

Kat sipped her tea. 'How do you know all this stuff?'

'The Ockley Cross College of Crime,' Finn said sardonically.

'Eh? What does that mean?'

'If you spend all day, every day, with criminals, you learn all sorts. I know how to pick a lock, smuggle drugs through customs, and intimidate a jury.'

Kat shook her head. 'Useful life hacks, eh?'

Finn laughed. 'You never know.'

Glancing out of the car window, he spotted something across the road that gave him an idea. 'Have you got a driving licence?'

Kat fished into her purse. 'Here you go. Three points for speeding last year.'

'Bank or credit card?'

'Both.' She showed him both her bank card and credit card.

'Great. How much money have we got left from the garage?'

'Lots. Hundreds.'

Finn opened the car door. 'Nice one. Come on.'

'Where are we going?' asked Kat as she got out.

Finn pointed to a car rental place opposite. 'We're not going to steal a car. We're going to rent one.'

They crossed the road.

'What? Why?' Kat asked as they headed for the main office.

'The police are looking for a stolen Porsche. Unless we get recognised, no one is going to know we've rented a car if we use cash.'

'Brilliant,' Kat said as they walked into the rental office.

Finn stopped by the entrance and said in a hushed voice, 'You'll have to do all the talking.'

'Why?' Kat whispered.

'I can't talk with my Geordie accent,' Finn explained. 'I'll stay by the door in case there's a problem.'

As Kat walked over, a young, nerdy-looking man peered up from his desk and smiled. 'Can I help?'

'I'd like a rent a car, please,' Kat said.

The nerdy man chortled. 'Well, you've come to the right place. Come and sit down and we'll just fill out some paperwork.'

Kat approached the desk and sat down. She reached into her purse, pulled out her driver's licence and credit card and put them down for him to see. 'Here you go.'

The nerdy man studied the licence and then looked up at Kat. 'Don't I recognise you from somewhere?'

Finn's heart went into his mouth. *Bloody hell.*

Kat looked over at Finn.

Shit! Play it cool, Kat.

Kat smiled. 'I don't think so.' She pointed to the driver's licence. 'My hair's completely different in that photo.'

The nerdy man smiled. 'Don't worry about that. I can see it's you in the picture.'

'Okay if I pay cash?'

'As long as I've got your licence number and a credit card number, cash is fine. I just need you to sign this agreement, and then you can be on your way,' the nerdy man said as he slid the rental agreement across the desk.

Kat glanced over at Finn. He gave her a reassuring wink – *Brilliant! We're on.*

CHAPTER 30

NICK LOOKED AROUND the canteen as he waited for his second coffee of the morning. It had taken him a while to get to sleep the previous night. The text conversation with Georgie had thrown him off guard a little. Lying next to his pregnant partner, he had felt guilty for not doing the right thing and ending the conversation earlier. Yet there was part of his brain that was addicted to the thrill of it. And he was an addict. Which meant he was drawn to anything that boosted his serotonin or dopamine levels.

'Black coffee. No milk. No sugar, thanks,' said a cheeky voice.

It was Georgie.

Nick felt his pulse quicken slightly. 'Morning.'

This is not good.

Georgie looked directly at him. Her eyelashes seemed longer than before. 'I need to apologise for asking if you were in recovery last night.'

Nick took a breath and moved his tray towards the till. 'No need to apologise. I'm very open about it.'

'Yeah, it's not easy to turn your life around and get it back on track.'

What a positive thing to say.

Nick waited for the coffees. 'No, I suppose not.' He was pleased and even flattered to hear it put like that. Some people just didn't know how to talk to him about recovery.

'What about your partner? She must be very supportive.'

'Amanda. She's in recovery too. I'm not meant to tell you that, but she wouldn't mind.'

Nick paid with his smart card, took the coffees and put them on the tray.

I don't want to talk to you about Amanda though.

Nick handed over the coffee. 'Here you go.'

Georgie took it and grinned. 'Thanks. I was only joking about buying me a coffee.'

Nick shrugged. 'It's all right. I think my sergeant's pay can just about cover it.'

'By the way, this doesn't count as us going out for coffee. I'm going to hold you to that when this case is over,' Georgie said as she touched his arm for a second and held his gaze a moment longer than was customary.

Oh my God. She is definitely flirting with me!

He glanced up and saw Ruth approaching. He felt uncomfortable. It was just him and Georgie together by the till but he felt like he had been caught doing something he shouldn't.

'What are you two up to?' Ruth joked as she grabbed a water from the refrigerator.

This feels very awkward.

'Nothing much, boss.'

'If you've finished, we've found the stolen Porsche.'

Nick was relieved that the conversation had moved on to the safety of the case. 'Where was it?'

'Retail park off the A5 near Llanberis. No reports of any cars stolen yet from there.'

Nick stirred sugar into his coffee. 'They have to be travelling in something.'

'Maybe they hitched a lift?' Georgie suggested.

'I'm sure they'd think there was too much danger of them being recognised,' Ruth said.

'CCTV?' Georgie asked.

Ruth shook her head. 'Still waiting for it to come over. Uniform have asked around. No one saw them.'

Nick put the wooden stirrer into the bin. 'Now we've got the evidence from the screwdriver, this might not even be a murder case anymore.'

Georgie looked at them both. 'Do they have any way of knowing that?'

Nick shook his head. 'No, but we need to talk to the CPS and see what they think about the new evidence. If Neal had a screwdriver to Kat's neck and was pushing it into her skin, then whether Kat or Finn stabbed him, it becomes self defence.'

'What if they knew that? It might change things?' Georgie asked.

Ruth unscrewed the cap on her bottle. 'And maybe they would give themselves up. Finn is facing a series of other charges. Assault, robbery, criminal use of a firearm. He's going to serve some kind of prison time, but it's nothing like facing a murder charge. Especially if he pleads guilty.'

'And as far as I know, Kat Williams has never been in trouble before. She might even get away with a suspended sentence. She only ran because she was scared and because Finn doesn't trust the police,' Nick said.

'Which isn't surprising after what happened to him.'

'Can't we use the media to flag it up?' Georgie suggested.

Ruth shook her head. 'We can't leak to the media that we think two suspects are only going to be convicted of manslaughter before they're arrested or charged.'

French came into the canteen. Nick could see that he had something urgent to tell them. 'God, I've been looking for you everywhere, boss.'

'What is it?'

'Phone call from a mobile phone shop at the retail park where we found the Porsche abandoned. A young couple went in this morning. They bought a pay-as-you-go mobile phone.'

That's a decent break, Nick thought.

'Tell me you've got the number?' Ruth said.

French waved the torn piece of paper that he was holding. 'Would I let you down, boss?'

Ruth took the scrap of paper. 'Let's give them a ring, shall we?'

AS FINN TOOK ANOTHER back road through Snowdonia, he glanced over at Kat who was fast asleep in the passenger seat. He watched her as the light and the shadows of the trees from outside danced across her face. She muttered something in her sleep as her chest moved up and down slowly. She looked so beautiful and so innocent. He knew how lucky he was to have found her. And now they were go-ing to build a new life together.

Indicating left, he took a road that was signposted for Penrhyn Castle. By Finn's calculations, they were half an hour south of Bangor and the Menai Bridge. From there it was only less than an hour to Holyhead where they would get the nine o'clock ferry. He was happy to get there early. Now that they were in their rented silver Vauxhall Zafira, they were virtually invisible. No one knew that they had rented the car and they had paid cash. The man in the rental place had only taken Kat's driving licence number and credit card details in case they didn't return the car. Ironically, that was exactly what they were going to do, having rented the car for three days. Drive onto the ferry. Then drive down from Dublin to Tipperary to stay with Sean. By the time the nerdy man in the rental shop realised the car hadn't been returned, they would be long gone. Kat was never likely to use her real driving licence or credit card again, so it was of no conse-quence that they had the details. All they had to do was to get false Irish plates and the car was theirs.

Finn was beginning to allow himself to get excited. The plan was really starting to come together.

Kat made a soft groan as she blinked. 'Have I been sleep-ing?'

'Yeah. You were well away.'

She took a long breath and stretched. 'I was dreaming about my mum. We were in the Arctic or somewhere. She was on this iceberg. I was holding her hand but she was drift-ing away. Then I had to let go.'

She reached down, took a bottle of water and had a swig. She passed it to Finn who did the same.

Kat stared outside. 'Where are we?'

'Hour from Holyhead.'

She shook her head and smiled. 'I can't believe we are actually doing this.'

Finn laughed. 'I know. It's mad. But we're not going to prison for killing that prick.'

'Like that woman said in the petrol station, they should be giving us a medal.'

Finn imagined their new life, hidden away in the Irish countryside. There would be no one there to judge them for who they were or what they had done. It was now so close that he was allowing himself to believe that it might come true.

Kat scowled as she listened to the radio. 'What the hell are you listening to?'

'Elton John. It's just the radio.'

'Yeah, all right Grandad.' She retuned to the radio and soon found a song she liked. *Vossi Bop* by Stormzy. She turned up the volume.

At that moment, the pay-as-you-go mobile phone rang.

Finn was startled. *How is that ringing?*

He saw the mobile phone number it was coming from. 'I don't get it. How has someone got the number of that phone?'

'Maybe it's a wrong number?'

'Maybe. Shall I answer it?'

As he took the phone in his hand, it stopped ringing.

He could feel the tension in his stomach. The phone call had definitely rattled him.

The phone burst into life again.

Kat glanced at him. 'Answer it.'

'Are you sure?'

She nodded. 'You can always hang up.'

Finn answered the phone. 'Hello?'

'Finn?' said a female voice at the other end. He recognised it from somewhere. She had a London accent.

'Yeah? Who is this?'

'It's Detective Inspector Ruth Hunter. We met when you were interviewed at Llancastell Police Station.'

Finn didn't say anything for a second. His heart was starting to thump in his chest. How had the police got this phone number? 'What do you want?'

'I need to talk to you about something. And I need you to listen very carefully. Is that okay?' Ruth said quietly.

'I suppose so.' Finn knew how this conversation was going to go. Ruth was going to tell him that he and Kat needed to hand themselves in before things got any worse.

'First of all, are you and Kat okay?' she asked.

Finn looked at Kat who pulled a face as if to say 'Who are you talking to?'

'Yeah. We're fine.'

'You're getting yourself into a lot of trouble out there, Finn.'

Finn took a breath. 'We're not giving ourselves up if that's what you're going to say. We didn't murder him.'

'I know you didn't.'

Ruth's response hung in the air for a few seconds. It wasn't what he was expecting her to say.

'What do you mean?'

'We've got the evidence here, Finn. We know that Crispin Neal held a screwdriver to Kat's neck or throat. We know that whoever killed him did it in self defence.'

Finn couldn't believe that the police knew this. He had assumed that he and Kat would be tried for murder.

'I didn't have a choice. He was going to kill us.'

'I know that. And it means that you and Kat wouldn't be charged with his murder.'

'You don't know that. You're just saying that to get us to give ourselves up,' Finn said.

'No, I promise you. I've spoken to the Crown Prosecution Service. You will probably face a manslaughter charge.'

'But we'll still go to prison, won't we?' he asked, trying to make sense of what Ruth was saying to him.

'I don't know the answer to that. Even though Kat would be charged with armed robbery, I think it's likely that she would get a suspended sentence. But I can't promise that.'

'What about me? I'm on licence. They could make me serve the rest of my sentence now.'

'Finn, I had a long conversation with Michael. And I'm so sorry about what happened to you when you were younger. It would be something that a judge would be looking at. Legally it's called mitigating circumstances.'

Finn didn't say anything for a few seconds. An idea had come to him.

'If we do hand ourselves in, then I want you to be there.'

Kat shook her head.

'Okay. That's fine. I'll be there. Where are you?'

'Close to Menai Bridge. But I need some time before we meet you.'

'Good. I will meet you and Kat at the south end of Menai Bridge. What time?'

Finn glanced at the clock in the car. It was now six. 'Eight o'clock.'

'Eight o'clock. I'll be there.'

Finn hung up.

Kat shook her head and shouted, 'What are you doing? You can't just agree that we'll hand ourselves over to the police without asking me!'

'We're not handing ourselves in.'

Kat looked at him. 'What the bloody hell are you talking about, Finn?'

Finn took her hand. 'Don't worry. We're not handing ourselves in. I don't trust the police and I never will.'

'But you've just told them that we're meeting them at Menai Bridge at eight?'

Finn smiled and shrugged. 'Yes.'

'For fuck's sake! Will you tell me what's going on?'

'Menai Bridge will be swarming with police from Anglesey and North Wales. Meanwhile, we'll be in Holyhead, getting on a ferry to Dublin. And they won't have a clue.'

CHAPTER 31

AS RUTH CAME OUT OF her office, she could see that IR1 was now full, noisy, and stuffy. She had called an emergency briefing prior to the operation at Menai Bridge. Finn and Kat possessed a firearm, and they had used it when robbing the garage and stealing the Porsche. Their arrest had now become a major operation. She was keen for it not to descend into the chaos that had surrounded the hunt for Raoul Moat by Northumbria Police back in 2010. That operation had ended in a six-hour standoff, police using an ineffective taser, and Moat shooting himself dead. Even though Northumbria Police force had been cleared of any wrongdoing by the IPCC, the Independent Police Complaints Commission, they were still perceived as having handled the manhunt, and the negotiations that led to Moat's death, badly.

Looking up, Ruth saw Drake sitting next to Chief Inspector Ian Clulow, who was the senior Armed Response Officer, ARO, in North Wales. Ruth had liaised with the Anglesey coastguard to have a rescue boat nearby. Menai Bridge stretched across the Menai Strait, which was a sixteen-mile sweep of tidal water that separated mainland Wales from the island of Anglesey. Even though it was relatively narrow, she knew that the differential tides caused very strong currents to flow in both directions, making it incredibly dangerous.

'Okay everyone, if we can settle down,' Ruth said as she strode over to the map. 'Our operation tonight is to arrest and detain these two suspects. Finn Starling and Kat Williams. As most of you know, they are wanted for questioning in connection with the death of Crispin Neal. I have agreed to meet them at the south end of the bridge at twenty hundred hours.' Ruth pointed to their photos. 'They are armed, and they have threatened to use the shotgun in their possession in two robberies. Even though I think it's highly unlikely that they will use the firearm, we are taking no risks. All CID officers are to wear bulletproof vests.' She then looked over at Clulow. 'There will also be AROs deployed across the bridge and ARVs at both ends. Any news on tracing the pay-as-you-go they're using?'

'Some time tonight, boss,' Garrow said.

Ruth rolled her eyes. 'Can we chase it? Any questions?'

French raised an eyebrow. 'What if they don't show, boss?'

'I had a conversation with Finn Starling earlier. Their primary reason for going on the run is that they felt they would be facing a murder charge. We have strong forensic evidence to show that Crispin Neal's death was a case of self defence. I've spoken to the CPS who agree that they will face a lesser charge of manslaughter. Once I explained that to him, and told him that Kat might only face a suspended sentence, Finn's whole attitude changed. They're tired, have very little money, and they have nowhere to go. I really believe they will hand themselves over to us. However, we do have a contingency for a no show. Nick?'

Nick got to his feet and went to the map. 'Finn and Kat's journey so far has been consistently to the north west of Wales. There has been no deviation.' He pointed to the red pins on the map that marked places they knew Finn and Kat had been. 'The logical end to the trajectory that they seem to be on is Holyhead. That would make sense to someone on the run. You can get to Ireland on a ferry without a passport, and might hope to disappear once you are on the other side. Officers from Anglesey will patrol Holyhead ferry port. If Finn and Kat have decided to throw us off the scent and make a break to Holyhead, they will be arrested there.' Nick looked out at the room. 'They will not be getting on a ferry tonight.'

IT WAS SEVEN O'CLOCK by the time Finn and Kat drove across the Menai Bridge. This suspension bridge was designed by Thomas Telford and completed in 1826. With its huge limestone pillars at either end, seven arches and sixteen vast steel construction cables, Finn thought it was an impressive sight.

The light of day was beginning to fade. Finn glanced left at the water that stretched away to the west towards Caernarfon and then, eventually, the Irish Sea.

Kat, who was busy texting something on the phone, pointed to where he was looking. 'You know Dublin is only a hundred miles that way.'

Finn's eyes widened. 'Really? It's so close.'

'I know. And we'll be there in six hours.'

Finn shook his head. 'I've always wanted to go to Dublin. I've never been abroad.'

'I went to Spain a few times when I was a kid and when my mum and dad were still together. Then they started taking us to Barmouth, which is very boring.' Kat glanced over at the dashboard. 'Slow down a bit. We don't want to get pulled over for speeding.'

Finn slowed the car a little. 'Sorry.'

They turned left. After a few miles, the road narrowed – it was virtually deserted.

'Once we get settled, maybe we can go up to Dublin for a few nights?' Kat suggested. 'They have loads of good bands playing there.'

'That's a great idea. I've had a text from Sean. He thinks he can get us jobs in the local pub.'

Kat frowned. 'Aren't we going to stand out like sore thumbs?'

'Sean says Tipperary is full of travellers. Plus, there are tourists and backpackers. People come and go all the time, so no one bats an eyelid. He said we'd be fine,' Finn explained. He thought what an incredible relief it would be to start somewhere new, and could already imagine holding a pint of Guinness.

'That sounds wonderful.'

Finn smiled at her. 'It's going to be perfect. And after what we've been through, we *deserve* a bit of perfect.' He gestured to the phone. 'What are you doing?'

'I'm writing a text.'

'To who?'

'That police officer that you spoke to.' Kat pointed to the phone. 'We've got her number from when she rang you.'

'What the hell are you texting her for?'

'You're going to think I'm stupid.'

Finn grinned. 'I think that already.'

'Hey! ... Look, I'm writing down everything that you told me happened to you when you were a kid. Then everything that happened with me and Crispin at home. And what happened when he got killed.'

Finn was totally confused. 'What for?'

'So she knows the truth.'

'She doesn't care about that.'

Kat looked at him with a serious expression. 'If anything happens to us, I want someone to have the truth. People need to know why we did what we did. I want people to know what you went through when you were younger. And I want her to know that Crispin would have killed us if you hadn't stabbed him. If anything happens to us, no one is ever going to know that.'

Finn furrowed his forehead. 'What do you mean, if anything happens to us? We're getting a ferry to Ireland. We're starting a new life together there.'

Kat smiled at him. 'I know that, babe. It's just something I want to do.'

He shrugged. 'Hey, if it makes you feel better.'

'It does,' she said, taking a small bottle of whiskey from a bag by her feet, twisting it open and taking a swig.

'Careful. I don't want you hammered on the ferry.'

Kat grinned and gave him the finger. 'Fuck off, Dad.'

Suddenly, Finn saw a flashing blue light in his rearview mirror.

You have got to be joking.

He shook his head. 'Shit!'

Kat spun around to have a look. 'I told you not to speed, you idiot!'

'Sorry. What do we do now?'

'You're not going to outrun anyone in this bloody thing.'

'Bloody hell!' Finn moaned, now regretting ditching the Porsche. At least, they could outrun pretty much everything in that. 'What shall I do?'

'You'll have to pull over. Hopefully, he'll just give you a warning about speeding and we'll be on our way.'

I bloody hope so.

Finn felt his stomach tense. He began to pull the car over and watched in the mirror as the police car tucked in behind them.

Why has he pulled us over? It has to be speeding, doesn't it? What if they actually know who we are?

Finn got out his wallet. 'He's going to want to see my driver's licence.'

Kat seemed jittery. 'What if he recognises us or your name?'

'I don't know.' Finn's heart was pounding. 'But if I was speeding, he will do a vehicle check and it will come up as a rental. There's nothing suspicious in that, is there?' Finn knew he was trying to convince himself.

'I don't think so.'

Finn watched the police officer get out of the car. He took a deep breath.

Keep it together, mate.

The officer began to walk up the road towards them.

'Here we go,' Finn said as he buzzed down the window.

The police officer, middle-aged and paunchy, stooped to look in through the window. Finn noticed that he had several shaving cuts on his neck and he smelled of coffee and cigarettes.

'Was I speeding officer?' Finn asked.

'Yes, sir. I clocked you doing fifty-three in a forty mile an hour zone,' the officer explained in a weary tone. He sounded like he wanted to be doing anything else in the world other than stopping them for speeding.

Phew! Speeding it is.

Finn smiled innocently and said, 'Sorry. I didn't realise. I won't do it again, I promise. We're on our honeymoon, you see. I guess I'm just a bit over excited.'

The officer gave Finn a look to reassure him that he really didn't care. 'Are you the owner of this vehicle, sir?'

'Actually, it's a rental.'

Just give me a warning and let us go.

The officer took a closer look at the inside of the car. 'I assume that you have all the necessary paperwork for the vehicle?'

Trying not to show how nervous he was, Finn gestured to the glove compartment. 'Yes. It's all in there. And once again, I'm really sorry.'

Come on. I've told you we're on our honeymoon. Don't dick us about.

The officer sniffed and then frowned. 'I can smell alcohol. Have you been drinking?'

Finn shook his head. 'No. I never drink and drive.'

Kat waved her half bottle of whiskey. 'Sorry. That was me.'

The officer seemed annoyed and his tone became officious. 'I'm going to need to see your driving licence and you're going to need to perform an alcohol breath test before I can allow you to proceed.' He glanced over at Kat. 'And I'll need to see some ID from you, Miss, as well.'

Bollocks! This is not going well.

Kat looked anxious. 'Of course. It's in my bag in the back, if that's okay?'

The officer didn't respond but took two steps back from the car. 'I'm going to need you to get out of the vehicle, sir. And then accompany me to my car where you'll be required to blow into a breathalyser. If you can bring your driving licence with you?'

Finn glanced over at Kat. What were they going to do? Finn hadn't drunk any alcohol, so the test wasn't going to be a problem. However, the longer the officer had them stopped, studied their driving licences, the more likely he was to become suspicious or remember that there was a young couple on the run in North Wales.

If only Kat hadn't opened that bloody whiskey.

Getting out of the car, Finn glanced over at Kat. She gestured to the officer, 'I'll just get my ID from my bag.'

The officer ignored her.

Finn continued walking towards the curb. He squinted at the blue strobing lights of the patrol car which dazzled him. He could hear the muffled sound of the police radio inside the car.

Looking up, he saw Kat approaching. She appeared to be carrying a blanket that had been in the back of the hire car.

What the hell is she doing?

The officer came from the car holding a breathalyser.

'If you blow into this continuously for at least five seconds please, sir.'

Before the officer noticed her, Kat had crept up behind him. Finn took an audible deep breath as he took the machine. He knew exactly what she was doing.

The blanket dropped to reveal that Kat was, in fact, holding the shotgun. She jammed it in the officer's back. 'I've got a shotgun. Put your hands where I can see them.'

The officer froze and slowly put his hands up. 'Okay, let's take this nice and easy, Miss.'

'Be quiet!' Kat snapped.

Finn dropped the breathalyser, moved quickly towards the officer's belt, and unclipped the handcuffs. 'Put your hands behind your back.'

The officer glared at him. 'You don't need to do this. I know who you two are now, and you're already in a lot of trouble.'

Kat pushed the barrels into his back again. 'Just be quiet!'

Finn took the officer's hands, put them together and then handcuffed them behind his back. 'Bet you wish you'd given us a warning and told us to go on our way?'

Grabbing him by his shoulder, Finn pulled the officer towards the car and opened the back door. 'Get in.'

The officer moved into the back of the car and Finn slammed the door behind him. He went around to the driver's door. 'I'm gonna move this off the road.'

He sat down in the driver's seat and took the steering wheel. The first thing he needed to do was switch the lights off. He peered at the dashboard. 'How do I turn the bloody lights off?'

'I'm not going to tell you that, am I?' the officer growled from the back.

Flicking a switch down, Finn saw the lights disappear. 'Bingo.'

He started the engine and drove the car about twenty yards along the road to a small turning which led into a field. Turning the steering wheel, he manoeuvred the car onto the bumpy surface of the ploughed field and then parked it behind a thick hedgerow.

He turned off the engine. 'Here we go.'

'You can't just leave me here!' the officer protested.

'Have a good night.'

Finn got out of the car, hit the central locking button, and tossed the keys away.

Jogging across the field, he came out onto the road where Kat was waiting in the car for him.

Finn got into the car. 'Let's get out of here.'

They pulled away and disappeared into the darkening half-light of dusk.

CHAPTER 32

RUTH AND OTHER OFFICERS from Llancastell CID moved into position at the south end of Menai Bridge. As she glanced west, she spotted the swirling white currents of the Menai Strait below. On its banks, where the rocks broke the surface of the water, small circular pools foamed and bubbled in angry circles.

Her stomach was tense. She wanted the arrest to go smoothly and for no one to get hurt. It wasn't as if they were dealing with career criminals. Finn and Kat were young people who were scared, desperate, and armed. That made them unpredictable and dangerous.

The wind off the sea and the nearby mountains felt bitter against her face and ears. As she looked back to the south, the grey and purple peaks of the Snowdonia mountain range loomed in a long, uneven line. For some reason, she found them unsettling.

As Ruth moved forwards onto the pavement at the edge of the bridge, she was accompanied by AROs dressed in their black Nomex boots, gloves, and Kevlar helmets over balaclavas. Carrying Glock 9mm pistols, more AROs moved purposefully behind the large limestone pillars on the other side that marked the beginning of the bridge.

Ruth adjusted the thick Kevlar bulletproof vest that she and the other CID detectives were all wearing.

She radioed the team of AROs, who had been positioned out of sight at the north end of the bridge, to check they were ready to go if anything went wrong. Marksmen were hidden up in a thick wooded area on the adjacent hills. Everyone was in place and ready for the arrest.

The North Wales Police Media Department had negotiated a media blackout to prevent members of the public being drawn to the bridge by live news reports.

Ruth glanced at her watch. It was now exactly eight o'clock. She murmured into her radio, 'Three-six to Gold Command. Officers in position two at target location, No sign of suspects, over.'

The radio crackled back. 'Three-six received. Officers in position one.'

Nick strolled over fiddling with the straps of his Kevlar vest. 'Are you sure we haven't switched vests. This is so tight I can hardly breathe.'

Ruth smirked. 'That's what happens when you have a baby.'

Nick frowned. 'What are you talking about?'

'You get tired and you get fat.'

Nick's eyes widened. 'Oh, that's lovely. Thanks for that.'

'Hey, it was you who said the vest was tight, not me.'

Nick pulled the sleeve of his jumper back. 'What time we on?'

'Eight, dead on.'

'You think they're going to show, boss?'

'Yes, I do.'

As the wind picked up, Ruth pulled up the collar of her coat. On an operation like this, time seemed to stand still.

I bloody hope they turn up.

Ruth peered over at the pavement on the other side of the road where Garrow, French, and Georgie were standing. 'What do you think of Georgie?'

'What do you mean?'

'As a copper? I can't seem to work her out. She definitely knows her stuff ...'

'But ...?'

'But I think she's got a ruthless streak. I've seen it before. She's biding her time because she's new, but when she gets settled I think her ambition is going to become very clear,' Ruth said.

Nick shook his head. 'I don't think she's like that. Don't get me wrong, she's definitely ambitious. But not at the cost of her colleagues.'

Ruth delved into her pocket and pulled out a cigarette. 'We'll see ... If they're going to keep us waiting, then I'm going to smoke.'

She lit the cigarette, took a deep drag, and then watched the swirling wind grab away the smoke as she blew out. She glanced down at her watch – *8.07pm.*

Bloody hell. I hate waiting with all the pressure of the AROs, coastguard, CID and marksmen.

Going over to lean against the railings, she gazed down the Strait. The water snaked slightly right and then hard left.

Nick joined her. 'Beautiful view.'

Ruth pointed west. 'If you keep going that way, what do you come to?'

'Caernarfon. Then the Irish Sea. And then Dublin.'

Ruth glanced at her watch anxiously – *8.11pm. Where are they?*

Nick raised an eyebrow. 'You think they're making us wait?'

Ruth started to get an uneasy feeling. 'I hope that's all it is.'

Garrow came jogging across the road with a look that told her something was up. 'Boss, we got a call log for their phone.'

'What have we got?'

'There is a call and three texts to the same number. A Sean Brennan. Last known address is Tipperary, Ireland. Finn and Sean shared a cell in Ockley Cross,' Garrow explained.

Nick glanced over at her. 'Looks like they were planning to go to Ireland after all.'

Ruth could feel her breath quicken with nervous energy. 'Maybe they still are? When was the last text?'

Garrow looked down at his phone. 'Six thirty this afternoon.'

Ruth's face fell. 'Bloody hell! That's half an hour after we spoke about meeting.'

Nick shrugged. 'He might have texted to say they're not coming to Ireland anymore.'

Ruth shook her head. It was now *8.15pm*. 'They're not coming. Finn thinks that agreeing to meet us here gives them a better chance of getting a ferry from Holyhead without being detected.'

'What are we going to do?' Nick asked.

Ruth reached for her phone. 'Jim, have you got that pay-as-you-go number?'

Garrow began to scroll through his phone. 'I can get it right now for you, boss.'

Ruth glanced at them both. 'Nick. Contact uniformed patrols at Holyhead and tell them to be even more vigilant. Then I'll ring Finn and ask him what he's playing at.'

CHAPTER 33

IT WAS NOW GETTING dark and Finn and Kat had just pulled into Holyhead port. If everything had gone smoothly, North Wales Police would be waiting over twenty miles away at Menai Bridge. He also hoped that meant any police or customs officers at the port would no longer be on high alert.

Kat looked along the dockside and pointed. 'That must be it.'

Finn smiled at her. 'Yeah. We'll give it ten minutes and then drive up there.'

Kat grinned and shook her head. 'Ireland here we come, eh?'

Finn attempted an Irish accent and said, 'Top of the morning to ya.'

Kat pulled a face. 'Yeah, I want you to promise me that you'll never do that again.'

They laughed. Kat leaned over and kissed him. 'I can't think of anyone else in the world that I would have wanted to go on the run with, Mr Finn Mahoney.'

Finn kissed her back. 'Well, that is handy, isn't it?'

The mobile phone rang.

Finn looked at it. This time he wasn't nervous. He already had a plan of how to string the police along.

'Hello?' Finn said, sounding as innocent as he could.

'Hello Finn. It's DI Ruth Hunter here. I was expecting you half an hour ago.'

'Sorry. We're about five or ten minutes away. We had to stop for petrol,' he said, making eye contact with Kat, who smiled back.

'You're not coming, are you?'

Finn felt a slight sense of anxiety. 'Yeah, of course, we are. I promise. What you said to me earlier. You're right. We'll be there in a few minutes. Don't worry.'

There were a few seconds of silence.

Finn could feel his pulse quicken. *What's she doing?*

'Finn, we know you're going to Ireland.'

Her comment hung in the air for a moment.

Finn took a deep breath. 'What? I don't know what you're talking about!'

'We know about Sean. And we know you're going to Tipperary.'

Finn's head began to spin. 'No. I don't know what ...'

'We know you're at Holyhead, Finn. And you think you're getting on that ferry to Dublin.'

Finn could feel his whole world crumbling. 'No. I promise you. We're going to be at the bridge any minute now.' He knew he was sounding desperate, but he couldn't help it.

Kat put her hand on his arm and mouthed 'Are you okay?'

'I've spoken to our officers at Holyhead. And customs. They're looking out for you. You need to hand yourselves in, Finn. Right now.'

Finn could feel his whole body shaking. 'We're ... going to be there.' And then tears came into his eyes. 'Please. We're going to be there. I promise you.'

'Finn, it's over. You're not going anywhere. Just hand yourselves over,' Ruth said very calmly. 'You're not getting on a ferry.'

Finn took the phone from his ear and ended the call. His hand was trembling. He closed his eyes as a tear trickled down his face.

Kat took his hand. 'They know we're here, don't they?'

Finn blinked away the tears. The phone rang again and he turned it off. 'I'm so sorry, Kat. I'm ... so sorry I got you into this mess. I've fucked everything up.'

Kat put both her hands to either side of his face. She looked directly at him. 'Don't be silly. We did this together. And we're going to get out of this together. Whatever happens, we're together and that's what counts.' She kissed him hard on the mouth. 'Now budge over. I'm driving.'

Finn sniffed. 'But there's only two ways off Anglesey. And that's across Menai Bridge or Britannia Bridge.'

Kat shrugged. 'Okay. Then that's what we'll do.'

As they got out of the car to swap seats, Kat stopped and stared at the huge black Range Rover Sport with blacked out windows that was parked about ten yards away.

A blonde-haired woman was standing by it talking loudly on her phone and smoking.

From where Finn was standing, he could see that there was no one else inside the Range Rover.

Kat smiled at him and gestured to the car. 'Are you thinking what I'm thinking?'

Finn smiled as he wiped his face. He nodded. 'Yeah. Why not?'

IT HAD BEEN TEN MINUTES since Finn had hung up. Ruth knew that Finn and Kat had little option now but to hand themselves in. The ferry port at Holyhead was on high alert. Menai Bridge was swarming with police. She did need to secure Britannia Bridge, the only other route from Anglesey to the Welsh mainland. The island of Anglesey wasn't big enough for them to hide undetected for long.

Ruth was angry at herself for thinking that Finn and Kat would give themselves up. It was a very expensive miscalculation.

'Don't worry, boss. They're stuck and they're going nowhere. We'll have them in custody before dawn.'

'Thanks, Nick. I wish I shared your optimism. Drake is going to go mad.'

'Not if you bring them in.'

'I want to bring them in alive. Now they're desperate, armed, and stuck on an island. And that makes me feel very nervous.' Ruth turned to Nick. 'They sent me a text.'

'What? What do you mean?'

'Kat wrote a text. It details everything that happened to Finn before the arson attack. It also describes Crispin Neal's attempts to sexually abuse her. It confirms what we suspected. Neal held a screwdriver to her throat. When she pushed him away, Neal went to attack them with it.'

Nick shook his head. 'They should never have been put in a position where they had to go on the run.'

'We have to bring them in safely. We owe them that much.' Ruth then buzzed her radio. 'Gold Command from three six, are you receiving, over?'

'Three six, go ahead.'

'Suspects are a no show at target location. I'm going to need two ARVs to head to Britannia Bridge and secure that as target location two, over,' Ruth said.

'Three six, received. Gold Command will advise, out.'

Ruth beckoned French from the other side of the road. 'Dan?'

French came jogging over just as the police helicopter with a spotlight came thundering overhead before circling back. 'What's going on, boss?'

'Finn and Kat set us up. They were planning on getting a ferry to Dublin tonight, but we've got officers at Holyhead,' Ruth explained.

French raised an eyebrow in surprise. 'Bloody hell! What do we do now?'

'I want you to take Jim and Georgie and head to Britannia Bridge. It needs to be secured. There should be two ARVs and AROs that need to be positioned on both ends. But I want us to remember that they are a very scared young couple, not a gang of hardened criminals.'

'Yes, boss. And then what do we do?'

'We wait. And hope they don't do anything stupid.'

Ruth looked at him. 'If we have the bridges closed, they're going to be stuck on the island with virtually nowhere to hide. So, we wait. And pray that they don't do anything stupid.'

Ruth saw Garrow running across the road towards them. 'Everything okay, Jim?'

'Boss, they've stolen another car at gunpoint.'

HAVING RULED OUT THEIR chances of getting a ferry, Finn and Kat sped south from Holyhead. Finn gazed up at the night sky and reached out for Kat's hand.

Kat squeezed his hand. 'I wish I knew what they all were.'

Finn pointed to a series of bright stars. 'I think that's Orion.'

Kat smiled. 'Are you saying that just to impress me?'

Finn shook his head. 'No. It's the only one I remember. That's the belt and that there is the sword.'

'And who exactly is Orion?'

'He's a hunter, isn't he? That's why he's got a sword.'

For a while, there was peaceful silence as they drove.

Finn took a deep, long breath. The night air was sweet and fresh.

Gazing at the darkness above, the sky looked like a pitch black curtain had been draped carefully over the sky. The silvery speckles had been scattered in small clusters and patterns. Finn got an overwhelming feeling of just how small they were, gazing up into the endless sky. How tiny and insignificant. It felt like a relief to be that unimportant after the events of recent days.

'I don't want to go to prison,' Kat said in a virtual whisper, breaking the silence.

'We're not going to prison, Kat. I promise you.'

'I don't want to spend years apart from you. I don't know what I'd do if that was going to happen.'

'It's not going to happen. We're staying together. And somehow we're going to get out of this.'

'Promise? I don't want you to do any deals with the police, okay? I don't want you to hand yourself over if they say that I'm going to be all right.'

'I won't. We're not making any deals with anyone.'

Kat smiled. 'I want to go somewhere hot. And I want us to walk down a beach and then drink a cocktail as the sun sets.'

'Sounds nice. We could get jobs there. And have a cheap, little apartment near the beach.'

'If I close my eyes, I can see us there.'

'So can I.'

Kat's eyes widened. 'Can we really go to a place like that?'

Finn smiled, leant over and kissed her. 'Of course, we can. You wait. We can go wherever you want. Anywhere in the world.'

Finn could hear a growing noise as if a storm cloud was directly over them.

Jesus! What the hell is that?

Kat frowned. The noise was now thunderous.

What's going on? It's like we're in a tornado.

Looking up into the dark sky, his jaw dropped. He saw exactly what was going on.

A black and yellow police helicopter was hovering about three hundred feet above them.

Shit! They've spotted us.

Kat glanced up, then looked at him and shouted, 'Finn!'

Suddenly, a bright light flicked on that dazzled onto them as they drove. It was a high intensity discharge searchlight from the helicopter.

'This is the North Wales Police. Pull your vehicle over to the side of the road,' boomed a voice from the helicopter's sky shout public address system.

Fuck that!

'This is the North Wales Police. Pull your vehicle over to the side of the road and stop.'

'Bloody hell,' Finn said.

'My hands are shaking. Look.' Kat held out her hands to demonstrate.

'Where are we going?' Finn said, thinking out loud.

Kat pulled on her hoodie. 'South. We've got to get off the island.'

'There will be police on both bridges.'

Kat shrugged. 'They can't keep both bridges closed permanently. Think of all the traffic that goes to and from Holyhead. They'll have to let traffic through.'

Finn glanced out of the window and saw the helicopter fly overhead and then circle back. He took a deep breath. 'That's if we even get to the bridges.'

'Shit. How the hell do we lose them?'

Finn turned onto the main road south. Stamping on the accelerator, the 3.0-litre, six-cylinder engine roared as they hit 80 mph.

Finn had a nervous knot in his stomach. How were they going to get out of this?

'I don't know,' Finn said as he peered up. He saw a very tight right-hand turn into a side road coming up. 'Hold on tight.'

Without braking, he turned the steering wheel sharply.

The back tyres screeched and he completely lost the back end of the Range Rover. Spinning the steering wheel back, he managed to regain control.

'I thought we were going to crash,' Kat gasped.

Finn blew out his cheeks. 'Me too.'

As they raced downhill away from the A55, Finn peered up into the sky. 'Where are you, you bastards.'

Kat was looking in the other direction. 'I can't see them. You think we lost them?'

Finn shrugged. 'I doubt it.'

Suddenly a black shadow came low across the sky in front of them.

'For fuck's sake.'

Finn knew the helicopter would have radioed their location. It wouldn't be long before there were police cars on their tail or even roadblocks. This wasn't good.

The helicopter hovered above them before flying ahead and circling back again.

Kat put her hand to her face nervously. 'We're never going to get away from them. It's over.'

'Don't worry. I'll get us out of this.'

Out of the corner of his eye, Finn spotted a sign - *Newborough National Nature Reserve and Forest.*

He gestured to the sign. 'Bingo!'

Finn turned the car sharply, following the sign for the forest. 'What do you find in forests?'

'Is this a trick question?'

'No.'

Kat shrugged and then peered out of the window nervously. 'What are you talking about, Finn? Trees. You find lots of trees in a forest.'

'Exactly.'

Finn followed another sign to *Newborough Forest.*

Up ahead, he could see exactly what he was hoping to see.

A huge forest of towering pine trees. He was no expert, but they looked like they were close to being 150ft high.

Finn shouted, 'Try following us through this, you bastards!'

Kat laughed. 'Woo hoo!'

As they reached the forest, the sky disappeared behind the huge canopy of trees above.

Finn slowed a little. There was a right-hand turn marked *Yellow Trail.* He turned off his headlights, slowed right down, and gazed up at the sky which was virtually invisible through the branches and trees.

Turning left, Finn pulled into a small car park and stopped.

For a moment, he and Kat sat getting their breath back and composing themselves.

Then they opened the car doors and stepped out.

Finn stood frozen, listening intently in the darkness.

Nothing.

Kat peered up at the sky. 'Oh my God. They've gone.'

CHAPTER 34

RUTH WAS NOW AT A TEMPORARY incident base at the south side of the Menai Bridge. They had been forced to open the bridge. There were ten thousand islanders who commuted daily to mainland Wales, with five thousand coming the other way. Uniformed officers were slowing cars down on the north side to check the drivers' identities before allowing them to cross the bridge.

The Chief Constable had been in touch with Drake, making it clear that he wanted a resolution to the situation. The media now had the story and the hunt for Finn and Kat was the lead story on the national BBC News. It was turning into a PR disaster for North Wales Police.

Taking a deep breath, Ruth gazed north towards Anglesey. *Where the bloody hell are you?*

As she was taking out a cigarette, Nick came jogging over. He was holding a map book.

'Boss, the chopper spotted Finn and Kat in a field off the A55 here. Just by a place called Trefdraeth. They followed them up the A55 but then lost them just here in the Newborough Forest.'

'Sod it ... If they're near the A55, I think they're coming south.'

Nick frowned. 'You think they're going to try and come back over one of the bridges?'

Ruth nodded. 'I don't see that they have any other choice. Where else can they go?'

Nick shook his head. 'I guess you're right. I just don't want anything to happen to them.'

He's changed his tune.

'I take it you read their text then?'

'Yeah. It's a tough read, isn't it?'

Ruth reached into her coat pocket, pulled out her mobile phone, and dialled the number. 'I'm going to have to try them again.'

'Hello?' said a voice. It was Finn.

'Hi Finn, it's Ruth. I wondered if you'd thought about what we talked about?' Ruth said gently.

'We're not interested.'

He sounds annoyed.

Ruth took a breath and then said, 'I've read the text Kat sent.'

There were a few seconds of silence.

'What do you want me to say?' Finn mumbled quietly.

'I'm so sorry about everything that happened to you, Finn. I can't imagine how you feel.'

'No, you can't,' Finn snapped.

'I need you to trust me.'

'Why should I? I don't know you. Every copper I've ever met has been a bastard,' Finn growled down the phone.

'And I'm really sorry that's been your experience. But there are some of us that actually do care. I don't want you or Kat to get hurt. But unless you hand yourselves in, that's exactly what's going to happen,' Ruth explained.

'Sorry ... I can't do that ...'

Ruth took a moment. She needed to find something that would resonate. 'You know Finn, I have a daughter about your age. If anything had happened to her, like the things that happened to you, I would have held her, protected her, and tried my best to help her get over it. But you had no one for so long. But now you have Kat. I know you would do any-thing to keep her safe, wouldn't you?'

'Handing her over so you can put her in prison isn't keeping her safe, is it?' Finn said.

'It's going to be the safest option.'

'Why? Why do you say that?' Finn was getting annoyed again.

'You're wanted for a series of serious crimes. You're in a stolen car with a firearm. You have the whole of the North Wales Police force looking for you. I have a horrible feeling that you and Kat aren't going to make it,' Ruth said, desper-ate for Finn to see some kind of sense.

'Yeah, well we'll see about that!'

The phone went dead.

Ruth looked sadly at Nick. 'They're not going to come in.'

THROWING THE PHONE angrily out of the window, Finn stepped on the accelerator. 'Fucking coppers.'

'What did she say?'

'Playing mind games, that's all. You know what they're like.'

Glancing up, he saw a sign to Bangor and another to Menai Bridge. It was 12 miles away.

They came to the top of a steep hill. As they went over its crest, the valley of the River Cefni stretched out before them bathed in moonlight.

'God, it's so beautiful here,' Kat said with a sigh.

'I've never seen anywhere like this before,' Finn said.

Kat smiled and put her feet up on the dashboard. 'I know. Everything just looks different, doesn't it?'

Finn looked over at her. 'Yeah. It's like someone turned the light on.'

'That's what my taid always said. North Wales is God's country.' Kat buzzed down the window, stuck out her head and let the wind blow through her hair. 'This feels amazing!'

Finn opened his window too and sat back as the wind battered against his face. It smelled so fresh and cold.

God, I don't think I've ever felt this alive.

He yelled at the top of his voice, 'YEEEEE HAAAA!'

Shifting off her seat, Kat crouched on the passenger seat. She placed her left leg out of the window and sat on the ledge so that half of her body was out of the car. She raised up her left arm so that it was horizontal.

Finn laughed. 'What are you doing?'

'WOOOOOOO HOOOOOOOO!' she screamed. 'I'm never going home, and I don't care!'

Finn grinned and shook his head. 'You're mental. You know that?'

She slid back onto the passenger seat, reached over and put her hand on Finn's. 'I'm so lucky to have met you. I want you to know that.'

Finn was surprised to see the serious look on her face. She looked like she was going to cry. 'I know. It's okay.'

'I've never met anyone like you, Finn Mahoney. I've had the craziest, wildest few days. And I wouldn't have wanted to be with anyone else in the world. I want you to know that.' Kat now had tears in her eyes.

Finn squeezed her hand. He loved her so much. 'I do know that.'

She wiped the tears from her face. 'It's important. In case anything happens.'

'Nothing's going to happen. I promise you.'

Kat leant over and kissed him. 'I love you.'

Suddenly, Finn saw flashing blue lights in his rearview mirror. He wasn't even surprised. Rather than feeling nervous, he took a deep breath and thought 'Bring it on.'

He pushed down the accelerator. 'As they say in all the best films, we've got company.'

Kat spun around to look. 'Now what?'

He pressed the accelerator so that it touched the floor. 'We outrun them.'

He glanced down at the speedometer – *85 mph.*

'How far are we from the bridge?' Kat asked.

'Less than ten miles. But if they know we're coming ...'

Looking up ahead, Finn saw two police cars, with flashing lights, had blocked off the road. 'Shit!'

'What are we going to do?'

'That's the beauty of being in a Range Rover.'

'What is?'

'This is.' Finn spun the steering wheel, drove off the road, and sped into a field.

The ground was uneven. A series of bumps threw them around the car.

Kat reached up and grabbed the handle above her. 'Jesus!'

Finn knew that the Range Rover's permanent four-wheel drive made it perfect for off road, unlike the police BMW saloon.

Tearing across the field, Finn could see that he was already putting distance between them and the police car.

Suddenly, he saw something out of the corner of his eye. A large police BMW X5 4x4 heading their way.

Bollocks.

Turning sharp left, the Range Rover threw mud and earth into the air.

He glanced at the dashboard – *55 mph.*

'Finn!' Kat yelled.

He had been so preoccupied avoiding the X5, he hadn't seen a shed right in their path. There wasn't time to stop.

CRASH! They hit the wooden wall hard. For a second, he couldn't see anything except for splintering wood and hay.

Then everything cleared.

Phew!

Glancing behind, Finn could see the X5 was only twenty yards behind them.

I think I can outrun it on the road, he thought. The Range Rover had a bigger engine than the X5.

Smashing through a low wire fence, Finn hurtled back onto a road heading south.

A sign read – *Menai Bridge 3 miles.*

Stamping on the accelerator, he felt the engine kick in. The X5 wasn't going to be able to keep up.

He heard a mechanical sound. At first, he thought there was something wrong with the car.

It got louder and deeper.

Then he recognised it. He had heard that thundering sound before.

The helicopter!

Glancing skyward, he saw the black and yellow police helicopter that had followed them earlier hone into view.

'Finn!' Kat said as she looked up into the darkness.

'I know.'

Kat glanced in the wing mirror and then over at Finn. 'Shit!'

Looking in the rearview mirror, Finn counted four police cars that were now in pursuit.

This is not good.

Finn noticed a line of blue metal railings either side of the road.

As they turned the corner, a large structure came into view.

Menai Bridge.

Finn slowed the car down and stopped. The helicopter was now circling above them with its spotlight.

Glancing in the rearview mirror, the police cars had stopped about fifty yards behind them.

Word must have got to the bridge that they were there. Police officers began to scuttle around, and a police car, with its blue lights flashing, pulled across the entrance.

Finn glanced right at the trees and woodland that edged the roadside and covered the clifftops. He then looked over at Kat. 'End of the road, I think.'

Kat shook her head. 'No. It's not. It can't be.' She took his hand, leaned over and kissed him hard.

'What are we going to do?'

Kat gestured to the bridge. 'We just keep on driving.'

Finn revved the engine. For a second, he glanced at the cruise control and then nodded. 'Okay. Sounds like a plan.'

CHAPTER 35

AS THE RAIN LASHED down, Ruth peered along the length of the Menai Bridge towards the black Range Rover which remained motionless at the far end. The raindrops bounced and splashed off the nearby pavement and dripped noisily from the steel structure above.

Ruth shivered as she watched the helicopter circle again, its beam swathing the car in a brilliant white light, before it ascended up into the darkness and disappeared into the cover of the low, black clouds. There was a storm coming, and the distant rumble of thunder was getting closer.

The shadowy figures of two AROs, with Glock machine guns at the ready, hurried into position about fifty yards from the stationary Range Rover, training their weapons on the target vehicle. An ARV had already pulled across to block the road at the entrance to the bridge. Its rotating blue light illuminated the painted steel barricades and enormous chains that swung in a giant U-shape from the limestone towers, giving the scene an eerie atmosphere.

Although it was difficult to see from where she stood, Ruth knew that there were several patrol cars parked up about a hundred yards behind the static car.

Finn and Kat were trapped.

What are they doing now? Ruth wondered.

Pulling the collar up on his coat, Nick jogged over. His hair was matted from the rain and his face was wet. 'Nice night for it. What's going on?'

'I don't know. They've been sitting there for about ten minutes now. I was expecting them to come out, but now I'm not so sure.'

Nick shrugged as he wiped water from his face and beard. 'They can't stay there forever.'

'No. And there's nowhere for them to go.'

'The chopper had to leave because of the storm. North-bound traffic is being diverted over to Britannia Bridge.' Nick squinted through the rain at the stationary car and pointed to the high steel barricades that partially obscured their view. 'I can't really see what's going on.'

'Yeah, I know. The barricades are in the way. I'm going to wander down there and get a bit closer. I'm the only person Finn knows. I don't want some trigger happy ARO making a bloody mistake.'

There was a flash of lightening that lit up the whole sky, illuminating the Snowdonia mountains in the distance behind her. Then a second or two later, the deep grumble of thunder.

Nick looked at her. 'I've known Kat since she was a baby so I'm coming with you.'

Suddenly, the Range Rover's headlights went out. The car was now just a dark shape, barely visible in the driving rain and darkness.

What did they do that for?

Ruth and Nick moved quickly and got half way across the bridge. Splashing through puddles, Ruth felt the cold water against her ankles. She stared down. The two hundred foot drop into the churning black water below made her stomach lurch with vertigo.

There was another flash of lightening which seemed a lot closer than the last. *How safe is it to be on a bridge, over water, in a thunderstorm?*

The car was about seventy-five yards away, but the darkness and tinted windows meant it was impossible to see inside.

There was another flash of lightening.

The lights across the bridge went out, plunging everything into darkness. The only light came from the blue strobing lights of the police vehicles.

Are you kidding me?

For a few seconds, everything was silent.

Then the sound of an engine starting.

Ruth looked at Nick. 'Shit!'

Being at the centre of the bridge, in the middle of a storm, in virtual darkness, was feeling precarious.

Squinting towards the far end of the bridge, Ruth could hardly see anything in the pitch black. All she could hear was the roar of an engine.

The lights on the bridge suddenly burst back into life.

Phew. Thank God for that!

Blinking to adjust her eyes to the lights again, Ruth peered towards the Range Rover.

Nick nudged her and pointed. 'Boss!'

The Range Rover, still with no lights, had set off towards the entrance to the bridge and was gaining speed.

Ruth gasped. 'Oh God, no.'

The AROs ran out of the way as the Range Rover smashed into the stationary ARV, hammering it out of the way. The noise of the collision was deafening.

As Ruth and Nick continued quickly along the bridge, she grabbed her radio and shouted, 'All units from three six. Do not fire on target vehicle. Repeat, do not fire on target vehicle. We need the stinger pulled across the road at the south end *now*!'

The Range Rover was only fifty yards from where Ruth and Nick were standing. It was hammering along.

It seemed to lose control.

It swerved right and hit the steel barricade.

The force of the collision sent the car into the air. It twisted as it sailed upwards.

For a split second, Ruth could see the underneath of the chassis.

Then she realised what was about to happen.

Oh my God, no!

She watched in horror as the roof of the car smashed down onto the edge of the bridge. It then turned upright and fell from the bridge and out of sight as it plummeted down into the black waters below.

There was the loud sound of metal hitting water.

Ruth and Nick were already running.

She grabbed her radio as she sprinted to where the car had disappeared. 'Three six to all units. Target vehicle has crashed and is now in the water. I need search and rescue teams in there immediately,' she yelled.

Ruth and Nick reached that part of the bridge which was now covered in smashed glass and metal.

Looking frantically down, Ruth could see the Range Rover was already two hundred yards downstream. It was virtually submerged as it was swept west by the strong currents.

Please God, no.

A moment later, it disappeared under the water and out of sight.

CHAPTER 36
Two days later

THE FIRST GLIMMER OF dawn began to seep through the window in Ruth's office. She grabbed her coffee and took a mouthful. She had now lost count of how many she had drunk in the past two days.

Despite the best efforts of the coastguard and a Royal Navy helicopter, there had been no sign of Finn or Kat since their car went into the water two days earlier. The tides had pulled the vehicle out towards the sea. Ruth had liaised with the North Wales Police Underwater and Marine Search Team. It had taken them 48 hours to locate the sunken car. There were no bodies found inside, and it was assumed that they had been washed out to sea by the current. She had dispatched a uniformed patrol to Natalie Williams' home to keep her updated.

Looking out at the team, she knew that the mood was sombre. Had it been a different case, there might have been laughter and even drinks. But two young people had almost certainly lost their lives, and no one was in the mood to celebrate the case coming to a close.

Picking up her files from her desk, Ruth went out of her office and into IR1. It was their last day in the incident room now the case was over. She couldn't help but glance at the scene boards which would soon be dismantled. She stared at the photographs of Finn and Kat. Maybe it was because her daughter Ella was only in her early 20s, but the case had really affected her. She knew everything that they had been through in their all too short lives, and it didn't seem fair.

'Good morning everyone. I want to thank you all for doing an excellent job on this case. I know we're all very tired and we didn't get the result that we wanted. It really is a tragedy. We have to console ourselves that we did a thorough and professional job.'

Garrow, who had been on the phone, glanced over and signalled that it was important. 'Boss, that was the North Wales Coastguard. They've found clothing floating in the estuary.'

Ruth nodded sadly. It only confirmed what they already suspected.

For the next ten minutes, she ran through what she needed the team to do that day. The main thing was to write up reports on what had happened as there would be a full inquiry.

Returning to her office, Ruth sat for a moment. She could still remember the sound of Finn's voice on the phone. The overwhelming distress when he realised that he and Kat weren't getting on a ferry to Ireland to start a new life. It was heartbreaking to think about.

A knock on the door broke her train of thought. It was Georgie. 'Boss, I've forwarded over the CCTV files from the bridge. You wanted to see them?'

Ruth nodded. She really didn't want to see them. 'Thanks, Georgie.'

Spinning around her office chair, Ruth clicked on Georgie's email and saw the CCTV MP4 files. It wasn't long before she managed to track down the clip showing the actual crash. She needed to check that there was nothing else North Wales Police, or she as SIO, could have done to prevent the loss of life.

Pressing play, she could see a view of the bridge from a camera mounted high on one of the towers. The Range Rover already had its lights turned off. However, Ruth also noticed something else. The driver's door of the vehicle was open.

What is that about?

Playing the footage forward, she reached the point where the Range Rover began to gather speed across the bridge.

The image of the car got closer and closer to where the camera was positioned, and therefore larger and larger in the frame.

Ruth squinted at the screen. There was something wrong with what she was looking at.

'What the hell is going on?' she thought as she did a double take.

CHAPTER 37

RUTH SQUINTED UP AT the cloudless morning sky before putting on her sunglasses. Shadows from the clock tower of St Stephen's Church in Llancastell fell across the wide, gravel path that led through the graveyard to the church doors. It might have been a sunny day, but the mood was appropriately sombre.

Ruth took a drag on her cigarette as Nick came over. He had been talking to Ben Williams who looked devastated by his daughter's death.

Ruth gestured towards Ben. 'Poor man.'

'He's in bits. He blames himself for not doing more to protect Kat,' Nick said sadly.

It had now been a week since Finn and Kat had lost their lives so tragically. The terrible news that their bodies had not been found in the Range Rover, when it was finally discovered on the seabed, had made the heartbreak worse. Forensic officers and the North Wales Police Crash Investigation Team had examined the car once it had been retrieved. The windscreen had smashed when the car hit the water. That explained why the car had sunk so quickly. It also explained why Finn and Kat's bodies hadn't been found. The car would quickly have filled with water and, if they weren't wearing seatbelts, their bodies would have been carried out into the Irish Sea. It was unlikely that they would ever be found. Ruth knew that having no bodies would guarantee a thorough coroner's inquiry.

It was Sunday, and friends and family had gathered at St Stephen's Church to celebrate Kat's life. Ruth and Nick were there to represent North Wales Police, but they were keen to keep a low profile. The national press and social media had blamed North Wales Police for what had happened. They had forced a young couple to commit suicide rather than hand themselves in. Crude comparisons to Romeo and Juliet had given the tabloid headline writers a field day.

As Ruth and Nick entered the cold, dark church, the song *Nothing Compares* by The Weeknd was playing. They went over to a pew close to the back of the church and sat quietly. Ruth hadn't been inside a church since Sian's funeral. The agony of that day came back to her for a moment. She and Ella had sprinkled earth on Sian's coffin as it lay in the ground. Ruth had felt pain like nothing she had ever experienced before as she looked at Sian's coffin, knowing that she would never see her again.

'Are you thinking about Sian?' Nick asked in a whisper.

'How did you know?'

Nick shrugged. 'Because I am ... I miss her so much.'

Ruth reached over and gave his hand a reassuring squeeze. 'We all do, don't we? And then sometimes I forget for a bit, and that makes me feel guilty.'

Nick gave her a half smile. 'I do that too.'

Feeling her phone vibrate silently, Ruth took it from her jacket pocket and looked at him. 'Better get this.'

It was an email from Stephen Flaherty with an attachment. His emails always made her feel uneasy.

Hi Ruth

I spoke to colleagues at Interpol. They believe that Saratov is living in Paris, where he is running an elite escort agency called 'Global Escorts'. I've been on to their website. I found a profile of a British escort that I want you to look at. Tell me what you think. Kind regards, Stephen.

Ruth opened up the attachment which showed a series of photos of a blonde escort, Sophia, in white lingerie. Her face had been pixelated out. Studying the images closely, Ruth couldn't tell if it was Sarah in the photographs or not. The age and body shape were about right. She went back and forth through them, searching her memory of Sarah and trying to match it to the images in front of her. It could be, but she wasn't certain.

What about the tattoo?

Sarah had a small tattoo of a series of musical notes on the inside of her right wrist. Using her fingers to increase the size of the images, Ruth looked again. There just weren't any photos that showed the inside of her wrist.

'Work stuff?' Nick asked, indicating her phone.

'No. Just a friend. Nothing important.'

Now wasn't the time to give it her full attention. She would have another look when she returned home.

CHAPTER 38

HAVING HELD THE MONDAY morning briefing, Ruth had gone outside for a cigarette before heading up to the sixth floor. Incident Room 1 had now been cleared of the scene boards, and everything to do with Finn and Kat's case had been boxed up ready for the inevitable inquiry. CID officers had returned to the regular office down the corridor and, until the next major crime came in, things were back to some kind of normality.

Wandering across to her office, Ruth was still thinking about the images that Stephen Flaherty had sent over. She had scrutinised them over and over again but had come to no conclusion as to whether or not they were indeed Sarah.

Nick came across to her. 'Can I have a word, boss?' he said in a hushed tone that implied this was something relatively serious.

As they went into her office, Nick closed the door and took a USB drive from his pocket. 'There's something I need to show you.'

For a second, Ruth was going to make a joke, but she could see that whatever it was, Nick was in no joking mood. Taking a seat, he slotted the USB drive into her computer and brought up its contents on the screen.

Then she saw a file marked *Bridge CCTV.* She wondered if he had seen what she had on the CCTV images.

Nick clicked the file and the footage came up.

Ruth leant forward and stared at the screen. 'I've seen this already, Nick.'

His brow furrowed. 'You've seen it already?'

Ruth shrugged. 'Yeah. I saw it on Friday afternoon.'

'Erm, didn't you notice anything strange about what's on there?'

Ruth took a few seconds to answer. 'The driver's door was open as the car came onto the bridge.'

Nick looked at her. She could see that he was on to her. 'You know exactly what I'm talking about don't you?'

'Why don't you show me what you mean,' Ruth said. She wasn't going to say anything until she saw exactly what he was referring to.

Nick clicked on the footage and played it forward to where the Range Rover was in full view of the camera. 'Here.'

Ruth nodded. 'Yeah. I saw it. There's no one driving the car.'

There it was on the screen. It was clear to see that there was no one in the driver or passenger seat.

Nick's eyes widened. 'Didn't you think that was a bit strange?'

'Of course.'

'Aren't we going to do something about it?'

Ruth looked at him. ''I don't know, Nick. For starters, I don't understand. How is that even possible?'

'I did some digging around. In a car like a Range Rover, you can set the cruise control while the car is in neutral. When you put the car into drive, the car will increase the revs until it reaches the speed you've dialled in. If you set it to 120 mph, then the car is going to accelerate very quickly.'

'You mean it drives itself?'

'Yeah. Once you've put it into drive, you could leave the vehicle and it would accelerate on its own.' He then gestured back to the computer. 'There's something else, boss. I pulled the CCTV footage from Holyhead of the ferry to Dublin from the morning after the crash.' He clicked the image and it started to play. The CCTV was grainy, but it showed passengers boarding the ferry. 'There's a young couple just here. He's wearing a baseball cap, she's wearing sunglasses, so you can't really see them properly.'

Ruth peered at the image. It was Finn and Kat. There was no doubt in her mind. 'Yeah, I suppose it could be them.'

Nick looked at her. 'Come on, boss. You can see it's them. They got out of that car when the lights on the bridge failed. It's woodland right by the road there. They hid in it and managed to get themselves back to Holyhead by the following day.'

Ruth nodded. She knew he was right. It was an incredible theory, but her instinct told her that he was right. 'It's an interesting hypothesis.'

'What do we do?' Nick asked.

'Have you shown this to anyone else?' Ruth asked.

Nick shook his head. 'No.'

'Are you going to?'

'Not unless I have to.'

'Why don't you give me the memory stick for safe keeping, eh?'

Nick took the USB from the computer and handed it to her. 'What are you going to do with it?'

'I'm just going to hang on to it. That's all,' Ruth said, and gave him a knowing look.

CHAPTER 39

IT WAS DARK BY THE time Nick came out into the car park at Llancastell Police Station. He was still weighing up what he had found on the CCTV from Menai Bridge and Holyhead. Was it okay for him and Ruth to have seen the evidence and not to have acted upon it? Did that go against everything that he believed as a serving police officer? It wasn't their job to pick and choose what evidence to use.

On the other hand, he had read Kat's text. He knew what they had been through. He was also aware that Crispin Neal had got what was coming to him. What if he had attacked Kat with the screwdriver? How would he feel then? Didn't Finn and Kat deserve to start a new life away from all the misery that they had been surrounded by for so long?

Nick's phone rang. It was Amanda. 'Hiya. You okay?'

'Yeah, I'm just on the way home.'

'I think I'm going to have to go to bed. I'm knackered,' Amanda said. Even though she sounded tired, Nick felt disappointed.

'I thought I was getting a chippy tea and we were going to watch that film?' Nick said, realising as he said it that he was being selfish.

'Sorry. I was looking forward to that, but I can't keep my eyes open.'

'No. Sorry. Get some rest. As long as you're alright. Megan's okay?'

'Fine. She went to bed early too.'

'Good night, babe. Love you.'

'Love you too.'

Nick finished the call and put his phone away. He glanced at his watch. It was too late to get to an AA meeting, which would have been the sensible thing to do.

From somewhere he could hear the sound of someone trying to start an engine. And by the sounds of it, the car's battery was flat.

Walking around the corner, he saw Georgie sitting in the driver's seat of her car and turning the ignition.

Again. Really?

Nick strolled over, trying not to feel any excitement at the thought of having to rescue Georgie again. 'What is it with you and cars?'

Georgie glanced up. 'Christ! You made me jump.'

'Talking of which, where are your jump leads? You've got a flat battery.'

Georgie put her finger to her mouth. 'Mmm. Jump leads. Pretty sure I don't have any.'

Nick shook his head. 'You're joking?'

'Really not.'

He remembered that he had cleared out his car at the weekend and left everything at home. 'Slight problem then because I've left mine at home.'

Georgie turned the ignition again and the engine grated. 'Bloody thing.'

'Yeah, that's not going to help much. Let me guess, you left your lights on?'

Georgie smiled. 'Hey, you should be a detective.'

'And by the smell, you've also flooded the engine.'

Georgie shrugged. 'I take it that's a bad thing?'

'It's not great.' Nick glanced at his watch. 'The good news is that it is early enough for you to get a bus this time.'

Georgie pulled a face. 'Ha, ha. You wouldn't leave me here.'

Nick grinned at her. 'Why not?'

'Because you enjoy my company. And you're a gentleman, so you'll drop me home.'

They looked at each other.

Nick gestured to his car that was parked nearby. 'Come on then.'

THE YOUNG BARMAN MOVED along the bar towards the next customer. O'Brien's pub was getting busy but there was hurling on the television, so it was to be expected.

'Hey, young Geordie fella. Two pints again, please,' said the old man as he leaned on the bar.

Finn smiled and gave him a mock salute. 'Right you are.' He went to the pumps and poured two pints of Guinness.

This was his fifth night of working at O'Brien's and he was just about getting the hang of pouring a decent pint of the black stuff.

Holding the two pints, Finn moved down the bar and gave them to the customer.

'Here you go. That's seven euros exactly.'

The man handed him the money and then gestured to the television. 'You like hurling, do you?'

Finn shrugged. 'I've never seen it before.'

'Right, good one.' The man laughed as though that was a hilarious thing to say, and he wandered away.

Looking over to the public bar, Finn spotted Kat handing over drinks and taking money.

Sean had kept to his promise, and they had really landed on their feet since they'd arrived. Even though it was a very friendly town, no one seemed to care who they were, where they came from, or why they were there. It really was perfect.

Finn felt someone pinch his bum. He turned around and saw that Kat had come around to grab two packets of crisps from under the bar.

He grinned at her. 'Hey, that's sexual harassment, you know?'

Kat laughed. 'That's okay, you can sexually harass me back later.'

'Where did you go earlier?' Finn asked. He had noticed that she had disappeared for a while.

Kat gave him a look that he couldn't decipher. 'I was sick again.'

He frowned. 'You must have picked up a stomach bug or something.'

She pulled a face. 'Yeah, I'm starting to think it's not that.'

He shrugged. 'What do you mean?'

Kat leaned towards him. 'I'm late.'

For a second, he didn't twig what she was talking about. Then his jaw dropped. 'Oh right. I ... you mean you might be ...?'

Kat smiled. 'Yeah, I might be.'

Finn's face lit up. 'That's brilliant isn't it?'

Kat looked a bit teary. 'Yeah, it's brilliant. Bloody scary, but if you think it's brilliant ...'

He pulled him to her, kissed her, and then swung her around.

There were a few cheers and whistles from the customers drinking at the bar.

NICK SLOWED DOWN THE car and stopped outside Georgie's house. 'Here we go.'

Georgie smiled at him. 'Thanks. You saved me again. I'm going to have to start giving you petrol money.'

'Well if it happens again, I'm going to start to think that you're doing it on purpose.'

'How do you know I didn't?'

Nick smiled. 'I'll bring my jump leads tomorrow and get you going.'

Georgie burst out laughing.

Nick grinned as he realised what he had said. 'Sorry, that didn't come out right.'

Georgie gazed directly at him and arched her eyebrow. 'Hey, it's fine. But I don't need jump leads to get me going.'

Nick took a breath. 'No? Well, I'm not going to ask you what does.'

'Having sex in cars is a big turn on.'

Did she actually just say that?

Nick tried to look indifferent. 'Okay, good to know.'

Georgie chuckled as she unclipped her seatbelt. 'Not really. I just wanted to make you feel uncomfortable.'

'Well, you certainly did that.'

There were a few tense seconds and then Georgie opened the door by a few inches. She turned to Nick. 'Do you fancy coming in for coffee?'

'Erm, no. I'd better ...'

Georgie sighed. 'Yeah, I know. You've got to get home. Sure there's nothing I can do to persuade you?'

CHAPTER 40

RIGHT. IT'S TIME TO do this, Ruth, she said to herself as she got out of the chair and headed back inside. Grabbing her laptop from the kitchen, she went into the lounge and slumped down onto the sofa.

Folding the blanket over her legs, Ruth stubbed out her cigarette and reached for her third glass of red wine. Normally she wouldn't have drunk more than two, but she was anxious. The attachment that Stephen had sent her of the blonde escort had been on her mind for two days now. Was the woman under that pixelated face really Sarah? Ruth knew she was driving herself mad by looking at the photos, but there was only one way to really find out. And that was why she was drinking more than usual. She needed some Dutch courage.

Flipping the laptop open, she waited for it to power up and then typed in *Global Escorts* as she had done a dozen times in recent days. She reached over to her purse beside her and pulled out her credit card. Her heart was starting to beat hard in her chest.

To gain full access to the site, Ruth now needed to add her details and a credit card. She filled out the contact information, typing the name *Harry Blake* for the name instead of her own. Having put in her credit card number, she pressed the *Enter* button and waited as the site processed her information.

Ruth took a breath and finished her wine.

A second later, the screen changed, and she was now inside the *Global Escorts* members' site. She typed in the details of the blonde English escort, Sophia, and waited. Sophia's homepage appeared with a description of what she could offer, along with a price list that ranged from an hour to a weekend. At the bottom of the page, there was another button marked *Bookings*.

The *Bookings* page appeared with a breakdown of the times and dates that Sophia was available this month. Below that were a list of ways that she could be contacted to book a rendezvous – online booking, email, or FaceTime. There was a separate button for each.

Ruth could feel her stomach tense as she considered the options.

Taking a deep breath, she clicked the FaceTime button.

A small screen appeared and there was the sound of a phone ringing.

With every ring, Ruth felt herself become more and more nervous.

Maybe I should hang up.

For a second, she moved the cursor to cancel the call.

Then the ringing stopped.

The small screen on her laptop flickered for a few seconds.

A face appeared looking at her.

Ruth's stomach lurched as she gazed back at the woman.

After a few seconds, she composed herself.

'Hello Sarah.'

Enjoy this book?
Get the next book in the series
'The Conway Harbour Killings' #Book 9
on pre-order on Amazon

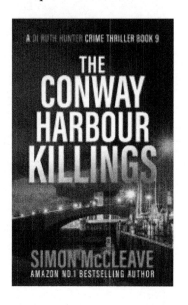

Publication date June 2021
https://www.amazon.co.uk/dp/B08X98W8TR
https://www.amazon.com/dp/B08X98W8TR
The Conway Harbour Killings
A Ruth Hunter Crime Thriller #Book 9

Your FREE book is waiting for you now

Get your FREE copy of the prequel to
the DI Ruth Hunter Series NOW
at www.simonmccleave.com[1]
and join my VIP Email Club

---

1. http://www.simonmccleave.com

NEW RUTH HUNTER SERIES

LONDON, 1997. A SERIES of baffling murders. A web of political corruption. DC Ruth Hunter thinks she has the brutal killer in her sights, but there's one problem. He's a Serbian War criminal who died five years earlier and lies buried in Bosnia.

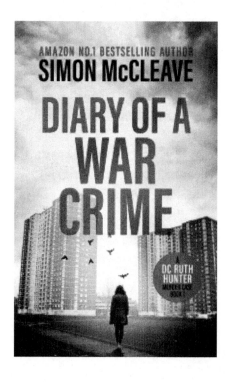

https://www.amazon.co.uk/dp/
B08T654J73

https://www.amazon.com/dp/
B08T654J73

AUTHOR'S NOTE

Although this book is very much a work of fiction, it is located in Snowdonia, a spectacular area of North Wales. It is steeped in history and folklore that spans over two thousand years. It is worth mentioning that Llancastell is a fictional town on the eastern edges of Snowdonia. I have made liberal use of artistic licence, names and places have been changed to enhance the pace and substance of the story.

Printed in Great Britain
by Amazon